The Banquet Ceases

MARY FITT

With an introduction by Curtis Evans

 Moonstone Press

This edition published in 2024 by Moonstone Press
www.moonstonepress.co.uk

Introduction © 2024 Curtis Evans
Originally published in 1952 by Macdonald & Co, London.
The Banquet Ceases © the Estate of Kathleen Freeman, writing as Mary Fitt

ISBN 978-1-899000-76-0
eISBN 978-1-899000-77-7

A CIP catalogue record for this book is available from the British Library

Text designed and typeset by Tetragon, London
Cover illustration by Jason Anscomb
Printed and bound by CPI Group (UK) Ltd, Croydon, CRO 4YY

Contents

INTRODUCTION

Ah me! My friend! It will not last, will not last!
This fairy scene that cheats our youthful eyes;
The charm dissolves; the' aerial music's pass'd;
The banquet ceases; and the vision flies.

—"He Complains How Soon the Pleasing Novelty of
Life Is Over," *Elegies* (1768), William Shenstone

He'd watch them all at dinner, eating, drinking, not having to think,
as he had to do, about their health; and he'd know that for him, and
for him only, in all that gathering the banquet was over...

—*The Banquet Ceases* (1949), Mary Fitt

William Shenstone, an eighteenth-century poet and landscape gardener
(he first coined the latter term), penned the lines quoted above in com-
memoration of the earthly life which passes away from all of us all too
soon. Shenstone himself died at the age of forty-eight, after having
impoverished himself designing the gardens at his family country estate
Leasowes and failed to achieve the literary renown which he had so
desired. 186 years after his death, however, crime writer Mary Fitt at
least graced Shenstone with a bit of posthumous fame by recalling one
of his memorable turns of poetic phrase in the title of her thirteenth
detective novel, *The Banquet Ceases*.

Like so many of Mary Fitt's detective novels, the action takes place
almost entirely at an English country house, this time Fairfield Manor,
home of mercurial millionaire industrialist Bernard Smith-Wilson and
his devoted mother. When the story begins, handsome, amiable war hero
Rupert Lavering and his lovely, charming wife Louisa are motoring to

Fairfield Manor, where Bernard, who before the late war had himself avidly pursued Louisa to no avail, is holding a banquet for a select company of guests. In addition to Rupert and Louisa, this company consists of Sir Matthew and Lady Risdon, a cynical, older middle-aged couple; Mabel Hetford, a put-upon dependent friend of Mrs. Smith-Wilson, and her two marriageable daughters, Clarissa and Lucilla; and the enigmatic Olivia Bannermore, a Smith-Wilson relation of some sort. There is also a large retinue of manor employees and house servants, a diminishing body in postwar British detective fiction, though not so much in Mary Fitt's crime corpus. The most significant of these are Holmes, Bernard's private secretary, and Barker, Mrs. Smith-Wilson's personal maid.

After ten chapters of intrigue, Bernard's dead body is discovered, quite classically, in his study. Soon Superintendent Mallett and Dr. Fitzbrown are on the scene, investigating yet another unnatural death. Bernard has been poisoned, but was the poison administered by his own hand or another's? One might almost think *The Banquet Ceases* was a between-the-wars detective novel rather than a post-WWII one, so many classic elements being affixed firmly in place; yet there are a few references which make clear the events in the tale take place after the Second World War. Most significantly, Rupert Lavering is a heroic war veteran, a recipient of the Victoria Cross, who has had trouble settling down in peacetime and is seen as a natural suspect by those gathered at Fairfield Hall when Death strikes. This character type appeared in much postwar British and American crime fiction, some notable British examples being Michael Gilbert's *They Never Looked Inside* (1948) (Gilbert himself was a WWII veteran and POW), Margery Allingham's *The Tiger in the Smoke* (1952) and Henry Wade's *Diplomat's Folly* (1951) and *Too Soon to Die* (1953).

We also learn the British Army requisitioned Fairfield Hall during the late war, during which time Bernard, fortunately for himself, thrived financially (even as his health declined), due to his manufacture of an invention of his friend Rupert which proved of great utility in the late war. Bernard's secretary Holmes, it turns out, is an "Anticrat," evidently a dubious, visionary radical political sect with ambitions of overturning the new world order. "There are only about twenty of them so far," explains Olivia. "They're against everything, it appears…"

Dr. Fitzbrown plays a minor role in *Banquet*, while Dr. Jones, his tetchy old nemeses from the prewar years, pops up briefly too. Mainly the investigative work is done by steadfast Superintendent Mallett, who has a rather unruly gang to deal with this time around. Will Mallett get his man (or woman)? Watch out for some twists in this devious tale.

Having feasted upon *The Banquet Ceases* "Ariel," the pseudonymous crime fiction reviewer at the *Huddersfield Weekly Examiner*, deemed the novel an "ingeniously devised" mystery with a particularly subtle use of psychology and a surprising denouement. Ariel found a number of the characters rather unpleasant people, affording "extensive scope for Miss Fitt's sardonic talent." The climax of the tale was indeed "decidedly unusual," agreed the *Liverpool Echo*. Even as the Empire crumbled, revolution engulfed East Asia and an Iron Curtain descended across the Europe, the British country house mystery endured in the capable hands of native crime writers like Mary Fitt. Thank goodness one could still depend on murder.

ABOUT THE AUTHOR

One of the prominent authors of the classical detective fiction of the Golden Age and afterwards was herself a classicist: Kathleen Freeman, a British lecturer in Greek at the University College of South Wales and Monmouthshire, Cardiff (now Cardiff University) between 1919 and 1946. Primarily under the pseudonym Mary Fitt, Freeman published twenty-nine crime novels between 1936 and 1960, the last of them posthumously. Eighteen of these novels are chronicles of the criminal investigations of her series sleuth, Superintendent Mallett of Scotland Yard, while the remaining eleven of them, nine of them published under the pseudonym Mary Fitt and one apiece published under the respective names of Stuart Mary Wick and Kathleen Freeman, are stand-alone mysteries, some of which are notable precursors of the modern psychological crime novel. There is also a single collection of Superintendent Mallett "cat mystery" short stories, *The Man Who Shot Birds*.

From the publication of her lauded debut detective novel, *Three Sisters Flew Home*, Mary Fitt—like Gladys Mitchell, an author with whom in England she for many years shared the distinguished publisher Michael Joseph—was deemed a crime writer for "connoisseurs". Within a few years, Fitt's first English publisher, Ivor Nicholson & Watson, proudly dubbed her devoted following a "literary cult". In what was an unusual action for the time, Nicholson & Watson placed on the dust jacket of their edition of Fitt's *Death at Dancing Stones* (1939) accolades from such distinguished, mystery-writing Fitt fans as Margery Allingham ("A fine detective story and a most ingenious puzzle"), Freeman Wills Crofts ("I should like to offer her my congratulations") and J. J. Connington ("This is the best book by Miss Mary Fitt I have yet read").

If not a crowned "queen of crime" like Allingham, Agatha Christie, Dorothy L. Sayers and Ngaio Marsh, Kathleen Freeman in her Mary Fitt guise was, shall we say, a priestess of peccadillos. In 1950 Freeman was elected to the prestigious Detection Club, a year after her crime-writing cover was blown in the gossip column "The Londoner's Diary" in the *Evening Standard*. Over the ensuing decade several of the older Mary Fitt mysteries were reprinted in paperback by Penguin and other publishers, while new ones continued to appear, to a chorus of praise from such keen critics of the crime-fiction genre as Edmund Crispin, Anthony Berkeley Cox (who wrote as, among others, Francis Iles) and Maurice Richardson. "It is easy to run out of superlatives in writing of Mary Fitt," declared the magazine *Queen*, "who is without doubt among the first of our literary criminographers."

Admittedly, Freeman enjoyed less success as a crime writer in the United States, where only ten of her twenty-nine mystery novels were published during her lifetime. However, one of Fitt's warmest boosters was the *New York Times*'s Anthony Boucher, for two decades the perceptive dean of American crime-fiction reviewers. In 1962, three years after Fitt's death, Boucher selected the author's 1950 novel *Pity for Pamela* for inclusion in the "Collier Mystery Classics" series. In his introduction to the novel, Boucher lauded Fitt as an early and important exponent of psychological suspense in crime fiction.

Despite all the acclaim which the Mary Fitt mysteries formerly enjoyed, after Freeman's untimely death from congestive heart failure in 1959 at the age of sixty-one, the books, with very few exceptions—*Mizmaze* (Penguin, 1961), *Pity for Pamela* (Collier, 1962), *Death and the Pleasant Voices* (Dover, 1984)—fell almost entirely out of print. Therefore, this latest series of sparkling reissues from Moonstone is a welcome event indeed for lovers of vintage British mystery, of which Kathleen Freeman surely is one of the most beguiling practitioners.

*

A native Midlander, Kathleen Freeman was born at the parish of Yardley near Birmingham on 22 June 1897. The only child of Charles Henry Freeman and his wife Catherine Mawdesley, Kathleen grew up and would spend most of her adult life in Cardiff, where she moved with her parents not long after the turn of the century. Her father worked as a brewer's traveller, an occupation he had assumed possibly on account of an imperative need to support his mother and two unmarried sisters after the death of his own father, a schoolmaster and clergyman without a living who had passed away at the age of fifty-seven. This was in 1885, a dozen years before Kathleen was born, but presumably the elder Charles Freeman bequeathed a love of learning to his family, including his yet-unborn granddaughter. Catherine Mawdesley's father was James Mawdesley, of the English seaside resort town of Southport, not far from Liverpool. James had inherited his father's "spacious and handsome silk mercer's and general draper's establishment", impressively gaslit and "in no degree inferior, as to amplitude, variety and elegance of stock, to any similar establishment in the metropolis or inland towns" (in the words of an 1852 guide to Southport), yet he died at the age of thirty-five, leaving behind a widow and three young daughters.

As a teenager, Kathleen Freeman was educated at Cardiff High School, which, recalling the 1930s, the late memoirist Ron Warburton remembered as "a large attractive building with a large schoolyard in front, which had a boundary wall between it and the pavement". The girls attended classes on the ground floor, while the boys marched up to the first (respectively, the first and second floors in American terminology). "The first-floor windows were frosted so that the boys could not look down at the girls in the school playground," Warburton wryly recalled. During the years of the Great War, Freeman, who was apparently an autodidact in ancient Greek (a subject unavailable at Cardiff High School, although the boys learned Latin), attended the co-educational, "red-brick" University College of South Wales and Monmouthshire, founded three decades earlier in 1883, whence she graduated with a BA in Classics in 1918. The next year saw both her mother's untimely passing at the age of fifty-two and her own appointment as a lecturer in Greek at her alma mater. In 1922, she received her MA; a Doctor of Letters belatedly followed eighteen years later, in recognition of her scholarly articles and 1926 book *The Work and Life of Solon*, about the ancient Athenian statesman. Between 1919 and 1926 Freeman was a junior colleague at University College of her former teacher Gilbert Norwood, who happened to share her great love of detective fiction, as did another prominent classical scholar, Gilbert Murray, who not long before his death in 1957 informed Freeman that he had long been a great admirer of Mary Fitt.

Freeman's rise in the field of higher education during the first half of the twentieth century is particularly impressive given the facts, which were then deemed disabling, of her sex and modest family background as the daughter of a brewer's traveller, which precluded the possibility of a prestigious Oxbridge education. "A man will do much for a woman who is his friend, but to be suspected of being a brewer's traveller... was not pleasant," observes the mortified narrator of William Black's novel *A Princess of Thule* (1883), anxious to correct this socially damning misimpression. Evidently unashamed of her circumstances, however, Freeman evinced a lifetime ambition to reach ordinary, everyday people with her work, eschewing perpetual confinement in academe's ivory tower.

Before turning to crime writing in 1936 under the alias of Mary Fitt, Freeman published five mainstream novels and a book of short stories, beginning with *Martin Hanner: A Comedy* (1926), a well-received academic novel about a (male) classics professor who teaches at a red-brick university in northern England. After the outbreak of the Second World War, while she was still employed at the university, Freeman, drawing on her classical education, published the patriotically themed *It Has All Happened Before: What the Greeks Thought of Their Nazis* (1941).[1] She also lectured British soldiers headed to the Mediterranean theatre of war on the terrain, customs and language of Greece, a country she had not merely read about but visited in the Thirties. During the cold war, when Freeman, passed over for promotion, had retired from teaching to devote herself to writing in a world confronted with yet another totalitarian menace, she returned to her inspirational theme, publishing *Fighting Words from the Greeks for Today's Struggle* (1952). Perhaps her most highly regarded layman-oriented work from this period is *Greek City-States* (1950), in which, notes scholar Eleanor Irwin, Freeman uses her "uncanny eye for settings, as is often seen in her mysteries", to bring "the city-states to life". Freeman explicitly drew on her interests in both classicism and crime in her much-admired book *The Murder of Herodes and Other Trials from the Athenian Law Courts* (1946), which was effusively praised by the late Jacques Barzun, another distinguished academic mystery fancier, as "a superb book for the [crime] connoisseur".

In spite of her classical background, Kathleen Freeman derived her "Mary Fitt" pseudonym—which she also employed to publish juvenile fiction, including a series of books about an intrepid young girl named Annabella—not from ancient Greece but from Elizabethan England, Eleanor Irwin has hypothesised, for the name bears resemblance to that of Mary Fitton, the English gentlewoman and maid of honour who is a candidate for the "Dark Lady" of Shakespeare's queer-inflected sonnets. Irwin points out that Freeman's "earliest literary publications were highly personal reflections on relationships in sonnet form". The name also lends itself to a pun—"Miss Fitt"—which it is likely the author deliberately intended, given her droll wit and nonconformity.

---

1   Under the heading of "Dictators", Freeman quotes Solon: "When a man has risen too high, it is not easy to check him after; now is the time to take heed of everything." Timeless words indeed!

While Kathleen Freeman's first four detective novels, which appeared in 1936 and 1937, are stand-alones, her fifth essay in the form, *Sky-Rocket* (1938), introduces her burly, pipe-smoking, green-eyed, red-moustached series police detective, Superintendent Mallett, who is somewhat reminiscent of Agatha Christie's occasional sleuth Superintendent Battle. The two men not only share similar builds but have similarly symbolic surnames.

Joined initially by acerbic police surgeon Dr. Jones and later by the imaginative Dr. Dudley "Dodo" Fitzbrown—the latter of whom, introduced in *Expected Death* (1938), soon supersedes Jones—Superintendent Mallett would dominate Mary Fitt's mystery output over the next two decades. Only after Freeman's heart condition grew perilously grave in 1954 does it seem that the author's interest in Mallett and Fitzbrown dwindled, with the pair appearing in only two of the five novels published between 1956 and 1960. Similarly diminished in her final years was Freeman's involvement with the activities of the Detection Club, into which she initially had thrown herself with considerable zeal. In the first half of the decade she had attended club dinners with her beloved life partner, Dr. Liliane Marie Catherine Clopet, persuaded Welsh polymath Bertrand Russell, an omnivorous detective-fiction reader, to speak at one of the dinners, and wrote a BBC radio play, *A Death in the Blackout* (in which Dr. Fitzbrown appears), with the proceeds from the play going to the club.

Presumably Kathleen Freeman met Liliane Clopet at the University College of South Wales and Monmouthshire, where Clopet registered as a student in 1919. Precisely when the couple began cohabiting is unclear, but by 1929 Freeman had dedicated the first of what would be many books to Clopet ("For L.M.C.C."), and by the Thirties the pair resided at Lark's Rise, the jointly owned house—including a surgery for Clopet and her patients—that the couple had built in St. Mellons, a Cardiff suburb. In the author's biography on the back of her Penguin mystery reprints, Freeman noted that a friend had described the home where she lived as "your Italian-blue house", though she elaborated: "It is not Italian, but it is blue—sky-blue." There Freeman would pass away and Clopet would reside for many years afterwards.

Born on 13 December 1901 in Berwick-upon-Tweed in Northumberland, Liliane Clopet was one of three children of native Frenchman Aristide Bernard Clopet, a master mariner, and his English wife Charlotte Towerson, a farmer's daughter. Although Aristide became a naturalised British citizen, the Clopets maintained close connections with France. In 1942, during the Second World War, Liliane's only brother, Karl Victor Clopet—a master mariner like his father who for a dozen years had run a salvage tug in French Morocco—was smuggled by Allied forces from Casablanca to London, where he provided details of Moroccan ports, beaches and coastal defences, which were crucially important to the victory of the United States over Vichy French forces at the ensuing Battle of Port Lyautey.

Even more heroically (albeit tragically), Liliane's cousin Evelyne Clopet served with the French Resistance and was executed by the Nazis in 1944, after British forces had parachuted her into France; at her death she was only twenty-two years old. In 1956, under another pseudonym (Caroline Cory), Kathleen Freeman published a novel set in wartime France, *Doctor Underground*, in which she drew on Evelyne's experiences. A couple of years earlier, Liliane Clopet herself had published a pseudonymous novel, *Doctor Dear*, in which she depicted a female physician's struggles with sexism among her colleagues and patients.

Kathleen Freeman, who was rather masculine-looking in both her youth and middle age (boyish in her twenties, she grew stouter over the years, wearing her hair short and donning heavy tweeds), produced no issue and at her death left her entire estate, valued at over £300,000 in today's money, to Liliane Clopet. In a letter to another correspondent she avowed: "My books are my children and I love them dearly." Admittedly, Freeman shared custody of her mysteries with that queer Miss Fitt, but surely she loved her criminally inclined offspring, too. I have no doubt that the author would be pleased to see these books back in print again after the passage of so many years. Readers of vintage mysteries, now eager to embrace the stylish and sophisticated country-house detective novels and psychological suspense tales of an earlier era, will doubtless be pleased as well.

CURTIS EVANS

The Banquet Ceases

I

The long, low, black car crawled up the lane.

The sun was still high; but the lane was in shadow, because it was bounded on both sides by high walls, and the walls were overtopped by bushes and trees and in places hung with ivy that brushed the sides of the car.

Rupert and Louise were quarrelling.

"Darling," said Louise, "you know I detest Bernard. I've always suspected him, where you're concerned. I think he's the most pernicious influence in your life. You know I think it; yet you persist in forcing me to meet him."

"Darling," said Rupert, watching the winding lane ahead and wondering what would happen if any car should be coming down, "I am not forcing you to meet Bernard. You know you would never have agreed to my coming here alone. Since I've known you, I never *have* been allowed to meet anyone alone; so that if I'm not to lose touch with *all* my friends—"

Louise put out a hand to the door-handle.

"Darling," she said, "please stop, here and now. I don't wish to go another yard with you. You may stay with Bernard for the rest of your life, or any other of your friends, for all I care. But *don't* pretend that I am here for any other reason than that you insisted."

She laid her hand, as she always did, first on the window-handle; and then, realising what she was doing, she transferred her grip to the right lever. The door, as it always did when Louise tried to open it, sprang ajar, and then stuck with a click, rattling as the car moved over the uneven surface of the lane.

Rupert stretched out an arm across her and shut the door again.

"Don't be so ridiculous!" he said. "I could stand all this if only you were ever truthful for one single moment. But you *will* turn everything into melodrama—"

"Melodrama!" gasped Louise.

"Yes, melodrama!" Rupert, red in the face, changed gear, noiselessly as always. "Here we are, practically on Bernard's door-step, and you talk of getting out. Where do you imagine you'd go, in those shoes—in that dress?" He managed to cast a look, not disapproving, at her over his shoulder. "We are some thirty miles from home."

Louise too glanced at herself, her white dress, her sparkling high-heeled evening slippers, her white furs, with complacency.

"It's like you, and worthy of your chivalrous nature, darling," she said, "to insult me when you know I can't get away from you, and then taunt me with my helplessness."

The car turned in between the high stone pillars of the entrance-gate and moved more smoothly over the newly-laid yellow gravel of the drive. Between the trees, well-cut lawns came into view, and then flower-beds; the summer bedding-plants glowed with all their brilliant colours in the full blaze of the evening sunshine.

"Oh!" cried Louise, always ready to be irrelevant. "How utterly charming! Look, darling! What work Bernard has had done here! You should have seen it a year ago, when the Army had just left! There wasn't a window-pane unbroken; and as for the garden—a perfect wilderness, my dear! I never would have thought he could have got it straight again so quickly. How exactly like Bernard!" She leaned back, and opening her fan of ostrich-plumes, fanned herself as the rays of the sun filled the car with golden, dust-laden beams. "He has an absolutely diabolical gift for getting his own way!"

Rupert slowed down. "How unjust you are!" he said. "You know very well that what gives him his power is his money; and if I had it, you wouldn't see anything diabolical in my ability to get *my* own way—which means *yours*."

Louise clasped both her long fine hands round his left arm; and in spite of the drag on the steering, he did not resist her.

"You don't do so badly, darling," she said cajolingly. "You give me *nearly* everything I want." She laughed a little, aware of her effect on him, and then went on briskly: "Now remember: I shall be frightfully angry with you if you drink too much. Not more than two cocktails before dinner, remember, and perhaps one whisky afterwards." She turned to gaze out of the window again. "Look, darling, at those glorious begonias! And look! He has had the pools cleaned out, and the lilies are still there! Oh, I'm so glad!" She turned back to Rupert. "Because, you know, Bernard likes you to drink a little too much always. In that way, he gets you just where he wants you. And you're so silly, darling, when you've had even one drink too many—quite sweet, of course, but helpless as a baby. You'll talk. You'll give yourself away. You'll promise Bernard anything, especially if I'm not there to hear."

Rupert brought the car to a standstill beside a pond of white and purple water-lilies.

"Darling," he said, his exasperation mounting again, "I am *not* helpless when you're not there. I have travelled all over the world without you. In the past seven years I've been through the Greek campaign, the North African campaign, the Italian campaign, and a few other such trifles. Finally, since the end of the war I've re-established myself in civilian life as a stockbroker and general financial adviser in a world of sharks, and I haven't done so badly so far, as you yourself admit. Therefore I think I may be regarded as no longer in leading-strings. So—"

"Ah!" said Louise. "How much better you got on when you were out of reach of Bernard's influence, didn't you? I'm sure you were perfectly splendid when you were storming Pantellaria. That's why I don't want you to get back into his orbit, don't you see?"

"My dear girl, don't be absurd," said Rupert with momentary gloomy candour. "How do you think I could have managed to start again on my own, without a bean, after all those years, and without any knowledge of the market? How do you think I could have afforded to marry *you*?"

"Rupert!" said Louise, startled at last. "You don't mean to tell me you borrowed money from Bernard?"

"Where did you think I got it?" said Rupert, exaggerating the bitterness in his tone as he saw its effect on her. "Did you think it was my postwar gratuity?" He touched her furs with one finger. "And where do you think the hot tips come from that buy you things like these?"

"Drive on, darling," said Louise, leaning back. "We shall be late after all if you don't." Her flippancy had gone, and so too had her absorption in the present; she spoke calmly, like a mother who wishes to silence her rather tiresome child while she thinks about tomorrow's meals. "So that was it! I wondered. But I thought it was your father's legacy."

"That went long ago," said Rupert, "before the war, in fact." But he too was not thinking of what he was saying. He drove on again at a crawl, and the terrace of the house came into view. "By Jove," he said, brightening, his gaze directed ahead, "isn't that old Bernard walking up and down outside?" The car moved forward more quickly. "It does one good to see him in his right setting. At one time I thought we'd never see him again at all."

"You mean you thought *he*'d never see *you* again, darling," suggested Louise, "nor I, nor anyone who cared about you. That did occur to me too, you know, when you were busy retaking Tunisia."

"No, no," said Rupert impatiently. "I'm not talking about that. I was quite all right, always. I was thinking of Bernard's illness." His voice sank to religious solemnity. "He was desperately ill at one time, you know. They had all given him up, I'm told. But he rallied—good old Bernard!—he rallied."

"He rallied!" repeated Louise in a significant murmur. Rupert heard her; but there was no time, no need to stop to feel resentment. Already Bernard had seen them—was coming from the porch towards the stone balustrade—was standing at the top of the lichened steps.

Rupert hailed him.

In a moment Louise, graceful in her white tulle dress as a swan with its plumage in display, was mounting the steps towards Bernard, taking his outstretched hand, and saying, before she accepted his arm:

"Why, Bernard, how splendid you look! How splendid to see you here! And are you quite, quite better?"

Bernard responded to Rupert's greeting; then he turned to Louise and gave her his whole attention.

"Quite, quite better," he said.

"Your illness—quite gone? No trace left behind?"

"Not a trace," said Bernard, smiling, "except that it has made me value life as I never did before."

"You mean, value your *own* life," murmured Louise, "I suppose. Only a few doctors and other altruistics value life nowadays."

"My dear!" Bernard mocked her gently. "Don't tell me that marriage has made a metaphysician of you—already!"

She did not answer. Bernard dropped his tone of banter: he did not want to enrage Louise just yet.

"Yes," he said soberly, "you're right: I value *my* life. But that doesn't mean I don't value anyone else's. You must do me that amount of negative justice, at least; I don't claim to be an altruist."

"But, Bernard," said Louise, interested immediately by his apparent sincerity, "you always did value your life. That's not an accusation."

They had almost reached that part of the terrace which was opposite to the porch, and the cool interior invited them, beyond the open doors, to come in out of the dazzling sunshine and God's good air, and be the civilised, sophisticated creatures for which nature had intended them. But by mutual consent they paused and turned away. Rupert, carrying two suit-cases, had already been seen and acclaimed by several ladies who were sitting at one of the open windows. He disappeared into the dark shadows of the hall. Bernard and Louise, resting their elbows on the balustrade, stood with their backs turned to the house and gazed outwards to where the terraced lawns dropped down to the lily-ponds, and beyond that to the high trees and the shrubberies that outlined the encircling wall.

"Yes," admitted Louise, as if he had challenged, "it's lovely. And it must be lovelier for you than for us, even, because you thought you'd lost it. But, Bernard, what's the use? The lovelier things are, the harder to leave them. And we have to, in the end." She spoke the platitude with all the courage and the feeling that its truth demanded.

"I don't agree," said Bernard coldly.

"Oh, but—!" protested Louise, as sure of her ground as if he had denied that fire burns.

He checked her rather impatiently.

"You," he said, "hate to give up what's lovely. I should hate to leave something that was unfinished—untidy—undone." He smiled suddenly. "I merely mean," he added in the tone of one bringing an absurd discussion to earth again, "I should have hated to die a year ago, when this place had been allowed to become a wilderness. I wanted to live long enough to put it right. If I had died under the operation, my ghost would have haunted it—especially the gardens—dragging surveyors' chains." He laughed, and so did she. "Shall we go in?"

"Of course," she said brightly, and turned; but he still lingered, looking at her appraisingly.

"How well you look!" he said, not without envy. "You haven't changed at all. I shall never be as well as that again. You've never been ill in your life, have you, either in body or in mind? No, of course you haven't. You never will be. Neither you nor Rupert ever could be anything but gloriously healthy."

Louise looked up at him in surprise: "But you said you were better!"
"Yes."

"Then why do you sound so——" she paused, hardly liking to risk saying 'envious', "——so sad?"

"Because," said Bernard thoughtfully, "even when illnesses are cured they leave scars."

Louise glanced at him again, startled, alert. But he was staring at the ground, his chin resting on one hand, his elbow on the other, a favourite pose of his. His dark chestnut-coloured hair grew up in a rich wave from his high forehead; she noticed with amusement that he had allowed a small dark-red beard to grow, a mere tuft of hair under the lower lip, as if to accentuate what he knew to be his rather interesting Mephistophelian appearance. She felt a rush of love for Rupert—and of compunction towards him, the compunction of a mother who has slapped her darling child in a moment of irritation, without sufficient cause. How could she have been so absurd as to tell him she detested Bernard? She was sorry for Bernard, sorry for the barrenness of his life, for the something about him that made it impossible for him to evoke real love, or rather to want it when he had by chance evoked it.

"Well, what does a scar matter," she said cheerfully, anxious now to go indoors and join the rest of the party, "so long as the wound has healed?"

She started forward, across the terrace towards the house; and Bernard followed her, his long lazy stride easily matching two steps of hers.

"They mark one off," she heard him murmur, "from other people."

But by now she was impatient of discussion. He had implicitly appealed to her for pity, and she gave it, but with the usual admixture of contempt. What an interesting creature he was, she thought indulgently, knowing him to be still potentially hers. No wonder Rupert defended him against her; for Rupert *was* chivalrous, fantastically so, and nothing could have been more unjust to him than her gibe of a little while ago. Bernard, for all his apparent blandness, had weaknesses; and Rupert rushed in to defend him. It was as simple as that, she believed.

Bernard, following her, wondered for how long she would remain disarmed.

2

Rupert had passed the open window of the smaller drawing-room, which was near the entrance, and commanded a view of it. His delightful laugh could be heard in the hall; it was a laugh that might have been called infectious, except that it made perceptive people stop laughing themselves for the pleasure of listening to it.

"He *is* married, isn't he?" said one of the two older ladies sitting in the window-seat watching the terrace. She spoke thoughtfully, almost regretfully.

"Who? Bernard?" Mrs. Smith-Wilson bridled. She had red hair, and she bore a striking resemblance to Queen Elizabeth, a resemblance of which she was well aware and which she accentuated by every possible device of dress and manner. It was from her that Bernard derived the bright tints in his much darker hair; but in him the flaming red of his mother's hair had been softened down by the blackness of his father's, to that chestnut which people found so unusual and so becoming. He had not, however, inherited any of his father's weakness, his mother found to her surprise. She watched him now, as he leaned over the balustrade with Louise in her white dinner-dress and white furs; and the evening sun picked out the red flame in his hair, too, and made it momentarily like his mother's. "Bernard?" said Mrs. Smith-Wilson. "Good gracious, no! Bernard will never marry. His health has been much too precarious. He would consider it very wrong."

"Not Bernard," said Mrs. Hertford patiently. It required patience to convey to Mrs. Smith-Wilson that not every woman was primarily interested in Bernard. "Rupert."

"Oh, Rupert!" Mrs. Smith-Wilson dismissed Rupert with the nonchalance which is the world's best weapon against charm, beauty or

brains. "Yes, he's married. He married Louise Molyneux six months
ago: very foolish, because he has absolutely nothing behind him."

"Really!" said Mrs. Hertford, turning her mild blue eyes towards
Louise and Bernard where they leaned and talked. "I thought his people
had money."

"Rupert's father left him a few thousands, I believe," said Mrs. Smith-
Wilson, arching her back and looking down her aquiline nose at Mrs.
Hertford. "But he lost it all in some little invention—something to do
with cars. Bernard says it wasn't Rupert's fault—that it was because of
the war and his being called up before he had things started. But then,
Bernard is always ready to make allowances. He was able to help Rupert.
He is too kind." She gave Mrs. Hertford a defiant look.

Mrs. Hertford showed no surprise at this, to her, preposterous
statement. She merely said:

"Rupert did very well in the war."

Mrs. Smith-Wilson winced angrily: "Rupert will always do well in
anything requiring animal spirits and recklessness."

"Courage," murmured Mrs. Hertford. "I think it's awfully brave
to land on an open beach and run towards people who are firing at you.
I know I should run the other way, like a hare."

Mrs. Smith-Wilson cast a glance at Mabel Hertford's short, stout
legs, and smiled.

"I'm not trying to detract from Rupert's bravery, or any other
man's," she said, with a show of great reasonableness. "If it weren't for
him and others like him, we old dowagers wouldn't be here."

Mabel Hertford winced in her turn. She was twenty years younger
than Mrs. Smith-Wilson, but she was the mother of two fine girls, now, no
doubt, joining their laughter with Rupert's in the hall outside; and so she
must be swept into the same category as her hostess: no more fun for her!

"No," went on Mrs. Smith-Wilson with increasing magnanimity,
"I grudge them nothing. Nothing can be too good for them, of course,

after what they've done and gone through. But"—she lowered her rather wrinkled lids over her still bright hazel eyes—"there are some who have not been given their opportunity."

Mabel thought: 'Oh, dear me, here we are, back at Bernard again!' She nodded sanctimoniously: "Of course, dear; I know."

Mrs. Smith-Wilson thought: 'You don't, you fool! What do you know about how it feels to have a son, a unique amazing creature who is yours and not yours; who needs you and doesn't need you; who is always, at every minute of the day, a surprise; and then to find that he is flawed, like a beautiful piece of Venetian glass with a crack in it? You with your two healthy, high-spirited daughters—what can you know about that? I know why you're here: you want to marry them off, if possible, to my son Bernard. Ha!'

Not more than a second passed as these thoughts shot through her mind. She disliked being called 'dear' by any woman, but above all by Mabel, whom she despised; and if Mabel had laid a plump sympathetic hand on her long thin one she would have started back as if the hand had held an adder.

"For all practical purposes," she said harshly, "Bernard can be considered cured. But his illness has left a mark on him. He says himself it has set him apart."

"You don't mean there's any possibility of a recurrence?" Mabel's blue eyes opened wide as she wondered whether Clara—or Lucilla—ought to look elsewhere without further consideration. A man with a damaged lung—but then again... Her thoughts trailed away, avoiding the pros and cons, refusing to admit that she was willing to speculate on the advantage of early widowhood and a fortune of—well, they credited Bernard Smith-Wilson with about a couple of million. What was a mother to do?

"I don't think so," said Mrs. Smith-Wilson. She was able to laugh inwardly at what she knew to be Mabel's dilemma, because she knew that nothing would persuade Bernard to consider either Clara or Lucilla as a wife. "Medical opinion seems unanimous that he has nothing to fear so long as he takes care. But his life is—mutilated. He would have liked, for instance, to have taken part in the war. He did so to the best of his ability, until he broke down. Overwork was the direct cause of his breakdown; and he overworked because he had to console himself for not being *there*, with the others—the strong and healthy."

Her nostrils were pinched as she breathed more quickly. "*He* would have liked to be there, storming beaches and directing battles, and living with other men, instead of—" She broke off for a moment, and continued more calmly: "Sometimes, during the long months when he was in bed in the nursing-home, I used to think that he would die, not of his illness, but by sheer exhaustion of spirit. It seemed to me, sometimes, when I sat beside him, that he was doing everybody's work in his mind—everybody's, from the highest statesmen and generals right down to the lowest Tommy peeling potatoes or trudging along the road—and I thought it would kill him. Well, it didn't: his will to live was much too strong. But it's something that he can never get over, because it can't be put right—it's past and done with. Such times will never come again."

"But surely," said Mabel, rallying from under the weight of Mrs. Smith-Wilson's vicarious regrets, "the works must keep him very busy, don't they? It has become such a huge concern!"

"Bernard has organised it so well since he took it over—since my husband died," retorted Mrs. Smith-Wilson, "that he has no need to do more than supervise. He often says it's as easy to steer as one of his own twenty-horse-power cars."

"And this place!" Mabel turned her head to look again out of the window. "All the improvements he's making!"

"Oh, a mere trifle!" said Mrs. Smith-Wilson impatiently. "Just enough to keep him occupied for an hour after breakfast every day. And in any case, here there was no planning to do. Bernard sees it always as it was when he was a boy—in the days of its glory. All he has had to do is to restore it."

But Mabel was no longer attending. She was watching Bernard and Louise crossing the terrace towards the house, Louise leading like a swan in full sail, Bernard, tall, thin and elegant, in attendance. Mabel was wondering: 'What happened? Did Louise throw Bernard over because he was ill? Or was there never anything serious between them? She has no money. I suppose she must have fallen in love with Rupert and got carried away.' She sighed to think of the brief bliss afforded by such a yielding to romanticism, a yielding she would not have excused in Clara or Lucilla.

"We all thought, at one time, Bernard might marry Louise," she said, appearing casual, but actually full of caution, for she was aware of the dangerous ground on which she was treading.

"Louise?" Mrs. Smith-Wilson's response was exactly what Mabel expected. "Never! Louise could never have made a wife for Bernard. She hasn't—she isn't—" Words failed her to express Louise's total inadequacy.

"They were seen about together a good deal at one time," said Mabel meditatively. "But then, that was after Rupert went overseas, wasn't it? I suppose she was engaged to Rupert all the time, and as he and Bernard are such great friends—partners, too, weren't they, before the war?"

"Certainly not!" snapped Mrs. Smith-Wilson angrily. "Bernard has helped Rupert a great deal in the past. He took over all Rupert's stock-in-trade, and saved him from bankruptcy, when Rupert went away. It was he who introduced Rupert to Louise. And now, you may be sure that if Rupert's on his feet again, it's Bernard who has put him there."

"Poor Rupert!" murmured Mabel, with unexpected rebelliousness. "What a pity he didn't stay in the Army!"

The talk and laughter outside in the hall rose high, as Bernard and Louise joined the other guests. Mrs. Smith-Wilson rose.

"Shall we go upstairs?" she said in a tone not of question but of command. "I'm having dinner served to you and me in my room this evening. I don't believe in imposing myself on young people. This is Bernard's evening—his house-warming party." There was a note of disapproval in her voice which did not escape Mabel. "We can come down later, perhaps. Come!—No, not that way; we shall go up by the private staircase. You can meet them all afterwards."

She led the way out by the other door of the small drawing-room, through the library, and up a narrow staircase leading out of the library by the farther door, past Bernard's study.

Mabel turned once, regretfully, as the sounds of laughter in the great hall receded. It was rather hard, she thought, when you had married at eighteen, and had produced two daughters who were not yet in their twenties, to have to submit to the dictates of a woman of sixty—to be taken in tow and convoyed away from the feast, like a little ship in charge of a battle-cruiser. Men of Rupert's age—men whom experience had in some respects matured beyond their years, though without robbing them of their enterprise, did not yet find her old. But this baleful tyrant of a woman knew just this, and took good care to isolate her.

She regarded Mrs. Smith-Wilson's straight back, her high lace collar fanning out beneath her red hair—tinted, no doubt, but with great skill, so that it did not show the greenish tinge usual when such a colour is artificially imposed—her long pearl ear-rings, the pearl tiara perched high on the array of close-packed curls; and she thought, 'Well, you are having your own way now; but I shall have *my* way, sooner or later.'

The heavy, nail-studded door between the bookshelves closed, and they began to mount the staircase; Mrs. Smith-Wilson, now that there was no one to see, helped herself up by means of her silver-headed ebony cane, for she suffered from rheumatism, which she hated to reveal. The cane tapped on the polished stairs. Otherwise, there was no sound except the sounds that came from outside, through an open window on the landing where the staircase turned past Bernard's study door; sounds of distant farm-machinery whirring in the corn-fields, and the rustling of the light breeze in the tops of the tallest trees.

3

Bernard led Louise into the large ante-room on the other side of the hall. He held her lightly by the fingers, so that he could present her to the company.

Bernard liked to do things that way. Louise, standing with him at the entrance, felt no embarrassment; instead, she felt a momentary elation. Bernard's touch on her fingers had relaxed as soon as he had made his purpose clear, so that now her hand merely rested on his, which was held rather high; and she became aware, with a thrilling sense of power, that this so-called house-warming party had really been assembled because Bernard wished to do honour to *her*. She was to be the queen of it; and though among this gathering there were women wealthier than she, better-known, better-dressed, certainly with more expensive jewellery and larger houses and more successful husbands, perhaps even more beautiful; yet she knew that her own *ensemble*, the total effect that she had, both as a person and as a pattern on the dim background behind her, had something that they couldn't rival—not for tonight, anyway. And this was because Bernard willed it to be so. He called out of her all that she had and was—except love, of course: her love was reserved for Rupert.

She looked eagerly round the room, taking in the company as clearly and coolly as they were appraising her. Some of them she knew more or less well; others were complete strangers. In the far corner, with a glass of amber liquid in his hand, was Rupert, talking animatedly to an interested group of women. His fair head was flung back as he laughed; he was telling them some anecdote, enjoying himself, as always, like a child, when he had an audience. He couldn't realise that when they watched him like that they weren't listening to his amusing story so much as engrossed in the pleasure he gave them merely as a spectacle. They followed his every gesture, they laughed when he did, and occasionally one of them would put in a word to egg him on.

Yes, Rupert loved society; and society loved Rupert. If only he weren't obliged, she thought, to come to earth and deal with serious things like finance, and law, and even marriage! He had done his duty by the world in exposing his body, time and time again, to be blown to bits in their interest; why couldn't they keep him now, to be happy and to make them happy, for the rest of his life? What was the use of giving him the Victoria Cross and then leaving him to become—a stockbroker? Louise, exalted for the moment above all selfish considerations, felt that she could forgo her own claims on him, even, if only she could see him happy in the way nature had intended him to be.

A slight pressure on her fingers reminded her of Bernard. He guided her now, from group to group, and presented his guests to her. She saw faces, faces—a fat man with a curled insolent upper lip resting on a full sensual lower one; a woman, tall and dark, groomed like a greyhound, with her hair smoothed back, and wearing enormous pearl ear-rings like blisters; men with military moustaches, men who were still a little detached from their civilian surroundings, who looked on gravely and politely and tried to talk, but brightened only when someone mentioned the flies in Alexandria; wives worldly, talkative, self-assertive; wives bored and boring; wives envious, and wives envied: here they all were, smiling at Louise because Bernard wished it, and Bernard was a bachelor worth a couple of million, and one never knew, did one? Those who didn't know who Louise was wondered if they were obliged to take her seriously; and those who did know her knew quite well that they needn't bother the moment Bernard was no longer at her side.

But Bernard remained at her side; and when dinner was announced, to everybody's surprise he gave Louise his arm.

4

Dinner, for the first quarter of an hour, was a heavy burden on the spirits of those not hardened to the ceremony of the banquet. The greedy were too much absorbed in food present and to come, and in making sure that they got through the due amount of wine, to have much time for their neighbours; and the talkers, at first, could not get the necessary attention for their topics and their stories, when the nearest listener might be seated on the other side of the table or separated from them by a gourmand.

Louise, sitting at the head of the table on Bernard's right hand, ate gravely a little of what was put before her, and waited until her neighbour, the fat man with the insolent-sensual mouth, should have dealt sufficiently with the *hors-d'œuvres* to be able to recognise her existence. Bernard also ate little, and drank nothing but water; he was listening to the lady on his left, evidently the wife of the lover of *hors-d'œuvres*, a long-bodied woman wearing a large diamond collarette, and having on her face an expression singularly like that of her husband. Bernard addressed her as Lady Risdon. Louise, with a start, remembered the name.

"How is your mother?" said Lady Risdon to Bernard, rather loudly. "I hope she's quite well. Or has she gone abroad, did I hear?" Her insolent golden-brown eyes flickered for a moment over Louise's bosom, and away.

"My mother is very well, thank you, Lady Risdon," said Bernard quietly. "She is dining in her room. She hopes you will go and see her later. She never comes down to dinner, you know, when I have guests."

"Oh, but on an occasion like this!" Lady Risdon could never let well alone.

"I assure you," said Bernard coldly, "it's by her wish, not mine."

"Very noble of her," said Lady Risdon, unconvinced. "I hope, when I'm her age, I shall have the grace to be so retiring."

A deep-throated gurgle came from Louise's right hand.

"You'll never retire, my dear," said Sir Matthew. "You're not the retiring kind, any more than I am. But then, of course, we haven't got a son like Bernard." The Risdons were childless, and it was a great grief to them; they could not bear to think of anyone, relative or stranger, or institution however deserving, as inheriting their wealth and their possessions. Therefore they never ceased, in public and in private, to taunt one another with this failure, which he attributed to her deficiency, and she to his past indiscretions.

Lady Risdon flushed; even her bosom beneath the diamond collarette grew red, while Louise watched her and thought, 'Well, it's too late now.'

"By jove, Bernard, my boy," exclaimed Sir Matthew, returning to his food now that that question was settled, "this is splendid smoked salmon you have here! Very difficult to get the right stuff nowadays. Do you send away for it?"

Bernard made a sign, and a new supply of smoked salmon was immediately at Sir Matthew's elbow, while Bernard explained:

"This is our own salmon, caught in the Dill, and smoked on the premises. We have our own curing-room, you know. You shall have home-cured kippers for breakfast tomorrow if you like. I get them sent here from the estuary, and cured with oak chippings from the estate."

"By jove, do you really?" said Sir Matthew. "You don't deny yourself much, do you, my boy?" His left elbow brushed Louise's bare arm, and he suddenly became aware of her. "My dear lady," he said, looking at her with interest, "let me give you a little more of this excellent smoked salmon," and before she could say no he had helped her himself from the waiting dish.

"Yes," he went on happily, devouring his own three slices in haste—for the next course was about to be served—"Bernard has always been a connoisseur of everything." He ran his green eyes along the edge of her white corsage. "He's one of the few fellows left that I know of who really believe in the art of living. And he can afford to pursue his hobby." He took up his glass. "What's this?" he said, holding up the wine and savouring it. "Very good. Very good indeed." He turned animatedly to Louise again. "Yes, one can always trust Bernard to have everything just right—right age, right time, right temperature." He smiled at her, indulgently and sentimentally, knowing that she was not for him. "Bernard has the two qualities necessary for success—or perhaps they're the same quality: infinite patience, inflexible will."

Bernard too looked at Louise, with a smile and a raised eyebrow.

"It's no use your trying to impress Mrs. Lavering on my account, Sir Matthew," he said, "She and I are old friends. Once upon a time I could impress her—a little—when she was a small girl and I was what used to be called—so rightly, I always think—a stripling. Or didn't I impress you even then, Louise? I'm afraid I can't pretend I didn't try."

Louise smiled, and a sudden dimple sprang up at the side of her mouth.

"You did impress me, Bernard," she said, "but I knew you were trying to, and that took a little off the effect."

Lady Risdon, having listened avidly until now, to get the gist of this conversation, thought it time that she was attended to.

"What were you doing," she said to Bernard, "when you tried to impress Mrs.—?" The name naturally escaped her.

"Do you remember, Louise?" said Bernard, isolating himself and her again.

"Do you?" she said, smiling back at him.

"Of course. But I still want to know if I succeeded." He turned to Lady Risdon. "It was 'ducks and drakes'," he said, "down on the river here, if you must know. Louise used to live nearer us then."

Sir Matthew, having quickly finished his turbot, had turned again to stare at Louise, this time with a more penetrating curiosity.

"Did I hear you say 'Lavering'?" he said, and cast an uncertain look at Bernard. "Not young Lavering the——?" He didn't know whether he ought to say 'the stockbroker' or 'the V.C.', or both, or neither. He decided to say neither.

"Rupert Lavering," Bernard confirmed. "He's here tonight. Haven't you come across him?"

Rupert, lower down the table, had the back of his head turned towards them, and was quite unaware that he was being spoken of. Round him the ice had thawed. On one side he had Clara Hertford in her pale-blue dress; and opposite was Lucilla in her pale-pink one. They and their neighbours were by now all enjoying themselves, following Rupert's lead. The rays of the setting sun, streaming through one of the tall windows, passed over his head, lighting up the satin legs and shoes of the portrait on the wall behind him; it was the portrait of a boy of seventeen, who had insisted on going to the wars two hundred and forty years earlier, and who had left his bones to whiten and his fine sword to rust on the field of Ramillies. But Rupert could not know how much luckier he himself was to live in modern times and to have come safely home.

Sir Matthew's interest in Louise, no less keen, had completely changed in quality.

"Really?" he said. "My word, young lady, you've linked up your destiny to a man of parts! He's shaping very well: hasn't quite settled down yet—and no wonder!—but we all have the greatest hopes of him." He glanced at Bernard. "Lavering's been handling a certain amount of *my* business lately, you know, so I expect we shall see more of each other. You must come down, both of you, and spend a week-end with *us* some time. Margaret, make a note of Mrs. Lavering's 'phone-number!"

Lady Risdon, satisfied now that this was merely a matter of business, something that it suited her husband to seem to be doing to please Bernard, smiled and nodded a gracious affirmation. She gave up bothering about Louise, and turned to the silent military man on her left.

"Well, Colonel, what do you think of Russia? Do you think they know enough about the atomic bomb to oppose our plans?"

Conversation was now general. The chicken was almost eaten. The fumes of the wines were in everybody's head; the sun's rays were level, striking the buttons on the satin chest of the young man who had been killed at Ramillies. Sir Matthew, having reduced Louise's status from that of Bernard's future wife to that of the wife of one of Bernard's *protégés*, and having finished, all too soon, his wing of chicken, turned to bestow what attention he had to spare between this and the next course upon his right-hand neighbour. Bernard was able to say to Louise:

"Well, do you forgive me?"

Louise looked inquiry.

Bernard explained: "For having separated you from Rupert for an hour."

"I think it was inexcusable," said Louise.

"Really?" Bernard, pretending to be concerned, raised himself to peer down the table. "He's enjoying himself, at any rate. Look at him! And so is everybody round him; look at the girls!"

"Oh, I wasn't thinking of Rupert," said Louise. "I was thinking of myself. I've no right to be here. You've put me in a thoroughly false position." And then, aware that she was losing the necessary lightness of touch under his scrutiny: "Every woman here is wondering why you've singled me out for this—this honour; and every one of them is hating *me*, not you."

She tried to laugh, but it was difficult. She was not looking at him— she could not—but she was very much aware of his appearance: his pale face, his high forehead with the wave of red-brown hair rising from it, his thin, disdainful mouth with that new tuft of hair that she disliked, growing under the lower lip; his raised, pointed eyebrows, his hollow cheeks, and, above all, his unwavering, relentless, exasperating scrutiny. With that stare he was taking some liberty with her, she did not quite know what; not the gross, ordinary liberty of the sybarite on her right: with that kind of liberty she knew well how to deal. This was something more penetrating, more destructive. And it was just because they were surrounded by people that she was helpless to protect herself against it; if they had been alone, she thought, he would not have dared. She added, not quite in control of her words:

"Perhaps that was what you wanted—was it?"

"No, Louise," said Bernard, and his voice, too, was not quite steady, "that wasn't what I wanted. But I've chosen the second-best—the only thing open to me. Oh, don't worry!" He spoke in the same low voice, scarcely moving his lips, so that she would have had difficulty in hearing him if her whole attention had not been claimed: "I merely mean, I had a fancy to have you beside me and no other woman on this occasion." He smiled. "It's more than a house-warming, to me, you know: it's a return from the grave. So won't you be indulgent, just for this once? After all, if I had had my own way, seven years ago, you'd now be as far away from me as possible, sitting at the other end of the table!"

Gradually again, as he spoke more lightly, her fears and her anger subsided. 'After all,' she thought, 'he has been dreadfully ill. And sick men have queer fancies. When I first knew him, he was young and strong, just as Rupert and I are now. I don't regret what I did to him then: it wasn't my fault if I couldn't fall in love with him in the first place, and it wasn't my fault if I fell in love with Rupert when he came along. But now, after what Bernard has been through, I must—I must be kind!' She tried hard to screw herself into an attitude of permanent kindness towards Bernard.

"You've been awfully good to Rupert and me," she was beginning, when her eye was caught, as it always was by any new thing, by a slight disturbance at one of the doors. Someone was whispering to one of the footmen, through the opening of the door, which he held ajar. The man, looking uncertain, closed the door softly and went towards the butler.

Louise's eyes followed him, and her voice trailed away, so that Bernard, noticing her preoccupation, turned an irritable glance in the same direction. The butler came softly towards Bernard and whispered in his ear.

"Oh, tell him to deal with it himself!" said Bernard. "He has his instructions. I said this evening I wouldn't be disturbed."

The butler conveyed the message back to the footman, and the footman conveyed it to the unseen messenger on the other side of the door. Bernard, scowling, did not speak. He crumbled a piece of bread in his fingers; and the ice which had been put before him melted slowly into a pool of custard.

But in a moment, as Louise had somehow guessed, it all happened again: the slight disturbance at the door, the colloquies, the even more tentative approach to Bernard. By now Louise was distracted with curiosity, besides being very sorry for the butler. This time the butler handed Bernard a note.

Bernard took it irritably and opened it. He frowned at it for a second. Then, "Give me a pencil," he said.

The pencil was brought.

Bernard scribbled a word, and returned the folded paper. The incident was over.

'Oh, how exasperating it is,' thought Louise, 'not to know what's going on!' Nobody but herself seemed to have noticed anything unusual, and of course it wasn't unusual for a man of Bernard's importance to be disturbed, even against his own instructions, by something terribly urgent. His private secretary, a pale, morose, very determined young man, fended off everything and everybody, even Rupert sometimes.

Everybody except Bernard and herself, it seemed, had begun smoking. That, too, seemed to isolate them from the others—to bring them together again. Bernard, relaxing a little, had turned in his chair and was looking at her now with a look she knew better how to encounter, because she was used to it—a look of open tenderness. This was something she rather enjoyed, this look of hopeless love: she admitted it. But ought he to allow himself to look at her like that, here among all these people?

'Pooh!' she thought. 'It doesn't matter. They're all too befogged with food, wine and smoke to see anything not meant for them.'

She turned to look for Rupert again, to see what stage of enjoyment he had reached by now. The back of his blond head was still towards her, and she noticed with amusement how Clara had seized the opportunity to lay her left hand on his left shoulder, so that really her arm was round his neck. Oh, of course, only so that she could lean across him to speak to whoever was on his other side; but still: 'I wouldn't have done that,' thought Louise, 'even at eighteen.'

Sir Matthew, rising ponderously—for he had managed to get quickly through the fruit tart as well as the ice, and even he was feeling the strain—gazed round the table. Gradually, as perception dawned, silence spread. He cleared his throat:

"Ladies and gentlemen."

The few voices that had run on into the hush suddenly ceased. He began again:

"Ladies and gentlemen."

There was another pause while he straightened himself and expanded his chest; his stomach protruded a little over the table, and he gazed downwards past it with well-practised timing to the end of his newly-lit cigar.

"At the present stage in this munificent banquet—for I can call it no less, though our own host with his usual—if I may so express myself—princely modesty calls it merely a house-warming party, a simple gathering of friends: at this stage in our evening's enjoyment, it falls to me as one of his closest associates in business—as one who has watched with admiration, and seconded to the best of his all-too-limited powers, his phenomenal rise to a position second to none in this country's galaxy of industrial pioneers: it falls to me, I say, to express on your behalf, not merely how grateful we are to him for the pleasure he has given and is giving us this evening"——there was a murmur of assent as Sir Matthew glanced down at the empty plates and drained glasses that could not be removed until he had finished speaking——"but strike an even more personal and intimate note, a note of deep regard, of affection."

His glance dropped again for a moment, together with the lowering of his voice; and when he lifted up his chin out of the cleft of his collar, he had his audience in the hollow of his hand.

"I want to say to my old friend Bernard—for he is my old friend, young though he is in years: he is a man with the wisdom and the mature judgment we usually—quite wrongly, often, I admit, my friends—associate with age." He smiled. "I want to tell my friend—our friend—Bernard Smith-Wilson, how truly, deeply, warmly we rejoice that he has been restored to us from that valley of the shadow through which we all must pass one day. We ask him to convey to his dear mother, our unseen gracious hostess, the heartfelt happiness we venture in our humble way to share with her, and to tell her that we join with her in our sincere prayer that he may be spared to her, and she to him, for many a long day."

He paused and cleared his throat.

Louise, conscious of a pricking in her eyes and a constriction of the larynx, was relieved to notice several of the other women equally embarrassed. In another moment she would have shed at least one tear, possibly two, and would have had to blow her nose. She was therefore much relieved to hear Sir Matthew's tone change.

"And now, my friends, I want to bring another name into this little address of congratulation." He turned, beaming, to Bernard. "This is all quite unarranged and unpremeditated; in fact, until a quarter of an hour ago I didn't know the young man was present. But I'm sure no one will be more delighted than our good host if I couple with his name that of his comrade and dearest friend: a man who also has come back to us from the valley of death, bringing with him the highest award his country can bestow on any hero—the Victoria Cross."

He raised his glass.

"I ask you, therefore, ladies and gentlemen, to rise with me and drink the healths of our host, Bernard Smith-Wilson, and our absent hostess, his mother, Mrs. Smith-Wilson; and also that of Rupert Lavering, V.C., and his young and lovely wife—may I still say 'bride'?—whom I have the honour to have beside me."

And so again Bernard and Louise were isolated, seated while everybody round them stood; and far from both of them, Rupert sat with his hand shading his eyes, and looked down at the table, red in the face, annoyed and miserable.

When the toast had been drunk, and the murmuring of names had subsided, Bernard, cool and pale, a little languid but infinitely courteous, rose and looked round the company.

"Ladies and gentlemen. On behalf of my mother—whom I hope some of you will meet presently—and myself, I thank you for your good wishes and kind thoughts towards me on my recovery. Especially I thank my old friend Sir Matthew Risdon for his eloquent expression of those feelings: so eloquent that I really would be feeling extremely sorry for myself if it weren't for the presence of this delightful company, in whose society no one could feel anything but happiness. I thank you all most warmly for being here." He paused. "I was particularly delighted to hear Sir Matthew couple with my name that of Rupert Lavering, and Mrs. Lavering, both of them among my oldest and dearest friends.—Rupert, old chap!" He held out a hand in Rupert's direction with an unexpectedly boyish gesture. "You must take over from here!"

But Rupert, still looking down with his elbow on the table and his hand shading his eyes, shook his head, and his whole body, with a shudder of agonised refusal.

"Very well, then," said Bernard, smiling faintly round at the company. "We mustn't try even a brave man beyond endurance. I've led your horse to the water, but he won't drink!"

"Give him brandy!" interposed somebody, and the tension was released in loud laughter, in which Rupert, at last raising his scarlet face from the shadow of his hand, joined.

"On behalf of Rupert, then"—Bernard made another gesture, and Rupert, sheepish and creased-looking through his embarrassment, consented to rise—"and his wife Louise"—another gesture, towards Louise: she rose, inclined her head, sat down quickly—"as well as of my mother and myself, I thank you for your good-fellowship; and I shall ask you without more ado to drink a toast to our honoured guests, Sir Matthew and Lady Risdon."

The toast was drunk; there was clapping and laughter, as coffee was served, and cigars and cigarettes again went round. The shadows were lengthening over the garden, and down in the valley a winding swathe of mist marked the river's course. The great chandeliers above the table were lighted; and before the windows could all be closed and the curtains drawn half a dozen moths had rushed headlong to their doom. The guests talked across the table, across one another. Louise felt lonely. Bernard was everybody's now; he was no longer talking to her. She wished she could run round the table to Rupert, and tell him how absurdly he had behaved, how absolutely true-to-typishly; and hear him indignantly deny that anyone could have done otherwise in such incredibly ghastly circumstances.

At last Bernard rose. She thought for a moment that he had forgotten her, he had been so deeply engrossed in his conversation with Lady Risdon, a conversation which appeared to be concerned with a builder's estimate for the erection of up-to-date pig-pens on one of Sir Matthew's farms. But just as she was wondering what was going to happen to her—whether she would be left over with Lady Risdon's military gentleman and would have to go and claim him—Bernard turned and offered her his arm.

"The bar's in the smoking-room," he said over his shoulder to Sir Matthew. "I don't allow the barbaric custom of 'ladies to the drawing-room'." He touched Louise's hand. "Come along, hero's wife! I must take you first to see my mother. Then you can do as you please."

Louise felt happy again.

"Enjoying yourself, darling?" she called out to Rupert as they approached the same doorway from opposite directions.

Rupert, with Clara clinging to his arm, made a grimace.

"Bernard, my lad," he said, "if I ever discover that you had any hand in that piece of flap-doodlery, your life really won't be worth an old champagne-cork!"

Bernard dropped Louise's arm for a moment to lay his hand on Rupert's shoulder.

"You'll have to see my mother for a minute, remember, before she goes to bed tonight—so keep sober! I'm taking Louise up first."

They parted.

5

"You don't mind, do you?" said Bernard as they passed the door of the large drawing-room, already full of women with a small admixture of men, and the door of the smoking-room, already full of men with a small admixture of women. Among the last, Louise, in spite of her preoccupation, did not fail to notice the tall sleek woman with the pearl ear-rings, and to think: 'That's just where one would expect to see her—perched up there on a high stool, surrounded by men who are more or less indifferent to her.'

They crossed the now dimly-lit, deserted hall; but they did not mount the wide staircase. Instead, Bernard led her, by the way she had forgotten, down a long corridor past the small drawing-room, and through a nail-studded door into the library.

A delicious sense of danger shot through her as he threw open the heavy door and stretched out a hand past her head to the light-switch. The curtains were drawn, as if this visit had been prearranged—or did they always draw the curtains before sundown? The room, dimly lighted at one end only, smelt heavily and pleasantly of leather bindings, old dry paper, and dust; the book-laden shelves stretched away from where she stood into the shadows at the farther end, the shadows they must traverse before they reached that distant door leading to the dark, narrow private staircase.

They had not gone many steps before Louise felt Bernard's hands on her shoulders. She turned: it was all inevitable. This was the moment when, she knew well, the wise woman gives way—lets the wave break over her; for the wave does break, and it is its strength that is broken while one waits and saves one's own strength. And anyway, she would never have condescended to resist: it would have been too absurdly undignified.

So she let Bernard draw her close to him, kiss her. When he released her, she waited for him to speak.

"I brought you here for that," he said. "That's what I came back to life for." He shot her an angry look. "I suppose you think I'm being melodramatic?"

Louise walked away from him and sat down in one of the deep leather chairs.

"I think you're mistaken," she said quietly. "I'm not what you think me. No woman ever is—and I'm a very ordinary woman."

Bernard came slowly towards her, and he too sat down. He wanted, now, to talk—to hear what she had to say—what effect he had had on her.

"To yourself you are," he said, "but not to me."

"You'd soon find me out if you lived with me."

This touched him too nearly. He struggled for self-control.

"Listen, Louise," he said at last. "I want you to give me that chance. I always wanted you to, and you would have, if I hadn't stupidly brought Rupert to your notice. Even then, I ought to have interfered. But you were in love with Rupert—any girl would be when first he swam into her orbit: he dazzles them all for a time, as you know. Still, I ought not to have let you marry him. That was a piece of stupid chivalry on my part, a relic of my moon-calf days."

Louise laughed. "Bernard, my dear!" she said. "You're not serious! What on earth do you think you could have done about it, even if you had tried? Rupert and I *wanted* to marry each other; we weren't children, even then, you know. I waited for him—how long was it?—seven mortal years."

"Yes—you waited for him," said Bernard earnestly. He was leaning forward now, pale with the effort of persuasion, clasping his hands together. "You waited for him, while the bullets were flying round him and the bombs bursting, and—well, how often did you see him in all those years? Once, wasn't it?—and for a few weeks only. Then he was off again, perhaps never to return. It wasn't Rupert you waited for—it was your hero."

"Well, and what was wrong with that?" said Louise sharply. "Didn't he deserve all I thought of him, and more? Hasn't he proved it? He'd be the last man in the world to agree, but—if any man ever deserved the name of 'hero', isn't it he?" She spoke the word scornfully, as Rupert would have wished; and she added, still more scornfully: "I'm not talking merely about his decoration: that was just one thing he did that they happened to see. Plenty of others have done the same and got nothing—so Rupert says. But everybody who knows Rupert knows that that wasn't the only thing he did—that that's how Rupert *is*, always." She trembled with annoyance at having been drawn into this fantastically unnecessary praise of Rupert.

"You mustn't be angry with me, Louise," said Bernard with unexpected mildness. "I know I've put myself into the invidious and dangerous position of seeming to attack Rupert. I assure you, I'm doing nothing of the kind. I'm interested in the truth, always. But I'm taking a big risk in assuming that you are, too."

"I haven't said I am," said Louise, unmollified.

"No—but you are. You'll listen. And you'll tell me the truth, even if you don't want to. You can't help it. That's why I—can't get over you at all." He checked himself, and then went on more firmly: "You've been married now for six months. Tell me truly: does Rupert seem to you a hero still?"

Louise stirred angrily in her big chair.

"Rupert hasn't altered," she said coldly. "He seems to me just what he always did."

"You're not answering my question," insisted Bernard. "You know I don't mean by 'hero' a man who has physical courage, or dash, or enterprise, or all those things that make up the popular ideal. I mean, does he still seem to you——?" But his own courage failed him.

Louise took up the challenge.

"You mean, am I still in love with him, don't you?" she said. "Do I still find him as glamorous and romantic as I did at eighteen? Have six months of watching him comb his hair every morning, and hearing him sing in his bath, and seeing to it that he changes his clothes, taken all the shine out of him for me? The answer is 'no', Bernard, I'm sorry. It makes no difference to me. At least——"

Bernard's eyes gleamed with hope as he heard in her voice the familiar note of uncomfortable reservation that marks the breaking in of the unwanted truth.

"At least," she said, "if the first raptures are over, something else is taking their place. I couldn't ever give up Rupert for you, Bernard. I find you more—well, more intriguing in some ways; but I find Rupert more lovable."

"Because you think he needs you," prompted Bernard unkindly.

"I suppose so," said Louise, pretending to take him seriously.

"You flatter yourself," said Bernard. "Rupert doesn't need you at all. Rupert will always have clusters of women longing to look after him, and any one of them will do, provided she's young and pretty and sufficiently devoted. Divorce him, and he'll marry again within a year. That's what I mean: I should never have let you marry him. But I thought it best to let you have your fling. Now it's over: you've had Rupert, and he's had you, and you know all there is to know about each other. It's only a question of time. Six months—a year: you'll come round to my views in the end." He laughed. "You'll have to, if you don't want to see Rupert in poverty. He's going to be extremely poor quite soon, I assure you, unless you let him go. I'll see to that!"

Louise thought that he was showing off: that this was his latest idea for impressing her. She smiled at his folly and obtuseness.

"And do you think," she said, "that I would be afraid to face poverty with Rupert?"

"No," Bernard retorted, "but Rupert would, even with you."

He saw that he had hurt her at last, and he drove home his point eagerly:

"Haven't you noticed? Rupert always had extravagant tastes. And being in the Army has helped, not hindered them. Men who don't know from day to day when they'll be blown to pieces don't bother about such out-worn philosophers' nonsense as self-discipline. Why should they? You're extravagant, too, Louise; but it's from choice. You could stop, if need be, and live hard. Rupert's rapidly getting to the stage when he couldn't. He's not afraid of violent death; but he'd be afraid of poverty. And the first thing he'd do if poverty threatened would be to turn on *you*." He laughed again. "I've heard him say several times lately, 'I can't afford it: I've got an extravagant wife to keep now.'"

"What an incredibly distorted mind you have!" said Louise calmly. "That's Rupert's idea of a joke. He's very ordinary, too, like me. That's why we get on so well together. Actually, he's rather proud of my extravagance."

"He won't find it a joke," said Bernard, "when he's faced with—bankruptcy."

There was a crude triumph in his tone that made Louise look at him with sharpened attention.

"You speak as if it were a fact," she said. "What do you mean? Is there something about Rupert's business affairs that I don't know? Something important, I mean: I'm not interested in the details."

Bernard got up and walked away to one of the bookshelves.

"Simply this," he said. "Rupert has been speculating rather wildly in the shares of a certain company whose name I won't mention. He's not the only one who thought they'd get their money back because of certain side assets owned by this company, and because of compensation to be paid when the firm's taken over by the Government. I hold—or held, rather—a few thousand pounds' worth myself. Rupert bought heavily, on the strength of some supposed inside information—"

Louise was about to interrupt, but he prevented her.

"And what's more, he's been advising all his clients to buy. Now, as you know, a man can perhaps weather a financial storm if only he can preserve his credit. Everybody likes Rupert; everybody knows he's a splendid soldier. But, my dear, in business men want something more than that. They want a cool head—sound financial judgment: the fox, not the lion, let us say. Rupert still has his name to make in the world of finance. People haven't yet acquired complete confidence in him. He looks rather boyish still—younger than he is. What credit he has is derived from—please forgive me for mentioning it—his association with me."

Louise said: "I heard this evening, for the first time, that you had lent him the money to start his business. I was appalled."

"Oh, that!" Bernard had taken out a book from the shelf and was turning over the pages. He waved a nonchalant hand. "That was nothing. I did that for old times' sake. It's not the money that matters so much—though, of course, Rupert would have to look a long way to find a backer if I dropped him. Still, he has charm and drive and personality; and he's a hero. He might succeed. But—he could never survive the loss of *credit*. I can't drive that home to you too often. If it gets known that he has given bad advice—and it will be known, tomorrow morning, no later, unless something intervenes—he'll be hounded right out of the financial market for good."

"I see," said Louise. "And just how much have *you* had to do with all this?"

Bernard shut the book with a snap and came towards her, smiling.

"Quite a lot," he said. "For instance, I've just instructed my secretary to tell my agents to sell my own last block of these shares tomorrow morning."

"And that will tip the balance against *us*?" said Louise.

"I think so: not but that I could cancel the order still if I liked—if *you* liked." He threw the heavy book aside, and came quickly to her. "Louise, don't let's play this stupid game any longer. I don't want Rupert to get hurt, any more than you do. I don't want to do it this way. Just give me your word, and I'll buy up the whole lot of them and no one will ever know. I'll be content to wait six months—a year, even—if you'll use the time to get rid of Rupert discreetly. You can, you know. Throw some girl in his path—Clara Hertford, for instance—and he'll be asking you to forgive him and release him in a couple of months. But remember, I said six months or a year—a year at the outside. I'm not patient any longer. I've been too near to extinction for that."

Louise held up her hand. However engrossing the immediate situation, she was always open to receive extraneous impressions.

"S—sh! What's that? I heard a noise."

She looked round, towards the darker part of the room, where two doors stood at right-angles: doors leading to the private staircase and to the corridor.

"Probably a mouse or a rat," said Bernard, impatient at the interruption. "There are plenty of them in this house, behind the panelling, since the Army have been in occupation." He bent over her and took one of her firm white hands, studying the tapering fingers and the rose-pink oval finger-nails. "No, I should never have let you marry Rupert," he said. "But I was uncertain of myself—of my health, even—and that paralysed my will, I suppose. I'm different now: I'm inflexible. Don't make me prove it, Louise. Why should you? You know I love you—and you love me: don't you?" He tried to draw her towards him. Eagerly he watched her face.

Louise withdrew her hand.

"My dear Bernard," she said with cruel distinctness, "if ever I had had the faintest tendency to do so, what you've said to me this evening would have cured me. Not that I ever had: I liked you and I was interested in you—I suppose chiefly because I knew you were in love with me, and that makes anyone interesting, to me at any rate. I still find you interesting, Bernard; but it's because I think you're crazy—living in a world of your own imagining, a feverish sort of world where *you* get all your own way with a snap of the fingers. I can only hope it's because you're not yet yourself. I try to remember your illness. I try to be sorry for you. But the truth is, I think this trouble has gone too far." She got up. "I told Rupert today, on the way here, I thought you were a pernicious influence in his life—and when I said it I believed I was exaggerating. But—well, I still hope I am. I can't believe you mean to do anything so—so completely mad and wicked!" Her breath came quickly.

Bernard stood quite still, regarding her from under bent brows. He looked sullen and chagrined, but no more to be discounted than a bull in a meadow.

"You'll see," he said, "tomorrow morning."

At one of the doors there was a rap. Bernard turned round sharply. The dark head and solemn face of Holmes, his secretary, appeared.

"I beg your pardon, sir," he said. "I've been looking for you. May I speak to you for just one moment?" His manner was determined: evidently he was sure of his ground.

Bernard thought for a moment. Then he said:

"I'll see you in my study in five minutes' time."

Holmes withdrew.

"So that was the note you got, while we were at dinner," said Louise. "Well, my dear, think carefully before you sell your shares. These things so often have the opposite effect to what one intends, you know."

She began to walk towards the door by which they had entered. Bernard intercepted her:

"If you change your mind, there's still time—until ten o'clock tomorrow."

"Never," said Louise. "Perhaps, if you do ruin Rupert, it will be all for the best. We can always emigrate to Kenya. I never did really like his being in the financial racket: one has to meet such terrible people!"

"Very well," said Bernard. "Go your way, Louise. You'll regret it. You'll come back to me one day. But the terms will be higher."

"Oh, don't be so ridiculous!" said Louise. She turned. "By the way, weren't you going to take me to pay my respects to your mother? And don't you think it might be as well if we had an alibi?"

"Of course." Bernard led the way back to the door that gave on to the private staircase. "This way."

The heavy door creaked on its iron hinges as he swung it outwards and held it for her to pass through.

6

The air in the smoking-room was by now very thick indeed.

Rupert sat at the bar on a high stool, next to one of the few women who had managed to remain and endure the atmosphere. She was the tall woman with the sleekly-dressed hair and the large pearl ear-rings who had attracted Louise's attention also. Rupert knew her only as 'Olivia'. He and Olivia had been sitting round on their stools facing one another for some time now. On Rupert's other side was the broad back of Sir Matthew Risdon, who had quickly tired of him and was now settling the affairs of Eastern Europe over his third glass of whisky.

"Are you staying the night?" Olivia was saying.

Rupert nodded. "Are you?"

"Oh yes," said Olivia. "They have to ask me. I'm a sort of relative—a poor relation." She was what is known as 'perfectly sober'; but her tongue was loosened by the Jamaica rum she obviously liked so much.

"You don't look very poor," said Rupert. He was not so 'perfectly sober' as Olivia, yet he was not drunk either. His face was rather red under his tan, and his laugh was rather louder and more frequent than was usual even with him. But he could see Olivia quite distinctly, and his speech was clear, though he found himself sometimes uttering things that he had meant to think only, as now.

"Bernard keeps me, more or less," explained Olivia. "He has a whole gaggle of us hanging on to his coat-tails. It's one of the penalties of success. He lets me pretend to be doing a little work for him sometimes."

"I didn't know old Bernard was so sentimental," said Rupert. "I know he helps people—he has helped me—but I thought he always exacted a *quid pro quo*."

"You're dead right there," said Olivia, pushing her glass across the shining black counter. "Another spot of rum and orange, please. Thank God for Jamaica! I think I must go and live there in my dotage.—But you see, Bernard knows he owes me something. There was a time—years ago—when I thought he was going to marry me." She laughed. "I had the best of reasons for this idea: he said so."

"Really?" said Rupert, interested. He could see Olivia's attractiveness, though she was too thin for his taste, and too bizarre; but he thought she might have done very well for Bernard. Still, he was rather shocked at her for speaking so frankly to a stranger.

"Then he dropped me," she went on, "just like that. Well, I mean to say, what was the use of my trying to do anything about it? I knew Bernard would set a higher value on those broken promises of his than any court of law would do. So I left it to him. And I was right. He pays me five hundred a year to do a little drawing for him; and he's grateful to me as well, because I've made it all so easy."

Rupert found himself uttering his thoughts again:

"You shouldn't talk like that to a stranger. Bernard would be annoyed."

"Oh, shucks!" said Olivia, incongruously. "Bernard's saddled with me for life, so long as I have his—letters."

"Where do you keep them?" said Rupert curiously, eyeing her tight corsage. She followed the direction of his look and laughed.

"Not in my bosom, you may be sure! Those days are over, my dear! There isn't room for even an airgraph inside the modern frock. And anyway, I wouldn't trust Bernard: he'd get me shanghai'd. No, no; they're all in my bank, with instructions what to do with them if I should disappear. There are times when I feel inclined to use them, all the same." Her mouth twitched and her eyes narrowed.

"I should stick to the income if I were you," said Rupert. "It takes a lot of capital to produce five hundred a year these days."

"I guess you're right, poppet," Olivia agreed. She pushed her glass across. "Just one more, and then I must be going. By the way, somebody told me the girl sitting on Bernard's right hand at dinner was your wife. Is that so?"

"Yes," said Rupert, remembering he hadn't seen Louise for some little while. Then it came back to him that he had seen her going off with Bernard, who had said something about taking her to see his mother. He was relieved. By the time Louise returned, he thought, he would have joined the others in the drawing-room: he had better not drink any more—though perhaps just a short one... He pushed his glass across, and took out another cigarette, after offering the case to Olivia.

"So that's why he didn't get her after all!" Olivia was saying, pleased and malicious. She studied Rupert with fresh interest. "Of course! I remember! I met you once with Bernard. You were in uniform. Bernard was a bit envious of you. You know, your wife was the reason why Bernard dropped me. I don't wonder: she's a very lovely girl."

"Yes, she is, isn't she?" said Rupert awkwardly. "Well, if you'll excuse me, I think I'd better be going to look for her." He slid down off his stool.

Olivia turned away indifferently.

"I should, if I were you," she said. "I saw her and Bernard going off together towards the less-inhabited part of the house just now. You don't make the mistake of trusting him, I hope?"

The blood sang in Rupert's ears, and a pulse beat hard in his neck where his collar pressed against it. But there was no point in replying; this hard, embittered, rather reckless young woman—for she wasn't as old as her sophistication tried to suggest—enjoyed hurting people, stamping on their feelings as others like to stamp on an insect in their path. It was her way of paying out the world for her own dissatisfaction.

'God!' thought Rupert, 'how awful to be married to someone like that!'

He stretched his legs, and pulled down his jacket at the back before starting on his journey. In prospect, it seemed something of an effort; and the room certainly was not very clear. Still, the effort must be made.

He took a step forward, and was aware of Holmes, Bernard's taciturn secretary, standing in the doorway. Rupert went towards him.

"Hullo, Holmes," he said with a nervous laugh. "How goes it? You're not working tonight, surely?"

Holmes gave him a brief glance, and, without smiling, at once looked away, craning his neck as if looking for somebody else. Rupert felt offended by this lack of response, which affected him as being extremely discourteous. Holmes was never forthcoming, never at all responsive even, when one met him in business dealings; but that was understandable—a 'keeping of one's place'—though to Rupert it often seemed absurdly overdone among business-men, this recognition of, and insistence upon, distinctions. Even in the Army there were in certain circumstances relaxations between officers and men which were nobody's business off the parade-ground. Bernard, however, was a stickler for discipline, and doubtless Holmes had to conform. But tonight, when all were relaxed and happy, what did this fellow want, with his long face and his uncompromising manner? Rupert, his resentment growing, turned to say something that would really put Holmes in his place; but Holmes had now passed him by, almost brushing him aside, and was standing beside Sir Matthew Risdon, deferentially trying to engage his attention.

"The trouble is," Sir Matthew was saying, "you get all these fellows, whose great-grandparents were serfs—used to being pushed around—"

He waved his left hand with the cigar between the fingers, almost catching Holmes in the chest.

"—used to tyranny of one form or another—the great landowner— the Church—"

He caught sight of Holmes.

"Eh?"

He realised that Holmes was trying to address him.

"You want me? What is it?"

He bent down his head, realising further that the message was confidential.

Holmes whispered something into his ear.

"What!" said Sir Matthew. "It can't be! I had the best information! Are you—is Mr. Smith-Wilson sure? Where is he? I'd better see him." He got off his stool and squared his huge shoulders purposefully.

"He's in his study, sir," said Holmes. "I'll show you the way, if you wish."

When they reached the door of the smoking-room, Rupert was still standing there. Holmes slipped past him; but he and Sir Matthew met squarely. Sir Matthew's face creased into folds of bullying anger.

"What do you mean, sir," he said, "lounging about here when your clients' business is going to the dogs? Damn it all, sir, I know you're a brave man, but that doesn't give you the right to play the fool with other people's money. Why didn't you keep out of business if you knew nothing about it, and stay in the Army?"

Rupert frowned. He saw the large, bullying face not far from his own; and he thought confusedly, 'What *is* this? Has everybody started a conspiracy to insult me?' But he controlled himself and said, stiff with fury:

"If you'll tell me what you're referring to, I may be able to deal with any complaint—though I should have thought this wasn't the time or the place—"

Sir Matthew made a guttural sound, something between a grunt and a growl.

"Good God, sir!" he said. "Do you think the world will stop revolving while you sit guzzling here and soaking up compliments?"

Rupert took a threatening step forward. By now the whole room was listening, and he could see the faces of men, curious, amused, scornful, delighted at the prospect of a row; and among these the face of Olivia, eager as a greyhound, with shining eyes, willing him to punch Sir Matthew on the nose. But already two or three of the company were at his side, ready to check him. He could feel a restraining hand on his sleeve. He shook off the intervener; but Sir Matthew had no wish to be knocked down.

"My good fellow," he said, in slightly less insufferable tones, "you must excuse me if I momentarily lost my temper. But a man doesn't care to hear in the middle of what's supposed to be a joyful evening that he's the poorer by several thousands of pounds. It was on your advice that I bought shares in the West United Coal Conversion Company only a couple of months ago. You said you had inside information. And now it seems that the bottom has dropped out of them—and everybody seems to have heard of it except you. You're my financial adviser—luckily only one of them. Where've you been for the past forty-eight hours not to have heard? If you can't see things like that coming, and warn your own clients in time, what's the good of you? In future, when I want to lose money, I'll do it my own way—not through an agent."

He pushed his way past everybody to the door, where Holmes awaited him, and then turned:

"I hope none of you other fellows are involved in this."

He bustled out, breathing heavily.

The other men, now that the row was over, retreated to their previous places, leaving Rupert standing alone. For him, the room swung round and round, and the soles of his feet tingled. He tried to steady and direct his racing thoughts. This blow had found him completely unprepared. He could not understand it. The previous day he had left his office with a light heart, knowing that all was well, looking forward to this banquet of Bernard's; not expecting anything out of it for himself except the pleasure of the company, the bright dresses, the lights, perhaps some music, some dancing, some flirtatious talk. Then, to his astonishment, his name had been coupled with Bernard's in Sir Matthew's speech;

everyone had gone out of their way to shower kindnesses on himself and on Louise. He had not asked for this; he had not wanted it. And now—what had happened? He knew he must pull himself together and get his thoughts clear.

He saw Olivia climbing down from her high stool. She came towards him, while the rest of the room, affecting to ignore him, went back to their drinks and their conversation. Olivia took his arm and led him outside.

"Listen," she said, as soon as they were a little way along the corridor, where the air was clear and the noise less, "you do know what's happened, don't you?"

Rupert passed a hand over his damp forehead.

"Wait a minute," he said. "The gatling's jammed at the moment, I'm afraid."

"But the Colonel isn't dead," she capped him. "Listen. I think I can help you—with a bit of real inside information this time. Don't say where you got it. It's probably too late to be of much use, anyhow; but it's best to know the truth, as a beginning. What you do with it is nobody's business." She led him farther from the company, towards the deserted hall. "This situation has been deliberately brought about by Bernard, for your undoing."

"Oh, nonsense!" said Rupert. "Bernard's my friend! If it hadn't been for him, I couldn't even have started again. Why should he want to ruin me?" He gave a feeble imitation of one of his laughs. "After all, it would be his own money he'd be losing!"

"What does the loss of a little money matter to Bernard," said Olivia, "in comparison with getting what he wants? Please yourself; don't believe me if you don't want to. But I'm telling you it was Bernard who held the bulk of those West United shares, through his various companies—Bernard who put about the idea that though they looked shaky they were sound. It was he who told you, wasn't it? And you believed him. Well, now it's Bernard who's been selling out, so fast that they're slumping, and nobody'll have them at a gift; and it's Bernard who has put about a panic rumour about their rottenness. You can be sure that what he's selling with one hand he's buying with the other—or should I say, another?—because Bernard has a hundred hands at least, like that monster, or giant, or whatever he was. Actually, the shares are fairly sound; his original tip was all right, though not as brilliant as he pretended. The people who hang on now will get their money back, and a little more."

They paced on farther. They were now in the hall, where the subdued light of the wall-brackets picked out warm circles on the tapestries and tipped the hanging helmets and swords, but left the corners unexplored, to be filled with the greater riches of the imagination. At the foot of the great staircase Olivia stopped and faced him.

"Now look here, my bonny hero," she said, touching him on the cheek with a long forefinger, "what *you* have to do is to clear out of here quickly—get back to town. You have a car. Can you drive it? Of course you can. Put your head in the wash-basin. I'll go along to the kitchen and get you some ice-cubes, and a Thermos of black coffee."

"What about my wife?" said Rupert, swaying. "My God, why didn't I listen to her when she was nagging at me on the way here?"

"Never mind her," said Olivia. "She can look after herself. I know that good old Anglo-Saxon jaw: nothing temperamental about *her* when it comes to the point."

"I wasn't thinking of that," said Rupert. "I mean, she'll wonder what the devil has become of me."

"Leave that to me," said Olivia. "I'll let fall a drop of the old henbane in her ear." Then, seeing his bewilderment, she laughed. "You can trust me, hero. All I meant was, I'll let her know where you've gone, and roughly why."

"All right," said Rupert, "I'll do it. But look here—hadn't I better tell her myself?"

"In that state?" Olivia was derisive. "She wouldn't let you go. Or she'd want to come with you. No; leave her here. I'll keep my eyes on her and see she locks her bedroom door tonight. You bet I will," she added venomously.

Rupert turned to go upstairs. With one foot on the bottom stair, he turned back.

"What the devil do you mean by that?"

"Oh, don't waste time!" said Olivia. "What's the only thing you've got that Bernard covets? Ask yourself that, and don't be a fool!"

Rupert began to show fight again.

"I'll wring his neck! Where is he? I've got to see him before I go!"

"Shucks!" said Olivia.

Rupert subsided. He thought for a moment, and when he spoke again his tone was firmer.

"Right! I'll take your advice. Go ahead. What do you tell me to do? I've a hunch it'll be all right. Anyway, I'll risk it."

"You can," said Olivia, "for the simple reason that my advantage happens to square with yours. This is what you have to do: drive straight up to town. Be at your desk first thing tomorrow morning—ten o'clock or whenever you're there. Whatever happens, whoever calls you up or comes to see you, keep an absolutely calm front on the matter—and advise them to hang on. If they insist on selling, buy up the shares yourself. Lay hold of every penny you can—mortgage your house—pawn your wife's jewellery—sell your grandmother's gold-plated dentures. You'll get it all back. When Bernard thinks you're sunk, he'll fix it so that the price rises again. It will, as soon as he stops 'bearing' it, anyway, because the proposition is basically sound; the company is scheduled for conversion, and their assets and their government compensation will cover the shareholders."

"I hope you're right," said Rupert. "I wonder how the devil you know."

"Ah!" said Olivia. "That's another story. Now get cracking, while I fetch the ice and coffee. Tell nobody you're going. If your wife barges in on you, lie to her—pretend you feel sick and need fresh air—anything. Be off—and for God's sake don't have an accident. I don't want your blood on my hands."

"Thanks a lot," said Rupert, restored. With renewed energy, he bounded up the stairs.

But when, twenty minutes later, Olivia knocked on the door of the bedroom which she knew to be allotted to the Laverings, there was no answer. She entered, carrying the coffee and the ice. Rupert, his collar and tie undone, lay stretched across a bed in a stertorous slumber.

Olivia shook him; but all that happened was that he rolled over with a muttered protest, and sank into deeper sleep. After a few minutes of contemplating him, Olivia put the Thermos-flask and the dish of ice-cubes on the bedside table and, shrugging her shoulders, went away, back to the smoking-room.

7

It was an hour later.

Olivia walked slowly and meditatively along the corridor, round an angle, down a few steps, up a flight of stairs, along another, narrower passage carpeted with cheaper material. She knew her way very well about this house, of which she had once expected to be the mistress.

She tapped at a door. Holmes opened it at once and let her in quickly.

"You shouldn't have come here," he said reproachfully, looking her up and down. "Someone might see you."

Olivia sat down and took a cigarette from her own bag.

"Where did you leave Bernard?" she said.

Holmes, busy with papers at a big roll-top desk, answered distraitly. His black hair was disarranged into oily curls, and on his face, pale and youthful and uncompromising, a line of sweat stood out along upper lip and forehead.

"In the study," he said sullenly, "with old Risdon. Risdon was in a flap because of the shares; and Smith-Wilson was in a vile mood for some other reason. It was like seeing a picador tormenting a fat white bull."

Olivia gave a hoarse crow, her nearest approach to a laugh.

"I wish I could have seen them!" she said. "Well, I've had some fun, too, in my way. I've given some good advice to the hero."

Holmes shot her a resentful glance from under his curls.

"God!" he said. "Men like him make me sick! If it weren't for them and their blasted heroism, which holds everything up, we could change the face of civilisation—so called—tomorrow. But when every Government has a bunch of mastiffs it can call into action with a snap of the fingers—"

"You wouldn't have liked it if the Nazis had got over here," remarked Olivia, "would you?"

"No, of course not." Holmes glanced at some papers, and after a moment's hesitation thrust them into a pocket of the attaché-case lying open on the floor beside him. "But it wasn't the Nazis that Lavering and his kind were fighting. They knew nothing about Nazism—or if they did, they didn't care, otherwise they'd have protested seven years sooner and on their own account, in the name of decency and common humanity; they wouldn't have waited until their Government whistled them up. But did they? Not a bit of it! They were well content to go on living their easy comfortable lives while other people were starved and tortured and beaten to death—"

"Oh, all right, all right!" Olivia waved aside his spate of words. "You don't like heroes; heroes wouldn't like you. So let's cut that part. All I came to tell you was, I've put the hero wise about Bernard's game. And if only the hero could have pulled himself together in time he might have done some neat footwork in Bernard's rear—I hope I don't mix my metaphors?"

Holmes went on with his sorting and packing. The attaché-case containing the papers and books was now full, and he opened a large suit-case and began emptying drawers.

"But he was too far gone," said Olivia, "in drink and general confusion of mind. I left him lying on his bed. I don't know what his wife will say when she finds him. By the way, what's become of her? I thought she was with Bernard." She frowned a little, though she spoke nonchalantly.

Holmes spared her a glance, understanding but unsympathetic.

"She was," he said, "after dinner—and just where you'd expect: in the library, with very few lights on. All the same," he added hastily, seeing her expression, "I don't think he'd been getting on very well with her. When I looked in, they were standing some distance apart, and she was staring at him in no very friendly manner."

"What did he say to you?" said Olivia sharply.

"Got rid of me, of course; told me to come to his study in five minutes. Then he escorted her up the private staircase to his mother's room."

"And did you go?"

"Of course. He seemed rather queer altogether—suffering from the effects of the dinner-party—but when I could get it across, I told him there had been a second message concerning West United—that Mr. Stammers had rung up in person to know if he really meant to sell, as that might mean a final crash. I need hardly tell you Smith-Wilson scarcely waited for me to get the words out of my mouth. He was as pale as death—quite white, though he had red rims round his eyes—and he said: 'How many more times have I got to repeat my instructions? I've told you to sell—sell the lot. And get out!'" Holmes paused to wipe his own forehead. "There you are: that's your capitalist—crushes whole families as you and I would squash a fly—"

"*You*," corrected Olivia. "I don't squash my flies; it spoils the paint. I use a fly-spray."

Holmes made an angry gesture.

"You're as bad as he is. You've no social conscience. All you care about is your own petty personal feelings."

Olivia got up, walked to the window, and drew aside the curtain. The moon was rising, guinea-gold among the group of tall firs. It was now nearly midnight, and evidently some of the guests had not yet left. A long, low black car came out from the house and crawled down the drive.

"Well, well!" said Olivia. "Somebody's forgotten his lights. Ah, he's remembered!" The red tail-light with its white window flashed on as the car rounded the curve leading to the first egress into the lane; but it was too late for her to have read the number, even if she had wished to. She watched, not thinking much about it, as the headlights lit up the branches of the trees overtopping the boundary wall and then disappeared.

Olivia dropped the curtain and turned.

"So you did—what?" she said.

Holmes grinned. "Exactly nothing, of course! Whenever he told me to 'bear' the shares, I've 'bulled' them, except for the ones I've bought and sold for myself and you. It's been good fun while it lasted. But of course it could only be done for these few days while he's been away. The cat'll be out of the bag tomorrow. And I'll be—quite a long way off." He regarded her curiously. "You don't mind facing the music?"

Olivia gave a crow. "Facing Bernard, you mean? I'll love it! I'll revel in it!" She rubbed her hands together. "I'll enjoy explaining to him, step by step, how he's been fooled. You must never come back; he'll kill you if you do. He may kill *me*," she added thoughtfully, as if the idea were not wholly displeasing to her.

"Pah!" exclaimed Holmes. "You're just a squaw-woman, for all your show of pride. You're just one of the decadent end-products of European literature, out of Homer by Froissart. You think you're Helen of Troy and Mary Queen of Scots rolled into one, don't you? Actually you're—a fit mate for Bernard Smith-Wilson, with his diseased lungs and his distorted brain—"

"Shut up!" said Olivia in a fury. "You clear out, before I change my mind! You and your half-baked theories are nothing to me. You just use them as an excuse for helping yourself to what doesn't belong to you, and what you can never get by any honest means."

"Honest!" sneered Holmes; but he turned away and began packing again.

Olivia quickly recovered her calm.

"So actually the hero has made a packet for himself and his clients," she said. "I didn't realise you'd been quite so thorough. I thought it was only this last lot you weren't going to sell. And the information you gave Bernard this evening, and he passed on to the Great White Hog, was totally incorrect?"

Holmes nodded: "Not just incorrect—the reverse of the truth."

Olivia laughed her queer, crowing laugh.

"Poor hero! How funny to think of his bewilderment when he wakes up tomorrow and finds how smart he's been! He'll think the other story was a bad dream. What a good thing he was too drunk to take my advice and rush up to town! A long sleep will do him much more good. It only goes to show what a waste of time it is to interfere in somebody else's affairs for their own good."

Holmes was not listening to her. He had now locked the suit-case and was running through the papers in his breastpocket: passport, tickets, wallet.

"I suppose you'll be joining your cell," said Olivia, "when you arrive. I hope it'll be the right kind of cell—or do I?" She rose. "I'll leave you now. How are you going to get those things to the garage without being seen?"

"There's plenty of time," said Holmes. "If anyone sees me—well, I'm supposed to be going back early tomorrow morning, anyway, and I'm just putting my luggage in the boot, to save time."

"So long as it's not Bernard you meet," remarked Olivia, going to the door.

"If I did," said Holmes sourly, "I'd know who had betrayed me. One should never trust a woman."

"You mean, a decadent end-product, don't you?" inquired Olivia from the doorway. "You're dead right there, my dear fanatic-turned-embezzler. No woman worth the name will ever throw herself over the ramparts for your sweet sake, that's sure. Oh, by the way, that reminds me: what are you doing about Barker? Letting her down, I suppose?"

Before Holmes could reply, she opened the door and was gone.

Holmes locked the door after her. Then he laid his overcoat and hat on the bed, and sat down beside them, looking dejected and defiant, with his wrist-watch on his knee in front of him, and his eyes fixed on its face.

8

It was a few minutes to midnight.

Louise, stifling a yawn, rose from the card-table before Mrs. Smith-Wilson had time to deal out another hand.

"I really must go now," she said. "I'm afraid my husband will be missing me."

"Nonsense!" said Mrs. Smith-Wilson; but Louise remained firm.

"The guests will have gone by now," she said, "except those who are staying the night." There was a certain wistfulness in her tone. Through the uncurtained long windows she could see the moon; and she wished, sentimentally, that she and Rupert were speeding down the lane and along the road over those thirty miles that separated them from their own comfortable home.

Why, she wondered, had she agreed to the suggestion that they should spend the night here? The answer was, of course, because Rupert seemed to wish it; and also she had thought that by now, and with him, she would be safe. How stupid, even for an idle moment, to have played with fire! 'Well,' she thought ruefully, 'I have already paid for my folly: two solid hours of cribbage with this old egoist!' People had come and gone throughout the evening; but she, Louise, had not been allowed to escape. She felt bitter to think that she, in her youth and beauty, and in her loveliest evening dress, had had to sit here all evening like a hypnotised schoolgirl and amuse Bernard's mother. Where, by the way, was Bernard? He ought, in common decency, to have released her long ago. Perhaps this was his idea of revenge.

"Well, if you must go," said Mrs. Smith-Wilson grudgingly. "You do look rather tired, I must say." Her tone was critical, not sympathetic.

"And your dress is badly crushed. I always think white's a mistake, especially in such a flimsy material. When I was a girl—"

Louise's thoughts, hostile and exacerbated, were concurrent with her polite words.

"Can I do anything for you? Shall I call someone?"

"No, I can ring," snapped Mrs. Smith-Wilson.

Louise was turning away with a murmured 'Good night' when Mrs. Smith-Wilson recalled her.

"Or yes, you can call that stupid woman, Mabel Hertford. Where has she gone *now*?" She peered round the room as if Mabel might be seen peeping out from behind a piece of furniture—as if hide-and-seek were one of her pixy little ways after sundown.

"I should *think*," said Louise, with careful self-control, "she *may* have gone to bed. It's about two hours since she went away. Or perhaps she thought she'd like to join Clara and Lucilla and see something of the party."

"Probably reading in her room." Mrs. Smith-Wilson nodded. "You might give her a knock. Oh no, you don't know her door." She implied that this was rather tiresome of Louise, but only to be expected in a woman who wore white tulle. "But you *can* give a tap at Bernard's study door as you go down the inner staircase. I can see his light." The study window projected, and Louise could see it too. "Poor boy! He works too hard; and with all these people here, it's so disturbing."

Louise smiled, in a final effort to be gone; and at last she slipped away, as Mrs. Smith-Wilson turned to stare at the study window.

'Call Bernard!' thought Louise as she closed the door. 'I'll see him, and you, in hell first!'

Cautiously she began to descend the private staircase.

9

"Well, dears," said Mrs. Hertford, as she mounted the wide main staircase with her two daughters, "we mustn't worry. We must wait to hear what Bernard has to say about it tomorrow. I'm sure he would never give us wrong advice."

"Oh, Mother!" said Clara pettishly. "Bernard never gives a thought to us in these business matters. Or if ever he did, he has forgotten about us now. Men do, you know."

"I know, darling," said Mrs. Hertford gently. "I *was* married once, though it lasted such a short time. Bernard is rather thoughtless and self-centred, I'm afraid; but we must remember his illness. His mother says it has set him apart."

Clara remained unmollified.

"I'm sick of Bernard's illness," she said. "It's an excuse for every sort of selfishness. For instance, this evening he asks us all here to a party; and as soon as dinner's over he goes away and never appears again. He and his mother are a pair: they both do exactly as they like, whatever name they may choose to call it."

They had reached the door of the girls' bedroom, and Mrs. Hertford came in with them. The girls were both dejected: Clara, who had the more vigorous character, was angry as well, and Lucilla, usually so effervescent, was subdued.

"And I don't think you're paying sufficient attention to this rumour that's going round, Mother," went on Clara, seating herself before the dressing-table mirror and, after a look of distaste, beginning to undo her hair. "I assure you, everybody was very excited; and Sir Matthew was furious. There was a dreadful scene between him and Rupert in the smoking-room, and no one has seen Rupert since."

"Dear me!" said Mrs. Hertford. "Has Rupert disappeared too? How strange!"

Lucilla chimed in: "He was quite tipsy, you know. We could hear them brawling from where we were sitting in the drawing-room, although someone went at once and shut the door."

Clara turned to her with a gesture of disapproval.

"What's the use of saying that, Lucilla? Mother never could believe any harm of Rupert. It was Rupert who advised you to buy those shares, wasn't it, Mother? You merely gathered that he was speaking with Bernard behind him. You didn't know for certain."

"Oh yes I did!" said Mrs. Hertford, two pink spots springing up on her cheeks. "I know more about all this than you think. You were only children when I first met the Smith-Wilsons, and Rupert as well—for Rupert was Bernard's best friend. And what did Bernard do? When Rupert joined the Army, Bernard stole his idea—his invention—and used it. Oh, I know Bernard's mother says Bernard bought it! That means he gave Rupert a small sum for an idea which he knew was worth thousands. That's what Bernard's like. He wasn't ill *then*." Mrs. Smith-Wilson would have been surprised if she had seen the fire flashing in Mabel's blue eyes.

"Well, Mother," said Clara angrily, "I think you might have told me all this before. I thought you wanted me to marry Bernard." She tossed her head, and began brushing her long hair. "You never hinted at anything against him before."

"No," said Mrs. Hertford, "I know I didn't. I wanted to do the best I could for you; and if you liked Bernard, and he liked you—well, we can't have perfection. If we waited for that, we'd never get married at all."

"Well," snapped Clara, still more angrily, "you needn't have worried, because Bernard is obviously still infatuated with Louise. You never would think that she was married to Rupert only six months ago. I think it's disgraceful—going off with him after dinner like that!"

Mrs. Hertford smiled.

"He didn't spend long with her," she said. "He brought her up to see his mother; and when I left them, they were sitting down to a long session of cribbage. I don't think she can have had a very exciting evening, either. I'm afraid I was rather naughty. Mrs. Smith-Wilson had asked me to get her a book, so I took the opportunity to go off to my room instead and have a little read." She glanced at the small gold watch on her wrist.

"What's happened to your scarf, Mother?" said Clara suddenly. "I thought you were wearing the beige one before dinner."

Mrs. Hertford's hand went to her throat.

"Oh dear me!" she said guiltily. "I must have dropped it somewhere. Or no—I suppose I took it off when I went to my room. Well, good night, darlings. I really must look in on Mrs. Smith-Wilson before I go to bed. She'll never forgive me if I don't."

"I should have thought that was Barker's job," said Clara. But Mrs. Hertford took no notice. She kissed them both effusively:

"Sleep well, dears. And don't worry too much about the shares. I'm sure it will all come right. Rupert would never let us down, no matter what Bernard might do. But," she reiterated, "I'm sure it will be all right."

She hurried away to her room.

When, a little while later, she put her head round the door of Mrs. Smith-Wilson's sitting-room and saw her still sitting there with the cards spread out before her in a game of patience, Mrs. Hertford felt a twinge of compunction. Mrs. Smith-Wilson looked up and saw her.

"Oh, there you are!" she said crossly. "Where *have* you been all evening—leaving me alone to receive all those people, and with that silly young Louise Lavering on my hands! And Bernard—where *is* he? The light's still on in his study, and you know he's not allowed to sit up late at night! He should have been in bed at nine. And has he had his milk and his medicine, I wonder? I suppose this tiresome party has put every sensible idea out of everybody's head."

"I don't know about his medicine," said Mabel, "but he's had his milk. I got him that myself. I ran down to the kitchen for it, as the staff was so busy and I thought they'd forget, as you say."

"That was good of you, Mabel," said Mrs. Smith-Wilson, mollified as only a reference to Bernard could mollify her, though she took care to preserve her moral ascendancy by a slightly grudging infusion in her thanks: "But I wish he'd go to bed. Could you tap on his door as you go by? I should like to see him. I didn't think he was looking well when he came here with Louise; noise and talk and smoke don't agree with him. He isn't strong enough."

"I think," said Mabel tentatively, "he has been rather worried and excited about some dealings of his on the share-market: I must say I didn't think he looked at all himself when I saw him. I gather there was some question of a sudden fall in those shares he was so interested in a short while ago; perhaps he's worrying about that. I'm sure I hope so—I mean, I hope he's dealing with the matter"—she laughed diffidently—"for all our sakes, because I sank a good deal of our own little capital in these shares, on Bernard's, or rather Rupert's, advice."

"Make your mind easy, Mabel," said Mrs. Smith-Wilson, waving a magnanimous hand. "You may trust Bernard—to the death. All will be well."

"I know it," said Mabel, with shining eyes.

Mrs. Smith-Wilson looked at her in sharp surprise. She was well aware that there was a resistance in Mabel to praise of Bernard; and she never ceased, therefore, to drive home her praise. But now, here was Mabel agreeing—going all the way with her—running ahead, waving a flag, so to speak! She wondered if Mabel was thinking, as earlier this evening, not of Bernard but of Rupert.

"Now Rupert, of course," said Mrs. Smith-Wilson testingly, "would be utterly useless in business if it weren't for Bernard. Rupert is so unreliable!"

"Rupert is so young!" said Mabel deprecatingly.

"He's only a year or two younger than Bernard!" snapped Mrs. Smith-Wilson.

"Young in spirit, I mean," insisted Mabel gently. "And that's remarkable after all he must have gone through."

Mrs. Smith-Wilson opened her mouth to speak of Bernard's illness, but Mrs. Hertford managed to stop her.

"Of course," she said, "I know Rupert relies on Bernard in business matters." She returned to the point: "It was on Bernard's advice that Rupert bought those shares."

"Then it will be all right," said Mrs. Smith-Wilson, closing the subject, "and you have nothing to worry about."

"Yes, that's what I told the girls." She got up. "Shall I ring for Barker, or is it too late?"

"Of course it's not too late! That's her job. And she'll have to rub my neck tonight, otherwise I shan't sleep at all. Sitting all those hours playing cards has brought on my fibrositis again."

"Shall I do it for you?" said Mabel kindly. "As I'm up, I might as well."

Mrs. Smith-Wilson put on the grudging look that presaged acceptance.

"If you'll just go and undo your collar——" said Mabel.

Mrs. Smith-Wilson rose stiffly, leaning on her cane.

Mabel sat down in the window-seat and looked out over the beautiful scene that was in such great contrast to the agitation in her own soul. She watched the lighted window of Bernard's study, a few feet below, the only light to be seen from here in the darkened mansion; and once she saw Bernard's shadow pass quickly across the curtains. He seemed to be waving an arm above his head.

Mrs. Smith-Wilson called out from her bedroom:

"Mabel!"

Mrs. Hertford went to her at once.

"I can't find my liniment," said Mrs. Smith-Wilson.

"You'll have to ring for Barker after all."

"Wait!" said Mabel. "Where is it usually kept?"

"On my dressing-table, of course!" snapped Mrs. Smith-Wilson. "It was there this morning."

"Have you looked in the medicine-chest?"

"No."

"Probably it's there. I'll look. What sort of a bottle is it? Oh yes, I remember." She went into the bathroom, which opened out of Mrs. Smith-Wilson's bedroom, and began searching in the small cabinet that hung on the wall. A moment or two later she came out, carrying a blue hexagonal bottle with a red label. "This is it, isn't it?"

Mrs. Smith-Wilson snatched it from her, drew out the cork, and sniffed. "Of course it is! Where did you find it?" she said accusingly.

"In the medicine-chest, dear," said Mabel mildly. "It was right at the back. It had fallen down behind the other bottles."

"Well!" Mrs. Smith-Wilson glanced round angrily, looking for a culprit or a scape-goat. "What can Barker have been dreaming of? She knows I need it every night—in fact, I can't think why she hasn't been in tonight to see to it. These women!—utterly thoughtless of everybody's comfort but their own!" She looked at the bottle more closely, and turned it upside down against the palm of her hand. "And look: it's empty! Clumsy fool! She must have knocked it over, and that's why she hid it in there." She handed the bottle back. "Well, I shall have to put up with the pain tonight—no sleep for hours and hours! But that's nothing new." She yawned. "Just run down, will you, and tap at Bernard's door? A quarter to one! Shares or no shares, *he* must have some sleep! What can he do about them tonight, in any case?"

Mabel put back the bottle in the medicine-chest and went away.

In a few moments she returned, and tapped at the bedroom door.

"Is that you, Bernard?" called out Mrs. Smith-Wilson.

"It's only me," confessed Mabel. She could never bring herself to say 'I', because this sounded too egoistical, she thought. "The study light is out now: I think Bernard must have gone to sleep."

"Did you look?"

"No: the study door was locked. But he has a divan in there, hasn't he? I didn't like to make any more noise, in case I wakened him."

"Very well," said Mrs. Smith-Wilson grudgingly. "But it's funny he didn't come to say good night to me."

"Shall I go and knock louder?" said Mrs. Hertford.

"No. You'd better not. Perhaps I'll go myself." She came out of the bedroom. "Poor boy! I expect he has fallen fast asleep—worn out with bothering about other people's interests. Well, good night." Her tone implied that Mabel could go now, and that she no longer wished to be disturbed, but it was all rather unsatisfactory, and Mabel could have done better if she had tried.

Mrs. Hertford went away, through the large sitting-room with its many tables and chairs, its many pictures and miniatures, and its portrait of Queen Elizabeth over the doorway.

She did not go again down the private staircase. Instead she turned into the corridor and went straight to her own room. The house was quiet. She undressed quietly, without switching on the light, so that she could enjoy the brilliant moonlight through the uncurtained windows.

Once she thought she heard a slight sound outside on the landing: a footstep, a floorboard creaking, something scraping the wall; and for a moment her heart wavered. She wondered if she ought to open her door and look out. But then, she thought, it might be one of the guests groping his way to the lavatory: after all that drink… 'Clara is right,' she thought; 'men are self-indulgent and crude.' And yet—were the abstemious ones so very much better? Rupert, in his sociability, was apt to drink too much, whereas Bernard, in everything he did, was calculating and controlled. But who could prefer Bernard to Rupert, except Bernard's mother?

Mabel's room faced the rear of the house, the courtyards and stables. Below her were the garages. Earlier in the evening the noise had been considerable when the guests began to leave, but one did not particularly notice. Now, in this stillness, every sound carried. She heard one of the garage doors being carefully rolled back, and presently the dry whirring sound of a car battery.

She went to the window. A small car was reversing out of the garage into the yard.

She waited, expecting to see the driver get out and close the sliding door; but he did not do so. He drove straight away, through the pillared entrance, and was gone.

Mabel looked at her watch: ten minutes past one. Again she wondered if she ought to rouse Bernard and let him know… But it was none of her business. Thoroughly sleepy now, she climbed on to her bed, and in a few minutes was fast asleep.

10

T he guests slept on late next morning. Two of them, however, were up and about quite early. They met on the terrace, in the pure morning sunshine; but neither of them felt gladdened at the sight of the other.

"Good morning," said Olivia, as Louise approached her. Olivia was already smoking; she looked smart and alert in a black suit with a white frill forcing its way out between the lapels. Louise looked tired—or was it merely worried? 'She has something to worry about,' thought Olivia.

"Good morning," said Louise, admiring the cut of Olivia's suit, but wishing that Olivia were not inside it.

"Lovely, isn't it?" said Olivia, leaning on the balustrade and looking out over the sunny scene. "A pity to leave it and go back to pavements and petrol fumes."

"Are you leaving this morning?" said Louise, without interest. "So am I, as soon as I've had breakfast and said goodbye to my hosts."

'Ah!' thought Olivia. 'She's taking him away before anyone has time to remember and get talking.' She said aloud:

"They're bringing my breakfast out on to the terrace. We can ask them to lay the table for another two—that is, unless your husband's having his in bed." This was perhaps not very kind; but she had added it out of curiosity rather than malice. She could not help wondering what this proud young woman had felt when she had come upon the hero sprawling across the bed.

Louise said quietly:

"My husband isn't here. He left late last night." She gave a somewhat defensive laugh. "Unfortunately he has taken the car, and that means, for me, a very awkward cross-country journey. In fact, I think I shall go up to town by train and meet him at the office. It's quicker than going home direct from here."

"He's left?" Olivia's incredulity was lively, but Louise did not notice it; or if she did, she took it for granted.

"He seems to have been involved in a rather unpleasant scene last night," Louise went on, grasping the nettle in her customary way. "I gather there was some kind of a slump in the stock market, and Rupert is being held responsible for not having foreseen it. Probably he felt he must be there early this morning."

"How very odd!" said Olivia, beginning to like Louise in spite of prejudice, as most people quite soon did.

A table had now been brought out and set in the dappled sunshine under a willow-tree that had grown up from below to a height over-topping the terrace. The table was laid for two. The two women moved towards it.

"Oh no, I don't think so," said Louise. "Rupert usually acts on impulse, and he likes to do things at odd times. But naturally I'm rather worried about it all. I wasn't there, you see. I was with Mrs. Smith-Wilson, playing cribbage." She laughed ruefully. "I pretended I couldn't play, but that didn't help: she taught me!"

Olivia had made up her mind.

"I didn't mean 'odd' for that reason," she said. "I meant, I had thought he was in no condition to leave."

Louise bit her lip. "I gather you were there. Yes, I know Rupert was rather—elated—yesterday evening. But I don't think it was so serious as all that. He's awfully high-spirited; and "—her own temper rose as she thought of what Rupert had been doing in the past seven years—"isn't it rather natural in men who had to go without so much for so long?"

They reached the table and sat down opposite each other before the grape-fruit with a cherry in the middle; Olivia looked across at

Louise and began positively to admire her and to feel protective. Louise in her indignation was even better-looking than in repose: the minimum that nature's gift had ensured to her was still and always beauty.

"I entirely agree with you," said Olivia. She ate the cherry while the footman served the coffee; and after he had withdrawn, she began; "I think your husband is entitled to take a noggin of rum for breakfast at the expense of the State for a whole year, if he wants to. But what I'm telling you is that, whether you like it or not, you must grasp that he was completely knocked out last night, and in no fit condition to travel—certainly not to drive a car. I'm sorry if I alarm you—but, you see, it was I who urged him to go, in his own interests; I who tried to help him to get sober; and I who took some black coffee to your room and found him, to my disappointment, sprawling across the bed, fast asleep—or apparently so."

"So that explains it!" said Louise. "When I went to bed soon after twelve I found Rupert's dress clothes lying about, and on the bedside table an empty Thermos and a glass dish with ice-cubes almost melted. There was a note saying he had decided to dash up to town: he had to be at the office first thing tomorrow. He said: 'Don't worry about me, and don't believe anything you hear'."

"Oh!" said Olivia. "I see. Then the black coffee cured him." But to herself she thought: 'He was shamming. He did that to get rid of me. He thought I might want something for my trouble.' But though she felt momentarily humiliated, she did not feel enraged. 'My behaviour was open to misinterpretation,' she thought. 'One must be fair. How could he possibly guess the truth? And besides, the man's a hero, and he must have to put on speed sometimes to escape the women. Perhaps he wants to be faithful to Louise.' She smiled ruefully. 'One sometimes forgets that the simple explanation may be correct.' To Louise she said:

"Then you haven't much to worry about. He can't have been nearly as helpless as I thought. I must say, at the time I wondered: he didn't seem to me to have taken enough to lay him out like that."

"All the same, I shall feel happier when I've rung him up and made sure he's arrived," said Louise.

They went on with their breakfast, and from then on they talked of other things. It struck Olivia as strange that Louise did not ask her anything further about the scene in the smoking-room. She let fall a remark about Sir Matthew Risdon; but something about Louise's manner made it clear that she did not wish to hear. She began a resolute conversation about books and plays; and Olivia, with an inward shrug, let her have her way.

11

An hour later, while Louise was absorbed in trying to get through
to Rupert's office, from which there still seemed to be no reply,
and while she considered Olivia's offer to drive her up to town without
waiting for the call, she became aware of agitated sounds in the direction
of the library.

She never could remember afterwards which sounds first reached
her consciousness: was it the shuffling of feet, the loud knocking, the
distant scream? But she did remember for ever the chill of terror that
struck through her, the terror of the unfamiliar, the unprecedented,
akin to that which one feels in the middle of the night when a shadow
moves, or a strange object touches one's hand or one's hair. Now, it
was the broad light of a sunny July morning; a moment before, through
the confused noises that were coming over the telephone, she had
been aware of country sounds, a lark singing. And then, every other
awareness was banished, and she knew that she was about to face some
undreamt-of fear.

The library door on the opposite side of the hall to where she was
standing was flung open, and one of the footmen, white as wax, followed
by a wailing maid, strode over to Louise and took the telephone-receiver
roughly out of her hand, though training made him murmur "Excuse
me, madam," through white lips as he did so.

"Give me the doctor quickly, for God's sake!" said the man, and
Louise, to her horror, heard him say:

"Is that Dr. Fitzbrown? Please, doctor, come quickly! We've just
found Mr. Smith-Wilson in his study—and I think he's dead."

He replaced the receiver, but Louise took it up immediately.

"Exchange! Exchange! Can you get me my London call, please? It's urgent—desperately!"

"Trying to connect you," said the unamiable voice; and in a moment Louise heard, with a relief that brought tears to her eyes, the always cheerful voice of Rupert.

"Darling, is it you?" she said. "Oh, thank God! I've been trying to get you for ages!"

"Darling!" said Rupert. "Why, good heavens, it's only half-past nine! I've walked in this very minute; jolly good work, I think! What's the matter? Didn't you get my note? I wasn't really boned, you know. Don't be annoyed. I had to come. I'll explain all when I see you."

She interrupted his voice, though to her it was more musical and sweeter than the sound of Apollo's lyre, to say:

"Darling, darling, come back here quickly! It's Bernard—they've found him in his study, and they think he's dead. I have a terrible feeling that you ought to be here."

"I'll come at once," said Rupert with the precision of an officer ordered to attack. "Expect me in two hours. And hold your thumb!"

The receiver clicked down, just as the pips announced the end of the three-minute call.

Louise sat down on the nearest seat, a high-backed settle running along the wall; and then, from the terrace, she saw Olivia strolling in. She was humming to herself.

"Olivia!" she called out. She did not know her other name, or, if ever she had known it, she had forgotten it now. Briefly and sharply, she broke the news.

Olivia gripped her by the forearms.

"Where is he?"

"In the study, I think."

"I must go there."

But when Olivia reached the door at the bottom of the private staircase she found the footman on guard.

"You mustn't go up there, miss," he said, opposing his bulk to her passage, "not until the doctor has been. He's—not fit for you or anyone else to see him."

"What has happened?" said Olivia. She showed no fear and no excitement. "Is he dead?"

The man nodded: "He's dead all right, miss."

"But he was perfectly well last night. What did he die of?"

"A fit, miss, I think. Though"—he shook his head with gloomy enjoyment of horror—"it's the queerest fit I've ever seen. His face is a bluish-grey—and he must have rolled about on the ground before he—"

He was working up to further details when suddenly, to his surprise, Olivia turned and walked away, without a word and without giving him time to finish his sentence. At the door leading into the hall she turned back again; and he was astonished at the expression of vindictive hatred on her face.

"Did you call the police," she said, "or only the doctor?"

"Only the doctor, miss," he said, gaping. "I didn't think there was any need—"

But Olivia was gone.

She crossed the hall to where Louise was sitting with closed eyes, leaning her head back against the settle, and, without a word to her, picked up the receiver.

"Give me the police," she said. "Hullo! Yes. Send somebody at once to Fairfield House. Mr. Smith-Wilson has been found dead. Yes; Mr. Bernard Smith-Wilson. Yes, I said 'dead'. In his study. This morning. In my opinion there has been foul play. You understand? You must give your chief, whoever he is, this message immediately. Have you got that? Right. Well then, can you take a second message? I want you to get in touch with the authorities and have the day route from Newhaven to Dieppe watched. If you can get them in time to have the train searched, so much the better. I want you to tell them to watch for a young man travelling with a forged passport. No, I don't know the false name, but I know his real name and his description. He's of medium height, with black, curly hair and pale face, clean-shaven, probably wearing some slight disguise. He's carrying various illegal documents and stolen money; but that's a trifle. He's Mr. Bernard Smith-Wilson's ex-secretary, and whatever he calls himself now, his real name is Ralph Holmes. I suggest to the police that they get him back here for questioning in connection with the death of Mr. Smith-Wilson."

She listened attentively while the message was read back to her, and said in business-like tones:

"Quite correct. Now step on it, will you?"

She replaced the receiver. After a glance at Louise, who did not open her eyes, she went slowly up the broad stairway to her room.

When she had arrived there, she took off her smart black coat and skirt and the smart white frill that protruded through the lapels, and put on a silk wrap. Then, laying her tall, slender body on the bed, she gave way to a fit of prolonged shivering.

12

Superintendent Mallett sat in Bernard's study, at his desk, the drawers of which he had been examining thoroughly. Below, a group of dejected people waited in the library until they should be summoned to an interview.

No one knew in what order they would be called. No one, except the murderer if he was there, knew exactly what had happened. All realised that this meant delay, an interruption of their pursuits, so important to themselves, a great deal of wasted time and fuss and bother over something that was past and done with.

Rupert had arrived, as he had promised, an hour or so before luncheon. At first his exuberance had cheered them all; but now, after another two hours' waiting, he also had grown impatient and nervy. He paced about the library, pulling out books from the shelves and putting them back after a glance, coming back to Louise for a short conversation, smoking too much, occasionally darting out to the smoking-room to get a drink. This, too, was the only thing that made waiting tolerable for Sir Matthew Risdon; and there was an awkward moment when he and Rupert met. But after a muttered greeting, the ice was broken and they fell into conversation.

"Very sorry, old boy," said Sir Matthew, "if I lost my temper last night. But it was a bit of a shock, you know."

"Quite all right," said Rupert heartily. He added more cautiously, not wanting to make Sir Matthew feel too much of a fool all at once: "I suppose you know there was no truth in the rumour?"

Sir Matthew gulped and nodded.

"Extraordinary!" he said; and leaning closer to Rupert out of the deep chair into which he had slumped, glass in hand, he whispered:

"You know Smith-Wilson himself was quite deceived? I saw him after I left you, and I assure you he was quite definite about it. He said he was selling all he had before the bottom fell right out of the market."

"Yes, I know," said Rupert thoughtfully. "I think he must have been deceived by Holmes, or at any rate misled. We shall see when they get hold of Holmes. But what I find so amazing," he went on, half to himself, "is why he didn't tell *me*. Why didn't he send for me first, when he got the first intimation? He knew I had only passed on his advice to you others. I hate to say it—he was my greatest friend, or so I thought—but unless there's some explanation I haven't thought of, it looks as if he'd forgotten all about me and my interests. I can't and won't think it was deliberate. What possible motive could he have had for ruining me?"

"Seems strange, certainly," said Sir Matthew, watching him interestedly with his small, cunning eyes.

"After all," expostulated Rupert as if to an unseen accuser, "he lent me the money to start again, when I was demobilised. I hadn't a bean, you know. I had run through all my money before the war, trying to perfect my invention among other things; and that, too, I had to drop in the middle. Bernard picked it up and put it into production; and it was on the strength of my share in it, now it's beginning to bear fruit, that I borrowed the money: a sort of advance on royalties, you know."

"Oh!" said Sir Matthew more cordially. "So you've got a contract? Then that's all right! You should soon be drawing a comfortable five thousand a year—though the Government will get most of it!"

"Good lord, no!" said Rupert. "There was no need of any contract between Bernard and me. We were *friends*. We'd worked together for four years. I couldn't have suggested such a thing, especially when he had come to my rescue. What could I have done out there—in Greece—Crete—Egypt—Italy?"

Sir Matthew put down his glass sharply on the arm of his chair. Such folly annoyed him.

"So you left the country without any legal agreement? Well, I don't wish to speak ill of the dead; but for my own part I'll say that I haven't got a friend in the world I'd trust so far. Rescue you, indeed! You mean he bought the thing from you outright at a cut price, used it while you were fighting for your country—and rescuing *him*—and didn't even give you a royalty agreement!"

"There was no need," persisted Rupert stubbornly. "He was my friend." But there was now a trace of uneasiness in his tone.

"Well, that's as may be," said Sir Matthew. "Have it your own way. No one can prove he wouldn't have treated you fairly over it. But you do realise, don't you, that his death destroys any claim you may have considered you had? The law doesn't recognise moral claims—and that's all you've got. Any Board of Directors would laugh at you."

"By jove, yes!" said Rupert, daunted at last. "I hadn't thought of it. Don't think me stupid—not as stupid as that, anyway—but the news of his death came as such a shock to me this morning when my wife rang me that I haven't had time to think how it affects my own position. Ah well! If it is so, it is so. I never did get anything out of it but a great deal of fun and boundless expectations. Still, I'll have a shot at getting my rights, for Louise's sake."

"That's the spirit!" said Sir Matthew cordially. But his thoughts were quite different, for he believed he had a pretty fair notion why Bernard had not told Rupert first the bad news about the shares.

13

In the library, the women, left alone, avoided one another.

Lady Risdon sat by one of the long windows, ostentatiously looking at a large book of coloured etchings by some modern Viennese artist, already a quarter of a century dead of tuberculosis at the age of twenty-eight. She did not like the etchings, but she had heard the artist's name, and she wished to be able to say a word of weight about them when next he was mentioned at a party.

Mrs. Hertford and her two girls clustered together in a corner apart, and talked in whispers loud enough to be irritating, about the previous evening and their last encounters with Bernard or his mother.

Louise read, or pretended to read, a book.

Olivia paced up and down, smoking and pausing now and then to look out of the window.

At last the door into the hall opened and Dr. Fitzbrown came striding through. Everybody started and stared; but he passed straight through without looking at any of them, and up the private staircase, taking the stairs two at a time. After his passage they all subsided back to their tedious pastimes.

Lady Risdon scraped her throat portentously, as her husband did before he addressed a public meeting, and placed her glasses again on her nose for a fresh scrutiny of the Austrian's strange devices.

Louise applied herself to an already-read paragraph in her calf-bound copy of *The Tower of London*, and found herself, in spite of her preoccupation, pitying Lady Jane Grey.

Olivia, seized with a shudder as if the doctor's passage had brought a cold wind, repressed her momentary emotion and began walking up and down again.

Mrs. Hertford and the girls told each other that that was Dr. Fitzbrown, and that he had come straight from the post mortem, and that 'we shall soon know now…'

"H-r-r-m!" ejaculated Lady Risdon importantly; and Olivia muttered under her breath: "For God's sake, shut up, *will you*?"

Louise, with fast-beating heart, read on:

'Monsieur Renard,' replied the Queen, 'I have reason to believe you have played me false. If I find you have deceived me, though you were brother to the emperor, you should lose your head…'

14

Dr. Fitzbrown came in and shut the door.

"Well," said Mallett, looking up from among his papers, "what do you find?"

"Poison," said Dr. Fitzbrown, sitting in an easy chair and stretching out his long legs. "Atropine. About two grains recovered from the bladder alone. He must have swallowed four grains at least."

"What's the fatal dose?"

"It's difficult to say. The medicinal dose is one two-hundred-and-fortieth to one sixty-eighth of a grain. But people don't often take it as a poison, except by mistake. I believe a man has been known to recover from a dose of just under two grains; but Smith-Wilson was in a poor state of health. Atropine poisoning causes oedema of the lungs, and his were none too good already."

"What's the general effect?"

"Death is caused by asphyxia, preceded by convulsions. There's terrible thirst—the throat and tongue are parched and leathery—temperature rises—pupils are widely dilated. At first the person's wildly agitated, even talkative; but he soon stops, because he can't swallow. Then a deep sleep follows, then convulsions, then death. Meanwhile his face grows livid. It's not a pleasant end."

"In what form is it most easily obtainable?"

Fitzbrown reflected: "Well, the common preparations are of course the belladonna tincture and extracts, used in various ways—as eyedrops, for instance, or to relieve colic or asthma, or as a pre-anaesthetic. There's also a liniment; and some people still use belladonna plasters, though they're not much believed in nowadays."

"Well," said Mallett, "there doesn't seem to be much possibility of mistake; and I suppose suicide is ruled out, too, by the nature of the poison?"

"It is, unless he was crazy," said Fitzbrown. "Who'd choose to die in torment and at length, when there are so many easier ways of dying?"

"Well, then, it's accidental death—or murder, and murder of a particularly cruel kind," said Mallett. "Which do you incline towards?"

Fitzbrown seemed unwilling to commit himself. Mallett continued:

"I should have inclined towards accident myself, if it hadn't been for the peculiar circumstances. Anyhow, I'm bound to investigate the other possibility, because this woman Olivia Bannermore has made a definite and violent accusation, and she certainly won't let the matter rest until she's been proved wrong—a very difficult thing to do. A most troublesome lady, by the way: I know the type. The ends of justice are nothing to her: she's thinking of some grudge she has against this man Holmes. What exactly she has in mind we shan't know until I can question her further."

"Any news of him?" said Fitzbrown.

"Yes. They stopped the boat train to Newhaven and took him off. He should be back here by tea-time."

"Have you any reason to think anyone wanted to poison Smith-Wilson?"

Mallett said: "Huh! Most people did, I should say! He wasn't a very appealing personality—and he was worth a couple of million, they say. If you're looking for a motive, what more do you want?"

"You mean '*Cherchez l'héritier*'?" said Fitzbrown; and when Mallett raised his eyebrows: "The heir," he explained kindly.

"No, I do not," said Mallett dourly. "I mean, everybody has his knife into the man with a couple of million."

"Dear me!" said Fitzbrown, nodding sagely. "A cynic, I see: no faith in lovely human nature. What can have caused such a change in you,

I wonder?" He changed his facetious tone for one more business-like: "Well, tell me what you've found out so far, if anything."

Mallett opened his note-book and turned back for a page or two.

"Merely the time-table of Smith-Wilson's movements," he said. "Dinner was at eight. There was a reception of the guests between seven and eight. Smith-Wilson received them alone: his mother was not present. She stayed in her room."

"Why?" said Fitzbrown, interested. "Is she ill? She's a patient of mine, off and on, but she hasn't consulted me for some time. She's a tough old bird and as obstinate as hell."

"Rheumatism was the reason given, I believe," said Mallett. "I haven't seen her yet, but I fancy the real reason was disinclination."

"Why should she be disinclined to receive her son's guests?" said Fitzbrown. "She looked after him devotedly during his recent illness— almost too devotedly, perhaps. Perhaps she doesn't like to see him getting around again and escaping her. Well, never mind. Go on."

"Dinner, with speeches, went on till nine-thirty. The guests then went to the drawing-room, or to the smoking-room where there was a bar. Smith-Wilson conducted one of the ladies upstairs to see his mother. Then he went to his study, where he had an interview with his secretary Holmes, at about five to ten. Then, in response to a message, Sir Matthew Risdon went to the study and had a talk with Smith-Wilson lasting about twenty minutes. I don't know, yet, what exactly they talked about; but Risdon says it had to do with certain movements on the stock market. He says Smith-Wilson was very much excited and upset. I shall go further into that presently. After that, nobody admits to having seen Smith-Wilson except Mrs. Hertford, who says she took it upon herself to go down to the kitchen and get him his usual glass of milk, which he took before going to bed; she thought that as there was this party, the servants would forget. She went down to the kitchen soon after ten, and after some little trouble with the cook, she got the milk and reached Smith-Wilson's study door at about twenty past ten, but did not enter because she heard voices. She went away, and returned a short while later, when she saw Risdon come out and go downstairs. She then entered with the milk and gave it to Smith-Wilson. We shall return to her presently, of course. Meanwhile I merely add that she too says she found Smith-Wilson very excited and, for him, talkative, so much so that she thought he was either feverish or a little drunk. She said his manner frightened her: he spoke violently and gesticulated, a thing most unusual with him, and seemed not to know quite what he was saying."

"What *did* he say?"

"I don't know. There wasn't time to go into that. The little woman was eager to talk, and I had to get rid of her and establish the outlines first, otherwise I should have been swamped with explanations. I saw the cook, though, and checked up on the times. The cook was very indignant at the idea that the milk had been forgotten: she says it was waiting on the kitchen table, and in a moment one of the men would have taken it up; Mr. Smith-Wilson had told them not to bother him with it till ten o'clock, because of dinner."

"H'm," said Fitzbrown. "And the milk-glass? Have you had the analysis?"

Mallett nodded: "Jones 'phoned me just before you arrived: no result."

Fitzbrown stared. He looked disappointed.

"You mean they didn't find anything?"

"Nothing at all. The milk was innocuous."

Fitzbrown remained silent for a moment, looking down. Then he said:

"Did they find any finger-prints?"

"Plenty, I expect," said Mallett. "Smith-Wilson's and Mrs. Hertford's, anyway; she doesn't deny she brought it, in fact she volunteered this information, so there wouldn't be much point—"

"But you haven't actually asked?"

"No. It was Jones who rang me, and he was concerned merely with the analysis. Still, for the sake of routine, I'll ring up now if you like, though it seems a waste of time now that we know the milk was harmless."

Fitzbrown made an impatient gesture. Mallett lifted the receiver. When he replaced it, his green eyes were round.

"Well?" said Fitzbrown.

"Nothing," said Mallett grudgingly.

"They found no finger-prints?" Fitzbrown was gleeful.

"No."

"Not even Smith-Wilson's? Or Mrs. Hertford's?"

"I told you: none at all."

"Then it wasn't the glass he used," said Fitzbrown. "It was planted there, and by someone who overdid the wiping process, or used a cloth or gloves."

"Obviously." Mallett was annoyed.

"And all you have to do is to find out who put it there."

Mallett gave an angry snort. Fitzbrown suppressed his pleasure at his good guess, though his eyes sparkled.

"So Mrs. Hertford was the last person who admits to having seen him," he prompted. "Well, we can't expect the guilty person to do as much for us, I suppose. The guests must have thought it odd, didn't they, that neither the host nor the hostess turned up to bid them good night? Didn't anybody go to look for him?"

"Apparently not." Mallett roused himself from his annoyance as a fresh hare presented itself. "But all the same, somebody *was* with him after Mrs. Hertford, if my last witness is speaking the truth. Mrs. Lavering says she left Mrs. Smith-Wilson a little after midnight, and passed down the private staircase from the first floor to the library. She went that way because she thought she might find her husband still downstairs; but she saw no one, and went upstairs to her room. This private staircase is the quickest way downstairs: it passes Smith-Wilson's study door. She says she heard him talking, very volubly and angrily. She thought she heard something like a thud, as though someone had struck the desk with his fist."

"Did she hear any other voice?"

"She says she didn't stop to listen. Her nerves were already on edge for various reasons, and she hurried down the stairs and away. I should think she's a trustworthy witness." He shot a challenging look at Fitzbrown from under his bushy red eyebrows: "She's the wife of Lavering the V.C., you know."

Fitzbrown nodded. "I know her: a very nice girl. Her husband's a very decent chap, too. Straight as a die, both of them, I should say."

"May be," said Mallett. "His behaviour last night was rather odd, all the same. He had a row with Risdon, and a couple of hours later he bolted off like a scalded cat, leaving a note for his wife to let her know he was going back to town-He didn't say why. The first she heard of the quarrel between him and Risdon was this morning when she overheard some of the staff talking. Lavering arrived back here this morning: he came as soon as he knew from her that Smith-Wilson was dead. So you see, he has some explaining to do, too. I haven't seen him yet."

"What time did he go?"

"Shortly after midnight, I gather: at least, that's what his wife says he says."

"That is, soon after she left Mrs. Smith-Wilson and passed Smith-Wilson's study door and heard violent talking?"

"Apparently so."

"I see. Have you talked to Mrs. Smith-Wilson yet?"

"No. I wanted to give her time to recover, poor woman; also I thought it best to wait till you came and I knew what was the cause of death. I gather she's quite willing to see me whenever I wish. So I think I'll go along now and get it over. I never like these jobs, you know." He heaved his large bulk out of Bernard's swivel-chair: "Do you mind staying here till I get back? I sent Coles off with a message, and I don't want this room to be left unwatched for a moment. Take a look round: you may find the missing milk-glass."

Fitzbrown watched him go.

When the gothic-pointed, iron-studded door closed behind him, Fitzbrown moved round to the other side of the desk and took his place in Bernard's swivel-chair. He was just going to begin a search, not so much because he hoped to find anything as in order to pass the time, when Mallett put his head round the door:

"Oh, by the way, Mrs. Hertford also claims to have passed the door after midnight; she says, about a quarter to one, she thinks. And she says that at that time the light was out and the door was locked. What do you make of that?" He withdrew, shutting the door.

"Well," said Fitzbrown after him, "either Mrs. Hertford is a liar, or the murderer was then inside the study—because the door wasn't locked this morning."

He planted his two elbows on the desk and stared across the room at the thick, dark-blue carpet, noticing every blemish—threads of cotton, cigarette-ash. Smith-Wilson did not smoke, but of course his visitors did, and several of them had been here yesterday evening. Then, swivelling round restlessly in the chair, he looked at the floor between his feet. A fragment of glass caught his attention, then another, then a little heap of splinters, as if someone had ground his heel on some glass object, almost forcing it into the pile of the carpet. Fitzbrown, removing nothing, got down on his hands and knees and began investigating, like a terrier with his nose to the trail.

He was rewarded. In the knee-space under the desk he found a small rubber bulb, like the press-bulb of a fountain-pen filler.

15

At the end of half an hour Louise could stand it no longer. The atmosphere of the library, with its preoccupied inmates, impinged on her so acutely that the remote sorrows of poor, deluded, valiant Lady Jane ceased to move her, then to hold her, and finally to reach through to her consciousness. At last she shut the book sharply and stood up.

"I'm going outside for a while," she said defiantly in the direction of Olivia, who was staring out of the window with her back turned to the company. "If the Superintendent wants me, I shall be in the garden somewhere."

Nobody bothered to answer.

Louise, thankful to escape, hurried away, across the hall, out at the front door, down the steps of the porch. She stood for a moment looking out over the prospect: the broad terrace with its clipped box-trees in green tubs and its stone vases planted with bright flowers and hanging ferns. Near one of these vases, under the willow-tree, she and Olivia had sat, so very few hours ago, yet in a different world: a world of petty worries and annoyances that had then seemed important and now were reduced to nothing by this horrible black nightmarish cloud overhanging them all. She walked on slowly, across the smooth flagstones towards the balustrade, enjoying the summer afternoon in spite of all her cares.

Here, just here, she had stood with Bernard—and now Bernard was dead. How horrible, how completely horrible and unexpected—and how opportune! 'It's terrible,' she thought, 'when someone you regard with dislike and fear is removed by circumstance. You feel as if you had caused it yourself. And yet—did I dislike Bernard? I said I did to Rupert—but was that true? It *was* partly my fault, that scene in the library. But I didn't seriously think he meant what he said.'

Her thoughts moved on, from Bernard to Rupert, as she went down the steps on to the path below the terrace, and along the path towards the lily-pools. Why, she wondered, had Rupert been at such pains to avoid her since his return? She had expected him to draw her aside, away from the others, and tell her all he knew—all that had happened yesterday, about which she was still in the dark. He had come back immediately, after receiving her 'phone call. He had greeted her with his usual enthusiasm, damped only a little by the circumstances and by the presence of the others. After luncheon, she had waited for him; he had followed her into the library with the others; and then—he had dashed away with a muttered excuse, leaving her once again.

So now, she knew only that Rupert had quarrelled with Sir Matthew Risdon over a financial deal in which Bernard had had a hand, and that Rupert had left soon after midnight, without letting anyone know, even herself—soon after she had heard loud talking in Bernard's study. And now, Bernard was dead, and they were saying he had been murdered...

16

Rupert jumped up suddenly.

"Excuse me," he said to Sir Matthew, "I really must go and look for my wife. I've got some explaining to do, you know, about last night!"

He laughed, apparently unaware that he had interrupted Sir Matthew in the middle of one of his long, ponderously-told anecdotes, and had thus proved that he had not been listening.

Sir Matthew watched him go, and envied him his power to leap to his feet like that out of a chair; but he did not envy him his wife, for it was so long since Lady Risdon had taken any interest in his movements that he had forgotten what it was like to feel the restraint imposed by affection; and though he had enjoyed those bonds for a short while, he now preferred the freedom granted by indifference.

He sighed, stretched out his stout, short legs, folded his stout white hands on his abdomen, and went instantly to sleep.

17

Louise heard Rupert's quick step behind her on the gravel, and turned. She was overjoyed to see him. She wanted above all things to hear his story. Yet she found herself saying in a voice by no means welcoming:

"Darling! Where have you *been?*"

"Hullo, darling!" Rupert was as cheerful as ever, and crossly she thought how delightful he looked with his fair hair shining in the sun: "'I've been to London to see the Queen.'" He came towards her with hands outstretched, and when she turned her cheek, he kissed her first on one, then on the other. "You're cross with me for going off without telling you; but really, darling, it was better so."

"At what time *did* you go?" said Louise, trying hard to sound more amiable than she was feeling. "I didn't get away from Mrs. Smith-Wilson until just after twelve——"

"Good lord!" said Rupert. "I told you, darling: that's about the time I left, too. You nearly caught me!"

Louise would not laugh with him, nor even smile.

"Bernard was still alive then," she said broodingly. "I heard him talking—arguing with someone—in his room, when I passed the door. You do realise, don't you, they think he was murdered?"

"Well, I presume they suspect foul play since they've got the police here," said Rupert. "But what was the cause of his death? Does anyone know?"

"The rumour is that it was poison," said Louise.

"Then it's more likely to have been suicide."

"So I thought. But Olivia insists that it was foul play. She is quite rabid about it. She says it was that man Holmes. He left the house in the middle of the night, too, you know." She watched Rupert closely. "He seems to have absconded with some money and bonds and things. He has been playing ducks and drakes with Bernard's affairs for some time."

"Well, then, that's all right!" Rupert endeavoured to cheer her up. "When they catch Holmes, we can all go home and forget about it."

"Aren't you at all *sorry* Bernard's dead?" said Louise wonderingly. "Don't you feel it's awfully sad, I mean, that he should die so young when he had so much to lose?"

Rupert looked puzzled.

"Of course I'm sorry!" he said wholeheartedly. "But really, darling, when you've seen fellows blown to bits beside you—fellows, you know, who'd never had much out of life at all—What's the matter?" He saw that her lips were trembling. Louise did not readily cry. "Darling, what is it? You weren't in love with Bernard, were you? I know he was always keen on *you*; in fact, last night—" He stopped.

"What about last night?" Louise spoke sharply, and any desire to cry was checked.

"Well," said Rupert reluctantly, "I was a bit tight at the time, and I may have misheard, but I understood that woman Olivia to say that Bernard's intentions towards you were serious—serious to the point of getting rid of me. I fancy I had some idea of coming to look for you and pushing his face in, but she stopped me."

"*She* stopped you!" Louise was thinking hard. "I can't make her out. Why did she take such an interest in you and your affairs? She told me this morning it was she who urged you to go. In fact, she thought you hadn't gone: she says she took you the black coffee and the ice-cubes soon after half-past ten, and you were fast asleep on the bed—in fact, darling, drunk and incapable. She frightened me to death. I thought you must have had an accident on the road."

Rupert looked, for him, exceedingly cunning.

"My dear," he said in superior tones, "that was an act. That thin, voracious type of woman scares me. I didn't want her hanging round me. Not," he hastened to add, "that I've any reason to think—"

Louise laughed for the first time.

"That's the most sensible thing I've heard you say since we've been married, darling!" she said. "Always beware of women, the fat as well as the lean. You're their natural prey. You're so *simple*!"

She put an arm through his, and began walking him further down the garden, away from the house, along the edge of the lily-ponds. They paused to admire the splendid nenuphars, white, yellow and purple, proudly riding on their rafts of dark green leaves.

"You're a fine one to talk," protested Rupert, "going off like that with Bernard! Did he make love to you?—No, don't tell me. I don't want to know. It seems to me, now he's dead, the fewer questions I ask about him the better. And I thought he was my friend!" He walked on, brooding on what Sir Matthew had told him: "Every stone I turn up seems to hide an adder! Old Risdon, you know, thinks we shan't get a bean out of my carburettor."

"What!" said Louise, her hand tightening on his arm.

"He says, now that Bernard's dead, I shan't get a bean," repeated Rupert. "I relied on Bernard's word, but there's no contract, and so—"

"Oh, I'm so glad, darling!" said Louise, letting go of his arm. He stared at her in amazement and some annoyance.

"Glad! But damn it all, darling, I was entitled—"

"Oh, I know, I know!" Louise almost sang for joy. "It's *very* hard on you, but you can easily invent something else if you give your mind to it. The important thing at the moment is, nobody can say *you* stood to gain anything by Bernard's death; in fact, you stood to lose—a fortune!"

"I don't see—" began Rupert. Then he did see.

He faced her, frowning, and the naso-labial fold that he had earned by laughter showed deeply now in his revulsion.

"You mean to say they could suspect *me?*"

"They can, and will, suspect everybody, darling," said Louise firmly, "you—me—the cook—the Risdons—Mrs. Hertford, and the girls even. To the police we're simply people who were here when Bernard died."

"But—surely a man's character goes for something!" said Rupert, outraged. "Damn it all, a man like me doesn't kill his friend—with poison! You don't mean to tell me they don't take one's whole—record into consideration!"

"No, darling," said Louise. "But I think they'll also take into consideration the fact that Bernard, having first cheated you out of your due reward, was then trying to ruin you because he wanted to steal your wife; and that you left the house at some time in the middle of the night without telling anyone. I'm the only person who knows you weren't in your room soon after midnight, and even I don't know exactly when you left. Does anyone? Unless someone saw you go, they've only your word for the actual time. And they've only my word for it that Bernard was alive and talking at that time, so far as I know. Oh, I *wish* you had waited to see me before you left! *Why* didn't you? Things always go wrong when you act without telling me!"

"It was Olivia's idea," said Rupert sullenly. "She thought it would be better if I cleared out quickly without worrying you."

"Oh, really!" said Louise. "And may I ask what right Olivia has to advise you about how you shall treat me?"

A voice behind them startled them.

"No right at all, my dear. Don't waste your time being jealous of me."

They turned to face Olivia, smiling at them with amused understanding.

"Actually," she went on, "it should be the other way round. Bernard was my target." She turned to Rupert. "I hope I didn't give you any cause for misapprehension last night? If so, let me explain, and put your mind at rest. I happened to see through Bernard's little plot to discredit you; and I knew what was his objective. So I took steps to thwart him. I had inside information about those shares: I knew that Holmes hadn't been carrying out Bernard's instructions to sell, and that you were all right so long as you didn't panic. That was my sole reason for helping you, I assure you."

She turned away; and then, as if remembering why she had followed them:

"Oh, by the way, they want to see you up there."

"Both of us?" said Louise.

"No—you." She nodded at Rupert. "Don't be alarmed: I think it's something to your advantage."

She turned away again, and they made no effort to stop her.

When she had gone too far to be overtaken, they prepared to follow.

"Well, *now* I hope you're satisfied!" said Rupert savagely.

"Oh, darling!" said Louise. "Please don't say any more! I feel the meanest worm on earth, or under it. Poor woman! How she must be suffering! I had no idea! It must have been terrible to love Bernard if he didn't want you. I think he could have been terribly cruel when he chose."

She took his arm again, fully conscious of the power within her, that made it impossible for Bernard or any other man to treat her as he had treated Olivia.

This time, when they reached the terrace, she sent him on alone.

18

Rupert walked rapidly through the library, past Lady Risdon, who did not look up, and the two girls, Clara and Lucilla, who did. He smiled at them cheerfully and called out a cheerful greeting. The girls looked wistfully after him as he opened the door and disappeared.

Even the passage up the dark, narrow stairway past Bernard's room could not repress his spirits. He might have lost a fortune, but he had discovered that Bernard had been nothing to Louise; and, what was more, that she really loved *him*. He had wondered sometimes, lately: they had quarrelled so much, and she had seemed so censorious—not without reason, but still, once she had liked him as he was, or at least had not seized on every little excuse, as she now did, to criticise him.

But now, all that was swept away; for what else but love could make a woman like Louise, fond of everything that money can buy—clothes, an elegant house, jewellery, expensive scent, a good time, in this very expensive modern world—what else but love could make her cry out with joy to hear that her husband had lost his one great chance of making a fortune? Rupert knew that he would never have another inspiration like that of his patent carburettor: the youth who had devised that, with patient thought and work and all the *élan* of self-confidence, was a different being from the man who couldn't sit down for five minutes in a chair without fidgeting; who couldn't read a book right through, or sit through a play; who needed a cigarette every half-hour and a drink every hour, and a constant change of place, people, activity. No: that had been his only chance, and he had thrown it away or allowed it to be snatched from him: entrusted it to Bernard, who had died. And Louise had cried out for joy! She loved him: she cared more for his safety than for anything he could do for her or give her.

With a quick, light step he reached the top of the stairway, and tapped on the door of Mrs. Smith-Wilson's sitting-room.

He entered.

The tableau that confronted him was enough to make anyone pause. Seated on a high-backed chair, the centre of the picture as always when she was present, was Mrs. Smith-Wilson, upright, undefeated, inflexible; she held her head high and looked grimly at the newcomer, as if she held the power of life and death over him and meant to exercise it. Behind her stood Mrs. Hertford, anxiously leaning forward to watch her; one felt that she had the *sal volatile* ready and that she would be disappointed if after all it were not needed. Standing at the window in her favourite pose, looking out, with her hands behind her back, was Olivia. At the other side of the room a table had been placed, and at it, with a number of papers before him, sat a small, white-haired man of legal aspect: Mr. Rainford, the Smith-Wilsons' family solicitor. Near him, Superintendent Mallett had deposed his very large frame as best he could on to a very small chair.

Rupert stared round the semi-circle in amazement, beginning with Mr. Rainford, and passing to Mallett, Mrs. Smith-Wilson, Olivia; and then all the way back to Mr. Rainford again.

"Come in, Major," said Mr. Rainford, when Mrs. Smith-Wilson remained monumental, and no one else spoke. He glanced at Mallett, who nodded to him to proceed. "Do please take a seat."

Rupert remained standing.

"You wanted to see me?" he said.

Their silent concentration worried him. He became aware of Olivia's back, ostentatiously turned, and of foolish, anxious Mrs. Hertford's nods and smiles of sympathy.

"Er—yes," said Mr. Rainford. It was soothing to Rupert to see at any rate one person he knew to be well-disposed towards him, someone who knew the true history of his relationship with Bernard. "We shan't keep you a minute, Major Lavering." His precise voice was a pleasure to hear. He looked down at his papers, bringing their edges together with his hands: "This is a very distressing occasion. H'm!" He cast a quick glance at Mrs. Smith-Wilson's immovable countenance, and returned hastily to his papers. "Mr. Bernard Smith-Wilson's sudden and tragic death has made it necessary for me to come here, at Superintendent Mallett's request, and disclose the contents of the will. It is not usual, as you know, to do so with quite such expedition; but the provisions of a testator, if the will is valid—and we have no reason to think otherwise—come into force at the moment of his death; and though these provisions cannot be carried out until the will has been proved, nevertheless the presumptive beneficiaries are entitled to know them at the earliest convenient moment. Owing to certain—peculiar—features of Mr. Smith-Wilson's death, Superintendent Mallett had asked me to come here and give you the gist of the contents of the will *now*."

He coughed again, aware of his importance. This was a moment that never failed to thrill him, as when an actor steps forward to deliver a famous speech, or an opera-singer to sing a famous aria, and the audience waits, breathless, for him to begin.

"The will is dated July 12, 1946, almost exactly a year ago. It was drawn by myself, acting on Mr. Smith-Wilson's instructions, and its provisions are in exact accordance with Mr. Smith-Wilson's wishes as expressed at that time. I have no reason to suppose that he altered them during the intervening twelve months.

"After the usual preliminaries, Mr. Smith-Wilson says:

"'I give to my mother Frances Jane Smith-Wilson my house and adjoining freehold property known as Fairfield Manor together with two hundred and fifty acres of land annexed to the said Fairfield Manor and all rents and other income derived therefrom.

"'I also give to my said mother the whole contents of the said house and adjoining property for her use and enjoyment during her lifetime.

"'I give to Olivia May Bannermore of 90 Sudbrook Gardens London and Yule Cottage Humbleford Wiltshire the freehold property known as Yule Cottage Humbleford Wiltshire together with all its contents and an annuity of one thousand pounds to commence from the date of my death and to continue during her life.'"

Mr. Rainford paused, and cast a look at Olivia's rigid back; but Olivia did not turn round or give any sign that she had heard. After a cough, Mr. Rainford continued:

"'I give to Mabel Susanna Hertford of 12 Uptown Street, Chode, the sum of five hundred pounds free of duty in recognition of her kindness to my mother, and to each of her daughters Clara and Lucilla I give the sum of one hundred pounds free of duty.'"

"Oh, how kind!" burst out Mabel tearfully, looking round the audience, which remained unresponsive. "How very, very kind!" She cried for a few moments over Mrs. Smith-Wilson's shoulder, provoking the latter to a sharp shrug, her first sign of interest.

Mr. Rainford adjusted his glasses again, and with an even more important 'H'm!' went on:

"'I give to my friend Rupert Lavering V.C. of 10 Merriel Buildings Cannon Street London the sum of twenty thousand pounds in recognition of his valuable services as an inventor and designer of the Smith-Wilson Thasson atomiser-carburettor the said twenty thousand pounds to consist of Preference Shares in the Smith-Wilson Engineering Company Limited reckoned at their Stock Exchange value on the day of my death. I also direct that the loan made to the said Rupert Lavering by me of five thousand pounds on June 21st 1946 shall be cancelled.'"

Mr. Rainford cast a hasty look round over the top of his glasses before adding:

"There are a number of other bequests, to servants and employees, and to ourselves as executors, which I needn't go through now. The last clause reads:

"'The residue of my personal estate after the aforesaid legacies and annuities have been paid I give to my said mother for her use and enjoyment during her lifetime and after her decease I give the said residue to Hugh Bernard Bannermore my illegitimate son by the said Olivia May Bannermore the said property to be held in trust for the said Hugh Bernard Bannermore and administered during his minority by the said Olivia May Bannermore and by the said Rupert Lavering if the death of my mother precedes the majority of my said son and after the death of my said mother I give to my said son the said property known as Fairfield Manor together with all its contents and appurtenances and together with the land attached thereto.

"'I feel sure that these provisions will compensate the beneficiaries for any trouble I may have caused them during my lifetime and will console them for my death.'"

"The witnesses," said Mr. Rainford, "to Mr. Smith-Wilson's signature are two of my clerks."

He sat back, folded up his glasses, restored them to their well-worn case, and thrust the case into his waistcoat pocket, as one who has come triumphantly to the end of his aria and now confidently awaits the applause.

19

Rupert was the first to break the silence.

"But I say, Mr. Rainford!" His voice was high with protestation. "There must be some mistake! Twenty thousand pounds! Good heavens, when I thought he was trying to get rid of me!" The words were out before he had realised their significance. "I mean, of course, in the business sense," he added unconvincingly, seeing Mallett's shrewd eye fastened on him. He wondered: 'What will Louise say now? Will she believe I knew nothing about all this?' The mere thought of Louise recalled him to a sense of his danger, and he determined not to say another word.

He need not have troubled: he was not the centre of attention. The size of his legacy was as nothing to the revelation that Bernard had, after all, a son and heir. Nobody bothered to answer Rupert's protest; and even Mallett's scrutiny soon left him, as Olivia turned from the window and bore down upon them with a very odd smile on her face.

She made straight for Mrs. Smith-Wilson, who had not spoken or moved.

"Yes, it's quite true," she said. "You're a grandmother. Aren't you pleased? You should be. He's quite like Bernard, and very much like you."

Then, as Mrs. Smith-Wilson did not speak or give any sign of having heard, Olivia flung a glance round the semi-circle of spectators and said:

"Please go away, will you, and leave us alone for a few minutes?" She looked Mallett full in the eyes. "There's nothing in all this for you—or if there is, you'll hear it later, from each of us. You can check up better that way."

"You'll find me in the study, ma'am," said Mallett to Mrs. Smith-Wilson. He made for the door, encountering Rupert on the way. "Come along with me, Major, will you?" he said. "I want to have a word with you, and now seems a good time." He took Rupert by the elbow and led him out of the room.

Mr. Rainford, after a hasty glance at Olivia, had already begun to gather up his papers. He bowed in the direction of the two antagonists, and hurried after Mallett and Rupert.

Mrs. Hertford hesitated behind Mrs. Smith-Wilson's chair.

"You too," said Olivia sternly.

Mrs. Hertford cast an inquiring look at her friend, as of one prepared to defend her to the death; but all the answer she received was a hostile stare and an impatient "Leave us alone, Mabel, please." So Mabel, too, scurried away, past the three men at the head of the stairs. The door closed.

"Well?" said Olivia with an insolent smile. "You didn't think he was capable of it, did you?"

Mrs. Smith-Wilson stirred a little, like a strong tree in the first breath of wind that presages the storm.

"I suppose the child *is* Bernard's?" she said, in a tone quite as insolent as Olivia's.

"Hah!" Olivia's exclamation was a substitute for a triumphant laugh. "Even if he weren't, it wouldn't matter, since Bernard acknowledges him. But you'd only have to see him to know."

"When was he born?"

"Seven years ago, on the sixth of April. Nice time of year, isn't it?—'When the birds do sing Hey dinga-ding-ding.'"

Mrs. Smith-Wilson was not amused: "Why didn't Bernard marry you?"

"He didn't want to. And since I'd been fool enough to give him all he wanted without, it was my own fault, wasn't it? But then, you see, at the time I thought he *would* marry me, in due course. And he would have, too, if circumstances hadn't changed."

"What do you mean?" said Mrs. Smith-Wilson. "Are you talking about his health?"

"His health?" This time Olivia really laughed. "There was nothing wrong with his health in those days. Don't you remember him as he was then?—always active, enjoying life in every way. No, it was just that he fell in love with someone else. And he never could get over it. It was the most powerful force in his life. I believe it was that that killed him, in the last resort. He wore himself out over it. He wanted this woman so much that it spoilt all other women for him—including me. He told me so; and that didn't make things very comfortable between him and me. Before that, he had been willing to marry me, especially if I produced a son for him; but afterwards he couldn't. I understood, in a way. I'm rather like that myself. I could never have looked at any other man but Bernard."

"Who was this woman?" asked Mrs. Smith-Wilson, ready to condemn, but not without curiosity.

Olivia regarded her superciliously. "What sort of a mother *are* you?" she said. "Didn't you know anything about Bernard? Never mind who she was: is, rather, for she's extant all right, and not so very far away. She's no siren. She's just a distractingly beautiful girl with masses of charm and complete honesty and a character of steel. She's married to a man she loves, a man worth ten of Bernard; but Bernard was still plotting to get her away from him, though that man was his best friend, who trusted him. Now you know what sort of son *you* produced. I only hope mine won't turn out to be the same—or do I? I'm afraid Bernard has tainted me: I admire the virtues, but I don't find them so frightfully interesting."

Mrs. Smith-Wilson's already straight spine arched backwards as she realised what Olivia was saying.

"What! You mean that young woman he brought in here and left with me this evening—Louise Molyneux? Oh no—of course she's married to Rupert Lavering now. You can't mean her? Don't be ridiculous! Bernard knew her when she was a little girl; and as for her husband, Bernard has done nothing but help him: he has set him on his feet again now that he's demobilised. He took him up before the war—made his fortune for him—"

"You mean," said Olivia, "he appropriated Rupert's brilliant idea without acknowledgment and without payment. Bernard has made amends in his will, I'm glad to see. If he had lived, it might have been a very different story." She held up her hand. "Oh, don't bother to argue. I was in his business counsels, right on the inside. He didn't want me as a wife, or even as a mistress, but he kept me near him as a confidante and sometimes as an adviser. He knew I had a good brain, and it never occurred to him not to trust me. There was always Hugh—your grandson, you know. You must get used to the name."

Mrs. Smith-Wilson leaned forward the fraction of an inch.

"Do you believe," she said, "that Bernard was poisoned? Or do you believe he took his own life?"

Olivia thought. "I believe," she said slowly, "he was poisoned."

"What makes you think so?"

"Because I think I know who did it. And—oh, God, I believe it was my fault!" Her voice was low, and the pain in it was unmistakable; but Mrs. Smith-Wilson pressed inexorably:

"How?"

Olivia put out a hand to the back of a nearby chair, and raised the other to her forehead.

"I'll sit down, if you don't mind," she said faintly.

Mrs. Smith-Wilson watched her sink on the chair, and waited without the least sign of sympathy for her to recover. After a few moments, Olivia raised her eyes:

"You know Holmes, the secretary?"

"Of course."

"He had been misappropriating the firm's money, in quite a big way. He belongs to some crazy gang across the Channel who call themselves Anticrats. There are only about twenty of them so far, and they have a room somewhere in Paris which they call their headquarters. Holmes 'represents' them in England. They're against everything, it appears, that anybody else had ever stood for in the name of decency. They believe in slave labour, and the segregation of women, and illiteracy in manual workers, and of course the unequal distribution of property, provided they get the lion's share. It's quite mad—but then things just as mad have succeeded, you know, because nobody took them seriously until it was too late."

She was no longer talking to Mrs. Smith-Wilson except incidentally. But Mrs. Smith-Wilson was listening attentively.

"You say he has been stealing Bernard's money?" she asked sharply.

"Not Bernard's," corrected Olivia. "The firm's."

"The same thing!" snapped Mrs. Smith-Wilson.

"Apart from a few thousand shareholders. Well, never mind. It doesn't matter. The point is, I knew what Holmes was doing, and I let him continue, until I had him in my power. Then I showed my hand. I wanted to use him, you see."

"What for?"

"Never mind that: for a purpose of my own, connected with Bernard—something Bernard was trying to do that I didn't like. Oh well, I suppose you'd better know. You're awfully curious, aren't you?—I knew that Bernard was trying to get Louise Lavering away from her husband. She married Rupert Lavering as soon as he was demobilised and while Bernard was still too ill to do anything about it. But Bernard came back to his idea as soon as he was better. Bernard never gave up anything he'd set his heart on. He planned to ruin Lavering temporarily and get his wife away from him, and then set him on his feet again—unless Lavering had drunk himself to death or shot himself meanwhile. Well, I'm pretty determined, too—and I'd made up my mind that Bernard would do no such thing. So I set to work to prevent it—not out of any kindly feelings towards the Laverings, but because, if I couldn't have Bernard, I didn't intend him to father anybody else's brats, over the head of *my* son."

"I don't blame you," said Mrs. Smith-Wilson, suddenly and surprisingly. "Well, go on," irritably. "What did you do?"

"I made Holmes fail to carry out Bernard's instructions, or else do the opposite. When Bernard told Holmes to 'phone his agents and say 'sell', I made Holmes say 'buy', and vice-versa. So you see—Mother—when Bernard thought he was ruining Rupert, he was making his fortune: making him a reputation as one of the smartest brokers in town. Poor Rupert! I don't know what he'll do without Bernard, because he's not smart at all—not in the business sense. He should never be in the business world."

"Well, I should think he wouldn't need to be, with the legacy Bernard left him," said Mrs. Smith-Wilson grimly.

"Restitution, Mother," said Olivia, for her quite gently. "Anyway, Louise will pull him through. She's got a sound business head on her. If he had been smart, believe me, he wouldn't be a hero: he'd have saved his skin and let some other guy get the V.C., which is often awarded posthumously, if you've noticed."

Mrs. Smith-Wilson did not contest this. They sat in silence for a minute or two. Then Mrs. Smith-Wilson said:

"So you think this man Holmes is responsible for Bernard's death?"

"You bet I do!" said Olivia viciously. "He was due to leave tonight, to join his anticratic friends. He was taking various assets belonging to the firm: bearer bonds, and some five-pound notes sewn up in his clothes, worth about twenty pounds each in Paris, I believe, if you can convince anyone they're not forgeries. He knew that Bernard would leave no stone unturned to track him down and punish him. Bernard wasn't hard, in small things; he was good to his employees, and quite willing to overlook various slips and failings. But he never forgave treachery. Holmes knew that—and he was afraid. He saw to it, somehow—I don't know how—that Bernard didn't live to exact vengeance. And I—fool that I was—I knew all this, and I let it happen! I let Holmes go, never realising that he couldn't afford to leave Bernard behind alive! I shall never forgive myself. But I've done the only thing left to do—I've got Holmes back. They've caught him. They'll be bringing him back here. He'll be confronted with his crime—and with me! He won't be able to deny it. He'll see me—and he'll see Bernard behind me, looking over my shoulder!"

In her excitement she had risen from her seat, and was looking out across the room as if she could see Bernard coming to meet her. Mrs. Smith-Wilson watched her sombrely.

"You're a strange girl," she said. "But I don't dislike you. I wonder Bernard didn't prefer you to that young woman who was here for so long last night. I thought he liked more character."

"Oh," said Olivia, relaxing, "don't make any mistake, my dear. Louise has got heaps of character. Don't be taken in by the golden hair and the big blue eyes. Even Rupert's afraid of her—and Bernard found her utterly fascinating because he couldn't move her. I wish *I* were as tough as she is, by jove!" She sat down again. "If I were, I'd be reigning here, and you'd be the dowager!"

Mrs. Smith-Wilson bridled a little, and grew red, as she said in her most ungracious tones:

"Well, since your boy's Bernard's heir, you'd both better come and live here. You'll have your own quarters, of course. I can't be bothered with children at my age. And he'd better take his father's name." She pressed her lips together in a thin line, and threw back her head haughtily.

"I'm damned if he shall!" said Olivia, equally pugnacious. "He's going through life as Hugh Bernard Bannermore, so long as I have any influence over him. He has done without his father's name for the first seven years of his life, and those are the most important, they say; so as I've had the responsibility, I'll have the credit also!"

They glared at one another angrily. Then Mrs. Smith-Wilson looked away.

"I envy you," she said. "*You* still have a son—to fight for." And, to Olivia's consternation, a tear rolled slowly down her cheek.

"Oh, for God's sake!" she said. "Don't you folk *ever* play fair?" And when Mrs. Smith-Wilson didn't answer: "All right, have it your own way!"

She jumped up and rushed out of the room.

20

"Sit down, Major," said Mallett, pointing across Bernard's desk to a chair.

Rupert would have preferred to pace about; but remembering that this would not create a good impression, he took the chair indicated and sat forward, clasping his hands and looking, in his effort to remain calm, intensely nervous. He wished he had not drunk so much the night before: it made his pulses race, and gave him noises in his head and a bad taste in his mouth. When he could move about or talk to someone, he forgot these symptoms; but now, in this quiet room, with this bulky police-officer watching him, he was aware of the twitching of muscles and the over-activity of nerves. He would have liked to smoke; but as Mallett did not suggest it, he steeled himself to refrain.

"You were a great friend of the deceased?" began Mallett in tones of false consideration.

"Perhaps his greatest friend," said Rupert. "At least, I thought so."

Mallett did not ask him what he meant; and Rupert did not add what he was thinking: that he had been Bernard's only real friend.

"How long had you known him?" said Mallett.

"Since I was a boy. His father bought this place fifteen years ago, when Bernard was about twenty. I remember he celebrated his coming of age here with fireworks. I was only a youngster at the time. He was six years older than I. Later on, when I was eighteen and attending an engineering course in the Technical College at Broxeter, I met him again. He was then in partnership with his father, in the Smith-Wilson Engineering Works. We became very friendly, and we saw a lot of each other. I was working at a new type of improved atomiser-carburettor for internal combustion engines, which would make it possible to use a cruder type of petrol than is now necessary, and would obviate the necessity for the refining of petrol as at present practised. Bernard took it up enthusiastically. He was no engineer, you know: he was a business man. But he had a flair for good ideas."

As Rupert talked of his special interest, he kindled, forgetting all his unease.

"He encouraged me," he went on. "He helped me to equip a workshop where I could work in the evenings. I did work intensively. I perfected my idea. Bernard paid for all the tests, and gave me the run of their engineering works there at Broxeter. It was all very exciting.

"In the middle, Bernard's father died—and it was found that he wasn't nearly as well off as people had assumed. This house here, for instance, was mortgaged heavily. There was a danger of foreclosure—or worse. The shareholders began to panic. Through it all, Bernard kept perfectly calm. If it hadn't been for his coolness, I believe there would have been a complete crash, and everybody would have lost their money. I could never have stood it myself."

He leaned back, now perfectly at his ease, and crossed his legs.

"Have a cigarette," said Mallett, proffering his case.

"Thank you," said Rupert, taking one. But he had forgotten his intense desire of a moment ago. "At that moment, I solved the last little difficulty of my design—and Bernard decided to bring the Thasson into all their commercial vehicles. It was a big decision. If the thing hadn't been all we claimed, the firm would have gone under. But it *was* all and more than we claimed. Since then, the Thasson has become a standard fitting on all Smith-Wilson motor engines; and though other firms have imitated it, they haven't yet made anything to equal it in performance."

"That's a remarkable story," said Mallett, interested. "You must have been very proud of your achievement."

"Oh, I don't know," said Rupert, becoming a little restless again. "Things happened so quickly, I didn't have time. First my own father died and left me a small legacy, and after I'd spent some of it on new equipment for my workshop, I went off for a European trip and forgot about engineering. I needed a rest, and Bernard didn't need me any more. All he had to do was to manufacture the things. I was away for the whole of the spring and summer of 1939; and I had only just got back, with a few days to spare, when war was declared."

"And you joined up at once?"

"Of course."

"Mr. Smith-Wilson was exempted?"

"Yes, on grounds of being in charge of work of national importance. And mind you, this was quite true. You'll find old Smith-Wilson engines, complete with Thasson carburettor, lying about in many a field and on many a shore all over the world."

"And what remuneration did you receive for your invention?"

"Well, directly, I suppose, very little. Bernard bought up all my stock that wasn't his already, and gave me a fair price for it. Originally I'd wanted to try to manufacture the Thasson myself, but when war broke out it became clear that he'd have to take the whole thing over. It was understood that I should get my rake-off in due course. At that time I didn't need money, as I was in the Army."

"And did you get your rake-off? The war has been over for two years now."

"Well," said Rupert dubiously, "we never really got down to a settlement. Bernard suggested that for a time I'd better go into the City: he didn't think I could settle down to engineering research again for a while, and I had forgotten most of what I knew. He lent me the money to set up a well-placed office; and he sent me clients, and he gave me all his own hot tips. He said I could make enough in five years to finance any kind of life I felt attracted to by then—engineering or farming or whatever I fancied. He thought that in five years' time I'd know better what I wanted to do. So I agreed. His advice seemed sensible; and besides, I wanted to get married."

"When did all this happen?"

"I was married last January—"

"No, I mean, when did you set up in business?"

"As soon as I could get fixed up—that is, last October. The arrangement has worked out pretty well so far. With Bernard's backing, I've done well—much better than I expected. At times I've tried to go into the matter of my share in the Thasson—but it's been difficult to pin him down. He had become so very important during the war years and so busy that at first he hadn't the time, and he asked me to postpone a final settlement, and to consider the loan he made me as a sort of advance on my share. Then he had that terrible illness from which he had only recently recovered, and I couldn't press him then or after. I would have done, though, if only for my wife's sake; but I'm glad I didn't now. As you know, he had made provision in his will, in case anything happened to him. I was completely overwhelmed just now when I heard."

"You knew nothing about it?"

"Not a thing—any more than I knew he had a son. He was a dark horse!"

"He certainly was," said Mallett, stroking his chin. "I'm wondering what else we shall discover. He knew your wife, I believe, before he knew you?"

Rupert frowned. "He knew her when she was small. But after that she went away to school and they didn't see much of each other until the summer before the war."

"That was before you yourself had met her?"

"I met her in August, 1939," said Rupert. "She was a great tennis-player, and so was Bernard, and he invited a party here, and she was one of them and so was I."

His eyes shone at the thought of those idyllic days. In a flash he saw Bernard, tall, slim, elegant, serving his swift, unpredictable balls with the apparent ease of long practice and indifference; and Louise, young, high-spirited, but dignified, taking one's breath away with her dazzling beauty—no *beauté de diable*, for she had it still, but, nevertheless, the beauty of seventeen, which when it exists still draws its tribute of truthful *clichés*. Rupert saw the trees, the sunshine, the courts kept green by careful spraying all summer and always freshly-marked; the house, the flower-beds, the lily-ponds where he and Louise had first walked together, when he had drawn her away from the rest, in love with her from the moment he saw her.

"Bernard introduced me to her—here," he added.

"There was some rivalry between you?" questioned Mallett softly. Rupert stared owlishly at him.

"Rivalry? Not on my part. There was no need. My wife never considered Bernard seriously; in fact, she disapproved of him, though she went about with him a little. Soon afterwards the war broke out, and I went away into training. At Christmas it was all fixed up between us."

"You mean you became engaged?"

"Not exactly. I didn't think it fair to tie her down when I might get killed any day. But it was understood that we—preferred each other." He frowned, deprecating any further attempt to prise open his heart.

"How did Smith-Wilson take this? Did he know?"

"Yes, he knew. Naturally he took it rather badly—as a bad disappointment, I mean. But it never affected our friendship. He plunged into business; I went to France. I came home, the usual way, *via* Dunkirk. In the autumn I was off again, to Greece, and so on. No, there was never a shadow on our friendship, so far as I knew, all those years."

Mallett heard the note of doubt creep in at the end of the sentence, and saw the cloud of uncertainty cross Rupert's very expressive face.

"Major Lavering," he said, leaning forward, resting his forearms on Bernard's desk, "you must be patient with me if I ask you questions that may seem irrelevant. In a case like this, one has to cast one's net wide. I'm not going to pry any further into your domestic affairs; but I shall ask you two or three simple questions, and I'll be grateful if you will give me straightforward answers."

"Go ahead," said Rupert, suspicious and alert.

"Do you consider that Smith-Wilson still cherished his original feelings for your wife?"

"Yes, I do. Nobody could help *that*."

"And you're positive that she in no way returned his feelings? I don't suggest anything clandestine—but you suggested just now that originally she went about with him sometimes, though she disapproved of him."

"She told me only yesterday," said Rupert vigorously, "that she thought him a pernicious influence on my life. She even said she detested him. Louise is fond of extravagant expressions of that kind. But"—he smiled—"don't count on *her*, Superintendent. She didn't kill Bernard. She's no more capable of it than—you or I."

"I'll put my question in another way," said Mallett with continued patience. "Do you think that Smith-Wilson's unrequited passion for your wife could have affected him to the point of suicide? You knew him well. He was a sick man. Did he ever seem to you despondent— moody—unduly depressed?"

Rupert's brow cleared.

"Good heavens, no!" he said. "Bernard was never depressed. He didn't know the meaning of the word. He might be angry—impatient— disappointed; but depressed—oh no!" He laughed. "I believe there's some suggestion that he was trying to ruin me in order to get Louise from me. Now *that's* more like Bernard. He was capable of that, in one of his moods. But he never gave in or felt sorry for himself, even when he thought he was dying. Bernard was never—resigned."

"Then you don't think he committed suicide?"

"I do not."

"Not for that or any other reason?"

"No."

"Ah!" said Mallett, leaning back. "Your opinion is of great value, though it doesn't settle the question, of course." He was thinking: 'This man is honest to the point of genius. If he were guilty, he would eagerly seize on suicide as an explanation.' He added aloud:

"Then you think someone killed him—ruling out the possibility of accident?"

"I suppose so."

"You have no views as to who it could be?"

"None."

"I'm told there was some sort of a scene between you and Sir Matthew Risdon yesterday evening over the fall in the price of some shares. Did you connect Smith-Wilson in any way with this transaction?"

"Not at first."

"Did you know that he had instructed his secretary Holmes to sell those shares and so depress the market?"

"No."

"And that Holmes had not carried out these instructions, for reasons of his own?"

"I know that now. I didn't at the time."

"Then you felt no sense of grievance against Smith-Wilson? You did not blame him at all for the difficulty in which you found yourself?"

"Oh yes, I did!" said Rupert, with unabated frankness. "I blamed him for not having let me know that the shares were wobbly: in fact, for having tipped me them as winners. I was very angry indeed. I considered it was not the act of a friend—and I was astonished as well."

"Did you go and tell him so?"

"No. I left without seeing him." Rupert spoke firmly, but Mallett's practised ear detected a reservation.

"At what time did you leave?"

"Shortly after midnight."

"Why did you wait so long?"

"What do you mean?"

"You left the smoking-room after your encounter with Sir Matthew Risdon at about ten p.m. After that, nobody saw you. Your wife, I gather, didn't see you between the end of dinner last night and your arrival this morning. You say you left shortly after midnight. Did anyone see you go?"

"I don't know," said Rupert. He thought: 'Here it is, just as Louise told me. She was right: I ought to have seen her before I left. Damn Olivia!' He added desperately:

"But I did leave at that time—and Bernard was alive then, if you're trying to prove I murdered him!"

"I'm not trying to prove anything," said Mallett. "I'm trying to solve this problem of Smith-Wilson's violent death. You say he was your friend: well then, answer my questions. It's the least you can do. What were you doing between ten o'clock, when you left the smoking-room, and midnight, when you say you left?"

"Well," said Rupert grudgingly, "I'll do my best. But you fellows are so quick to jump at every little circumstance that sounds at all unusual, that one's afraid to mention anyone's name for fear of arousing your suspicion against them."

"Have no fear," said Mallett. "You're more likely to do so by remaining silent."

"Well, then——" said Rupert, and stopped. After a moment's thought, he began again abruptly: "Have you talked to Miss Bannermore?"

"Not yet, except in so far as she accuses Holmes. Did she see you leave?"

"Not that I know of," said Rupert. "I was merely trying to account for the interval, as you asked me."

"Go ahead."

"Miss Bannermore heard the row between myself and Sir Matthew, and she took me aside afterwards and told me she had inside knowledge about these West United shares—that they were really quite sound. She advised me to leave at once, in order to be at my office first thing today and deal with any clients who might have heard the rumour put about by Bernard and might panic, and so cause a slump where none existed. I agreed to go; but I had had a few drinks and wasn't quite up to driving, so she said she'd bring me some black coffee and ice cubes to my room. I went there, and lay down on the bed for a while, to cool off and get sober. I fell asleep. When I woke up, soon after ten-thirty, I found the coffee and ice beside my bed. I drank the coffee and began to feel better." He stopped again.

"Well?" prompted Mallett. "That brings us to, say, ten forty-five. What happened between then and midnight?"

Rupert looked across at him, tortured.

"Must I tell you? I can't see what it has to do with all this. I assure you, Bernard was alive when I left. I didn't see him, but I heard him talking."

"You did?"

"Yes. My wife heard him, too. She must have missed me by inches, coming down the stairs. I haven't yet told her that I was there, too."

"Why not?"

"I have a reason." Rupert looked dogged.

"Obviously," said Mallett dryly. "And it must be a pretty good reason, too, if you're willing to risk suspicion yourself rather than reveal it. I know of only one such reason—and that's a woman."

"What do you mean?" Rupert grew red, and Mallett saw that the shot had gone home.

"Come now! Who kept you from ten forty-five till nearly twelve? You may as well tell me. I shall find out in the end."

Rupert shook his head.

"Was it Miss Bannermore?" said Mallett.

"No."

"Sure?"

"Of course I'm sure!" Rupert said explosively. "I've told you: I never saw Miss Bannermore after she brought me the coffee."

"Oh, so you did see her then? I thought you said you were asleep."

"Well, I——" Rupert gave up the attempt.

"I see," said Mallett. "You were sleeping with one eye open. Well, then, who's left? It surely wasn't Lady Risdon," he said with heavy jocularity. "One of the young ladies perhaps? Ah well, never mind: I understand your feelings What's more important is: you passed Smith-Wilson's door, you say, shortly after twelve. How was that? It surely wasn't on your way."

"No," said Rupert glumly. "As I was leaving, I had an impulse to go and see him and ask him why he had acted as he did, if he was still my friend. It was stupid of me—but I get these ideas sometimes, and I wanted to settle the matter. He was the only one who could really explain."

"How did you know he was still awake? All the guests had gone by then. Smith-Wilson was an invalid: I'm told he usually goes to bed early. Didn't you expect him to have retired as soon as he was free?"

"Yes. But I thought that last night, as he'd had to stay up late because of the party, he might still be here, perhaps after saying good night to his guests." He evidently though this reason unconvincing, for he added: "And then I——I saw the light still on here in his study. This room juts out, as you see, and one can see the window from the other rooms in the front of the house."

"Where is your own room?" said Mallett. "Facing front or back?"

Rupert hesitated: "Back."

"Then where were you when you saw this window?"

Rupert remained silent.

"I see," said Mallett, "the same story! Well, I shan't press you. There's no need, yet. So you allege that you came to this door, heard someone talking, and withdrew. Whose voice did you hear?"

"Bernard's."

"You're sure? Anyone else's?"

"No. It was Bernard's voice, and he was talking rapidly. No one else could have got a word in. He was like that when he got wound up sometimes. At least, he used to be, in the old days, especially when he'd had a few drinks. But since his illness, I've never known him do it; he daren't, I imagine."

"Did you hear what he was saying?"

"Not a word. He wasn't talking loudly. He was talking fast—urgently. The door's supposed to be sound-proof, but as you've probably noticed, what it does is to muffle sound. Also, I didn't stop to listen—I didn't want to hear. I just crept away, thankful to have missed him after all, because it would have meant another row, and I thought he probably wasn't equal to it. I went straight down and to the garage, got my car and drove away."

"You've nothing more to add—no suggestion as to who might have been watching you, perhaps, from any of the windows?"

Rupert shook his head.

"I tried to get away without being seen. I didn't switch my lights on, even, until I had passed the gates, and I turned off by the side gate into the lane. I didn't pass the lodge. But if anybody saw a car leaving at that time with no lights on, that was me."

Mallett nodded.

"You still refuse to say who you were with between ten forty-five and eleven forty-five?"

Rupert was about to speak, when they were both diverted by discordant sounds coming from below, through the open window. Mallett turned hastily and leaned out.

"It's Holmes," he said. "All right, Major, I'll see you again later." He waved Rupert to the door.

Rupert went off, exasperated and preoccupied, down the narrow polished stairway to the library.

'This is no good,' he was thinking. 'I shall have to make a clean breast of the whole thing to Louise. She's right: nothing I do ever goes well when I haven't consulted her. But I didn't want to worry her.'

His hand was on the latch of the library door, when suddenly, from the other side, such a clamour arose, such a shouting of men's voices and a shrieking of women's, that all other considerations fled before the need for action. Rupert flung open the heavy door and hurled himself into the fray.

21

A quarter of an hour before, Dr. Fitzbrown had passed through the library, striding through, as he always did, with an eye on his objective and no time to spare for incidental encounters.

Nevertheless, he had paused on the threshold of Mrs. Smith-Wilson's door to let Olivia go by; and he had turned to look after her in some surprise, for she did not greet him or even ignore him. She passed him with half-averted face, and he saw that she was not in control of herself. If she had been any other young woman, he would have said that she was crying. She did not go down the stairway to the library; instead, she turned away as if to her own room.

Fitzbrown tapped at Mrs. Smith-Wilson's door and walked in.

Mrs. Smith-Wilson, too, had not recovered her rigidity. There were no tears in her eyes now; but she looked ruffled, excited, elated almost; and Fitzbrown remembered the new relationship suddenly revealed to her; the news had reached him almost immediately. He came forward, and spoke rather roughly, as was his manner with the wealthy or the wayward.

"You should be resting," he said. "Have you been having a scene with that young woman?"

She nodded at him, triumphant. "You've heard the news? She's going to bring the boy here to live. And he's going to take Bernard's name. I insisted."

"Good!" said Fitzbrown dryly. "It's about time. A pity *she* can't, too. It's going to make things a little awkward for her, isn't it? Or are you proposing that she shall become his aunt or his governess?"

He sat down beside her, as if for a professional examination, and absent-mindedly took out his watch. She laid her hand on his arm.

"You mustn't be too hard on Bernard," she said. "He was a man set apart. He couldn't have lived long, in any case, and he knew it. That was what made him so—reckless."

"Yes—with other people's happiness," retorted Fitzbrown.

"With mine, too," said Mrs. Smith-Wilson. "It's a long time since I've had any real influence over Bernard."

"You brought him up badly," said Fitzbrown, but not quite so roughly. "You never taught him he had duties to others. I suppose that was the secret of his success. And anyway, there was nothing wrong with him to begin with. If he had taken *my* advice, he could have lived to be eighty. But no: he must live his own life, overworking, rushing about, never stopping to consider the strain he was putting on the only piece of machinery that really mattered—his own body. And then, after avoiding me for years, knowing what I'll tell him, he comes to me at the last minute, when all I can do is to hand him over to the surgeon. *That's* his tragedy—not what's happened now."

Mrs. Smith-Wilson listened to him as he fumed and raged.

"You're a born dictator," she said, "just like your father. He always wanted to run all our lives."

"Only because he knew the truth."

"Maybe. But I didn't always do as he said, and I've survived."

"You're tough—but not so tough as you think."

"True enough," said Mrs. Smith-Wilson, looking sharply away.

Fitzbrown thrust a hand into his pocket and drew out an envelope. Carefully he shook the contents forward into the fold made by the flap, so that they were visible.

"Do you recognise this?" he said abruptly.

Mrs. Smith-Wilson bent forward, peering at the envelope through the glasses she raised to her eyes:

"Small bits of glass—and a rubber bulb. Yes, I think so: looks like one of those things I use for my eyedrops. Why?"

"You use eyedrops?" said Fitzbrown, startled.

"Yes, of course. Why shouldn't I?" She bridled. "Only now and then, when I want to look my best."

"Who gave you the prescription? You didn't get it from me."

"Oh, Bernard got it somewhere," she said indifferently. "In London, I think. Why?"

"Belladonna."

"I know. What of it?"

Fitzbrown jumped up.

"Don't you know," he said, "that belladonna is a poison—and the poisonous element in it is atropine? Has nobody told you that the poison Bernard died of *was* atropine?" He paced to the window and back. "Where is the stuff? Have you still got it? Who used it on you? Did you do it yourself?"

"Sometimes I did. Sometimes I got Barker to do it. If there's any left, it's in my medicine-chest there in the bathroom. You can look: it's not locked. But I don't think there is any. Barker was looking for it yesterday evening—I thought of using it, as we had visitors, though I don't as a rule—but she couldn't find it." She stiffened. "Good heavens! You're not suggesting somebody stole it, to use on Bernard!"

Fitzbrown had hurried into the bathroom at her mention of the medicine-chest, and she could hear him rummaging among the medicine-bottles. He came back to her slowly:

"I don't see it there. Did Bernard ever borrow it? Have you ever known him to use it? Has he ever had anything wrong with his eyes?"

"I don't think so. He complained sometimes of a smoky atmosphere, especially since his illness."

"Could he have borrowed it yesterday evening?" said Fitzbrown. "It can have very queer effects on people who are allergic to it, even when dropped in the eyes."

"I don't know. He didn't get it from *me*."

"But he could have taken it without your knowing. I found these bits of an eyedropper, and this bulb, under the desk in his study. He had trodden the glass into the carpet. It was the red rubber bulb I noticed first. I picked it up, and then I saw the splinters of glass. I thought at first it was a fountain-pen filler; but when I examined the pieces, I found traces of atropine. I came straight back here to tell Mallett, but he's engaged. So I came along to see you. When did you last use these drops, do you remember?"

"Yes, I do," she said with sudden and surprising vigour—for until then Fitzbrown had had the impression that she was not listening very closely. "I remember perfectly. It was last Friday, when I had my bridge party."

"Bridge party?"

"Yes." She eyed him haughtily. "I usually have a little bridge party once a week, when my rheumatism isn't too bad. You have no objection, I hope?"

Fitzbrown shook his head with a smile.

"Last week," she went on, "there were just the four of us: Lady Risdon, the vicar, and—let me see—who was the fourth?"

"Bernard?" suggested Fitzbrown.

"No, no. Bernard never played bridge. He hated games of chance. And it wasn't Sir Matthew: he couldn't come. At least, he came later, to fetch Lady Risdon, and looked on for a while. Then he and Bernard went off to the study to talk. Mabel Hertford was here, too, but of course she can't play. Now what *did* happen? Oh yes, I remember! The vicar had promised to bring his wife, but she made some excuse—something tiresome about one of the children—and so I got Bernard to send for Holmes."

"Bernard's secretary?"

She nodded:

"A very disagreeable and uncouth young man—and now I hear he's a thief as well. I'm not surprised. But he was useful that afternoon. He played quite a good hand, too. He and I were partners against the vicar and Lady Risdon, and they were not match for us—no match at all. He won twenty-five shillings. He didn't speak a word, I remember, except to bid and to say 'Thanks' when he was paid."

Fitzbrown gave her a sidelong look.

"You know what Miss Bannermore is saying about him?"

Mrs. Smith-Wilson looked back at him sharply.

"About his stealing?" She caught his meaning. "Or that it was he who did this thing to Bernard?" She nodded. "Yes, I know."

"She told you?" said Fitzbrown, watching her closely.

"She did." Mrs. Smith-Wilson's hands, gnarled with rheumatism, crisped together in her lap.

"What makes her say so?" said Fitzbrown.

"She thinks it goes with his dishonesty—his fear of what Bernard would do when he discovered it."

"What's your opinion?" said Fitzbrown.

Mrs. Smith-Wilson, lost in grim thought, did not at first answer.

"Do you think Holmes was capable of it?" Fitzbrown pressed her.

"Yes," she said slowly, "I think he was capable of it—though I would have thought he would have preferred violence to poison. I didn't like him. I told Bernard so. But Bernard said he knew all about Holmes: that he was full of theories, but they didn't amount to very much, he considered."

"Huh!" said Fitzbrown. "Bernard was always sure that nobody's theories were strong enough to conflict with his wishes, once they came under his influence. Now about this belladonna: you used it, you say, that afternoon, before your visitors arrived. Who administered the drops? Did you do it yourself?"

"Sometimes I did—but only if no one else was there. Barker usually did it, and sometimes Mabel Hertford if she happened to be there."

"Who did it that afternoon? And where? Where was the bottle kept, by the way?"

"In the medicine-chest, or on my dressing-table. Let me see: I think it was in the bedroom. Now was it Barker, or did I do it myself? No, I remember it was Barker's afternoon for going to the clinic in Chode: a frightful nuisance, but I had to let her. She goes to have some sort of light treatment for her rheumatism: a lot of nonsense, I say. A bottle of liniment would do her more good, unless she invents it all in imitation of me, which I always suspect. Well, of course I make her take that day as her afternoon off, in case she has any ideas of—"

Fitzbrown interrupted: "So she was out that day."

"Yes—most inconvenient." With difficulty Mrs. Smith-Wilson appeared to withdraw her mind from this recurrent irritation. "So I must have used the eyedrops myself—or was it Mabel? I forget. Anyway, it doesn't take a moment."

"Was anyone else there?"

"No, I don't think so. Who else could there be? Unless perhaps Bernard looked in for a few minutes beforehand. How can I possibly remember? Now I think of it, I believe Bernard was there when we began, because I seem to remember that the vicar arrived first, without his tiresome wife, and it was then that I asked Bernard to send for Holmes."

"When did Holmes arrive?"

"Oh, soon after. Or no: I remember he kept us waiting. Lady Risdon had arrived, and we were all waiting."

"Could Holmes possibly have known of the existence of these eye-drops? Were they mentioned at all? Was there ever a moment when he could have seen the bottle or got hold of it? Or do you think Bernard borrowed the bottle and the dropper for some reason and forgot to return them? Have you used them since?"

"I think so. Let me see." Mrs. Smith-Wilson, apparently flustered by the hail of questions, made no attempt to deal with any but the last.

"Now you mention it, I remember I asked Barker to get them yesterday evening, and she couldn't find them. But then, that girl is such a muddler, there's nothing unusual in that. She mixes up everything in the medicine-chest. The things that are wanted are always at the back. Only the other day—or was it yesterday?—"

But Fitzbrown, with a curt request for permission, had jumped up and hurried into the bedroom, and so into the bathroom which led out of it. He came back, carrying two bottles on a handkerchief laid on the palm of his hand.

"Is this the one?" he said, pointing to a small bottle labelled 'The Eyedrops'. "It was on your dressing-table behind everything else." When Mrs. Smith-Wilson agreed, he pointed to the other. "And this one? This was at the back of the medicine-chest. When did you last use this?"

She peered down at the blue liniment-bottle with its red label.

"Why, that's the liniment for my neck! But it's finished. I wanted it last night—or rather early this morning. We couldn't find it, and I wanted to ring for Barker, but Mabel Hertford hunted about and found it at the back of the cupboard. I meant to ask Barker about it today, though I knew she'd pretend she knew nothing about it. But the extraordinary thing is, she hasn't turned up. Imagine that, on this day of all days!"

"You got this on my prescription," said Fitzbrown. "I remember giving it to you, a couple of months ago. Do you know the principal ingredient?"

Mrs. Smith-Wilson stared at him, alert.

"Atropine," he said. "I must take these to Mallett at once." He hurried to the door. "You'd better lie down. I'll tell them to send you your tea at once."

Mrs. Smith-Wilson watched him go. Then, rising stiffly, she walked across the room to the bell and rang it violently.

No one came.

She rang a second time, and then a third.

Still no one came.

Angrily muttering to herself, she hobbled back to her chair. She had just seated herself when the door opened and the rather frightened face of Mrs. Hertford appeared.

"Can I get you anything?" she said, coming a little way into the room. "I heard your bell ringing in Barker's room, and I thought——"

"Come in and shut the door!" commanded Mrs. Smith-Wilson. "Where *is* Barker? That woman! Just at a time when she ought to be doing everything she can for me—heaven knows I've done a great deal for her!—she seizes the opportunity to absent herself without telling me! Typical of the servant-class! She's gone home, I suppose, to get out of all the trouble! I shall dismiss her as soon as she comes back. Meanwhile, you and the girls must stay."

"Of course, dear," said Mabel soothingly. "We'll do everything in our power, you may be sure. But I must say I'm surprised at Barker. I know she was a bit careless and scatterbrained at times; but I never would have suspected her of such—callousness. I did think she was genuinely attached to you. I call her conduct utterly selfish and"—she flushed—"immoral."

"Rubbish!" said Mrs. Smith-Wilson. "There's no such thing as a genuine attachment where money enters. Did Barker ever have anything to do with Holmes, did you notice?"

Mrs. Hertford stared. "Holmes?"

"Yes, Holmes! Dr. Fitzbrown has just been here, and he has found those eyedrops that Barker mislaid, and also that liniment-bottle, and he says they both contain this poison—the poison that——" Her strong, irritable voice faltered. She went on: "They believe it was Holmes. Olivia thinks so, and she knew Holmes well. If they could prove some link between Holmes and Barker, they'd know where he got the poison. Fitzbrown has taken the bottles away to show to the Superintendent. We shall soon know."

She folded her hands once more on her lap, and set herself to wait, apparently until the answer should be found. "I believe the woman's run off with Holmes!" she added with scorn.

"Shall I see about your tea?" said Mrs. Hertford after a pitying and rather nervous look at her.

Suddenly, from below, up the stairs leading from the library, came confused sounds: shouting, shrieks, footsteps, doors slamming.

Mabel hurried to the door and stood listening at the head of the stairs.

22

When Rupert threw open the library door, he did not stop to think: he took in the scene in a flash, and acted.

He saw, near at hand, Louise, the two Hertford girls, and even Lady Risdon, all standing up in attitudes of horrified expectancy. He saw Olivia, rigid, waiting. He saw Holmes, grimacing with fury, struggling with the two men who were holding his arms. Holmes was shouting at Olivia, calling her by the few foul epithets that rise so readily to every man's lips when his hatred for a woman is stimulated. He managed also to say: "I'll get you for this!" when his guards wrenched him back so violently that for a moment pain silenced him. He turned furiously on them:

"You fools! I didn't kill Smith-Wilson! *She* did—and then she set a trap for me: got me to clear out, and then betrayed me! But I'll get you!" he muttered, suddenly lowering his voice as he turned back to Olivia; and with a sharp twist he freed his arms. Olivia, white to the lips, stood her ground: there was nothing else she could do.

It was fortunate for her that Rupert had started to run the length of the library the moment he saw Holmes' face. He flung himself between them with such force that he and Holmes fell some feet away, rolling over and over, until they reached the bookshelves. Holmes struggled and writhed with the despair of a baulked panther; but Rupert, having the superior hold and the greater weight, held him down. The two policemen, exasperated at having been outwitted, seized on their helpless prey with brutal roughness and dragged him to his feet. But all the fight had gone out of him. When Mallett entered, and then Fitzbrown, Holmes was leaning back, dazed, against a complete set of the *Gentleman's*

Magazine bound in calf, and down his pale face large tears of pain were rolling.

Rupert, glancing at him, felt compunction. He had difficulty in not telling the fellow to cheer up, but he remembered that Holmes had been about to attack a woman, and he remained silent. He walked away, ignoring Olivia, and joined Louise.

"Are you all right, darling?" she said, feeling his forearms anxiously as if she expected to be able to detect a breakage.

"Yes, thanks," said Rupert brusquely. "What the devil did Olivia want to get in Holmes's way for? Damn it all, does she think people *like* being betrayed?"

Louise looked at him in surprise and some interest. Why, she wondered, did he speak with such feeling about a stranger, a worthless little cheat and pilferer? Was he thinking of betrayal nearer home? Sometimes she thought that Rupert was not as easy to read as he appeared.

By now Mallett had reached the group by the bookcase, and made a brief inspection of the victim. He nodded at his men.

"Bring him along." And as he passed Olivia on his return journey to the staircase, he said curtly: "You'd better come, too, Miss Bannermore. We may need you—unless you don't feel able to stand it. Don't let this fellow's threats intimidate you. You're quite safe now."

"*Now*," repeated Olivia with malicious emphasis, looking round her, at Rupert, at Holmes, who was still glowering, and then at the crestfallen policemen. "So nice to know!"

She began to traverse the length of the library back to the door; and as she passed Rupert, she murmured:

"Thanks, hero."

Rupert turned away, and the procession filed past: Mallett, fuming and bustling; Olivia, pale and unhurrying; and Holmes in the grip of the two men, who were forced to modify their pace to Olivia's in order not to collide with her, and who filled up the occasional pauses by giving

Holmes another shake. They held him, now, with a grip of iron; but he was unresisting.

As Mallett reached the door, Fitzbrown, standing there, drew him aside and whispered something into his ear. The others, Olivia leading, passed on.

What Fitzbrown was saying to Mallett was:

"Listen: I've got reason to believe that the poison was administered in two doses—a small dose early in the evening by means of an eye-dropper, and a bigger dose much later, probably in a glass. I'll explain later; but meanwhile, find out if Holmes had anything to do with Barker, Mrs. Smith-Wilson's maid."

Mallett nodded. "What's the connection?"

"Just this: there were two preparations containing belladonna in Mrs. Smith-Wilson's rooms—eyedrops, and a liniment made up to my prescription for her fibrositis. I had forgotten about it, but I've got both bottles here. I'll take them back right away and have them examined to make sure. The point is this: Mrs. Smith-Wilson is very vague about how and when she used them; but one thing emerges—her maid Barker had access to the medicine-chest, and when she was there she administered any medicines Mrs. Smith-Wilson used."

"Where is this woman?" said Mallett irritably, looking after the retreating procession now half-way up the stairs. He held the door, eager to follow and get to work on Holmes.

"That's just it," said Fitzbrown. "Where is she? Nobody seems to have seen her today—or, in fact, since she got Mrs. Smith-Wilson ready for dinner yesterday evening. The presumption is, she's bolted; and the question arises, did she arrange to bolt with Holmes?"

Mallett nodded, and he and Fitzbrown separated. The doors at each end of the library closed behind them, and peace descended.

23

Rupert and Louise were left standing together among the leather chairs. The two Hertford girls had vanished, nobody noticed when or where. Louise, still a little uneasy about the extent of Rupert's knowledge or the accuracy of his surmises, turned to begin a new attack on him, when they were both startled to hear a deep voice behind them saying:

"Aren't you the young man my husband had that stupid scene with last night?"

Lady Risdon, her book still in her hand and her finger in the place, was surveying them both through her eyeglasses. She came forward.

"Congratulations on your prompt action just now. Really, I thought nothing could save that young woman from some very rough handling—which she had thoroughly earned, I don't doubt. Who is she? Another of Bernard Smith-Wilson's secretaries? Odd of him to ask her here."

Rupert glared at her.

"Not funny at all," he contradicted. "She was Bernard's mistress. She ought to have been his wife. At any rate, she's the mother of his son and heir."

"Rupert!" gasped Louise. "I don't believe it!" She was furious with him for having withheld this news for a single moment, and for having blurted it out thus in front of the tiresome woman, before whom one could not display all one's curiosity; furious with Bernard, too, for his unfaithfulness and his deceit.

"Please yourself," said Rupert sulkily. "He has left him the residue of his estate, after he's finished with the rest of us."

"Good gracious!" said Lady Risdon, mildly amused. "Who would have thought it? What will his mother say?"

"His mother knows," said Rupert shortly. "She took it quite well, so far as I could see. I admire her. She's got guts."

"But Rupert," Louise expostulated, "where have you been all this time? Why didn't you come and tell me? The reading of the will must have been finished ages ago! I saw Mr. Rainford leaving."

Rupert rounded on her.

"I've been with Superintendent Mallett," he said. "And he's been trying to pin Bernard's death on to me. You were quite right: I was safe enough so long as I didn't profit. But, you see, Bernard left me twenty thousand pounds."

He walked away to one of the windows, and stood staring out, his hands in his pockets, as if he had announced not a legacy but a debt from which there was no escape.

Louise, for once, was silent.

Lady Risdon broke in cheerfully:

"Well, that's quite nice, I must say—very useful to two young married people like yourselves. When Risdon and I started life together, we had about a quarter of that sum between us, and we thought ourselves not badly off for a start." She turned to Louise: "Wouldn't you like some tea? I should like to get out of doors for a while, out of this gloomy place. I wonder what's become of my husband. It looks as if we shan't get away for hours. Probably we'll have to stay the night. Matthew won't care, so long as he's comfortable and well fed. Do you think your husband could be induced to go and find one of those great useless fellows and get him to bring us some tea outside on the terrace?" She laid the book carelessly on one of the round tables.

"Rupert!" said Louise, appealing to his back.

Rupert said: "I'll try," and went off.

Lady Risdon and Louise followed slowly.

"You know," said Lady Risdon, laying her heavily-ringed hand on Louise's arm, "you two young people are lucky: you're still sufficiently interested in each other to quarrel, and you don't care much who's looking on."

"Is that a proof of interest?" said Louise. "If so, Rupert and I must be absorbed in each other."

"You are," said Lady Risdon. "All this tragic atmosphere doesn't mean anything to either of you except—how is it going to affect the other?" She laughed, a deep, well-satisfied gurgle. "Oh yes, quarrelling's a very good sign—at first. But don't carry it too far. Men get tired of spice in every dish."

They walked through the open hall doors into the porch and stood at the top of the steps, looking down across the terrace to the garden, which lay shimmering and silent in the sun. From the distance, the whirr of a motor lawn mower ignored the interruption of ownership: masters may die, but in summer the grass grows.

"And is he jealous of you, too?" said Lady Risdon. "But of course he is, my dear—a pretty girl like you!"

Louise winced at the growing familiarity. 'Why,' she wondered, 'do older women presume so much on their impregnable position and our politeness?' She did not want to share her relationship with Rupert. But Lady Risdon wasn't interested in Louise's views.

"Then again," she went on, "you shouldn't plague him too much, you know. If you do, he'll just go off and do the same—and then where will you be? Women usually return when they've had their flutter—but once let a man get a taste for other women and he doesn't come back. Your husband's going to get plenty of temptation, I assure you!" She laughed and added indulgently: "But you're too young and too sure of yourself, now, to believe me!"

Louise felt herself getting hot. Her temper was rising, and yet she shrank from the further intimacy that any retort would involve. She believed she knew very well to what Lady Risdon was referring: she was criticising her, Louise's, indiscretion of the previous day, when she had allowed Bernard to make her the queen of the evening in front of all his guests. She did not quite see, even now, what she could have done to avoid it, because she had not known what was coming; but she remembered her own discomfort at the dinner-table, and she remembered Lady Risdon, hard, worldly, inexorably censorious, sitting on Bernard's left hand, opposite to herself. Was it likely that Lady Risdon would forgive the 'chit of a girl', as no doubt she called Louise in her mind, for having been her supplanter in the seat of honour? That it was none of Louise's doing made no difference. Louise knew well enough that to women of Lady Risdon's type the woman ### always in the wrong, except when that woman is herself.

In a shaded corner of the terrace, under a profusely blooming American Pillar rose, a maid was placing a table and a moment later, through one of the french windows, out stepped a small party: Sir Matthew between the two Hertford girls, Rupert with Mrs. Hertford.

Lady Risdon brightened.

"Ah! So your husband's been successful! I knew he would be!"

She started off down the steps towards the party, not troubling to wait for Louise.

Louise turned and went indoors again, to seek the peace and coolness of the library.

24

Sir Matthew, with Clara and Lucilla hanging on his words, strolled across to look out over the balustrade.

"Ah well, poor old Bernard!" he said, in the complacent tone of one sure of another twenty years at least of this good life of eating, drinking, spending money and enjoying respectful attention. "*His* troubles are over! Perhaps it's all for the best: in his state of health one wouldn't care much about living or dying. And yet, when I saw him last night, I wouldn't have guessed what he intended. He seemed interested enough in the future then."

"Oh, but, you know," exclaimed Lucilla, "the police are sure, now, he was poisoned by somebody else!" She lowered her voice. "Everybody seems to think it was Mr. Holmes. But *we* think it was Miss Bannermore. You know they had a son, don't you?—she and Bernard, I mean. Isn't it dreadful? It all came out in the will. Mother says—"

Sir Matthew rubbed his eyes.

"Good heavens, is that so? I see I'm well behindhand with the news. The fact is, I've been asleep since—I won't say since when—and I've missed all the gossip among you ladies. So Bernard has a son, eh?"

"Yes," went on Lucilla, ignoring her sister's frown, "and he's to inherit the property after Bernard's mother. So what could be more likely than that—"

"Lucilla!" Clara's voice was peremptory. But Lucilla, defiant with Sir Matthew's encouraging eye on her and his protecting bulk between, persisted:

"Well, after all, Mr. Holmes accused her openly just now in the library in front of everybody, and she didn't deny it, did she? And

Mr. Mallett took them *both* away for questioning. Oh, I think she's a terrible-looking woman! I'm terrified of her, at any rate: I think she looks *evil*! And she's mad about men—isn't she, Sir Matthew? You saw her last night with poor Rupert in the smoking-room: she wouldn't leave him alone!"

Sir Matthew looked uncomfortable: he did not care to be reminded of this incident.

"Please don't listen to her, Sir Matthew," said Clara, trying not to show the anxiety she felt, lest she should incite Lucilla to further flights of indiscretion.

"Oh, but I saw her!" persisted Lucilla. "I saw her taking a Thermos flask and something on a plate to his room last night—and it was after half-past ten! She didn't stay long, it's true—but she went in. I saw her!" She looked over her shoulder to where Rupert and her mother were standing. "Ask Rupert if you don't believe me!"

Rupert and Mrs. Hertford had now reached the tea-table, and Lady Risdon had joined them.

"Rupert!" called out Lucilla, running across to them. "Isn't it true Miss Bannermore brought you something hot to your room last night? The others won't believe me!"

Sir Matthew and Clara followed slowly.

"She doesn't mean anything," Clara was murmuring urgently to him. "It's just her age—and my mother has always spoilt her. She's always been the baby."

"Yes, yes, of course," said Sir Matthew, his eyes fixed ahead. He hastened his step a little, to make sure of hearing and seeing.

Rupert turned, surprised, to Lucilla.

"Why yes, of course," he said mildly. "Why shouldn't she? You know I was rather tight when I left the smoking-room—and I had to drive to London. Why, Lucilla, what are you so excited about, all of a sudden? You're too young to have ideas like that, you know!"

Although he spoke indulgently, there was an underlying irritation in his voice that warned Lucilla not to go further. She blushed, and looked hurt.

"Oho!" Lady Risdon joined in the view-halloo. "So that's how it was! Out of the frying-pan into the fire!" She twinkled at him roguishly; but she said no more, and an uneasy silence fell.

"Excuse me," said Rupert abruptly. "I think I'll go and find my wife." He strode away, with exasperation in his every movement. The others stared after him.

"Oh dear!" said Mrs. Hertford, greatly agitated. "I'm afraid he's dreadfully offended! Lucilla, darling, you shouldn't have said anything. You don't understand how very easy it is to annoy him!"

"I told her, Mother!" began Clara self-righteously. Lucilla, scarlet with rage and shame, turned her back on her sister. Sir Matthew broke in soothingly:

"Oh, come come, ladies, you mustn't exaggerate! No harm's done. You're letting trifles get on your nerves. But—I say, my dear, what on earth did you mean by that cryptic last remark of yours?" He turned to Lady Risdon with avid curiosity.

"Oh, nothing much," said Lady Risdon, still staring after Rupert as he ran up the stone steps and disappeared between the stone columns of the porch.

"Do tell us!" Mabel put in anxiously. "Is it something to do with Miss Bannermore? Lucilla shouldn't have said so in front of Rupert—it was silly of you, darling, but never mind, I'm sure he'll soon forgive you—but *I* saw her, too, taking the Thermos flask to his room. In fact, she came into the kitchen to ask for it just as I was leaving with some milk for Bernard. But go on, Lady Risdon: what did *you* see? I can't help feeling we ought all to say *all* we know, in this dreadful situation. After all, how are the police ever to find out the truth if we don't give them the facts? And I feel we can't do better than pool our knowledge—"

"Very noble of you, I'm sure," interposed Lady Risdon dryly.

Mabel gave her a dubious glance. "I mean to say," she went on, still more flustered, "if it's only for his poor mother's sake—Bernard's, I mean—"

"Naturally," said Lady Risdon.

Mabel was looking at her with urgent inquiry, as were Sir Matthew and the girls. Clara had forgotten her anger, and Lucilla her chagrin. After a moment's consideration, Lady Risdon began in her rather deep, deliberate voice:

"Well, upon my soul, I don't know if I should tell you, but as you're all so anxious to hear, last night, I was rather bored with the company in the drawing-room, and I came upstairs before everybody left, at about a quarter-past eleven, to say good night to Mrs. Smith-Wilson. I talked to her for five minutes or so—Mrs. Lavering was there, playing cards with her—and then, feeling sleepy, I came away." Lady Risdon half-yawned again at the recollection. "I didn't go downstairs again. I went straight to my room, along the corridor. As I passed one of the doors, I heard voices." She looked round at her audience, and satisfied with the rapt attention she had secured, she continued: "The door was ajar, but the light wasn't on, and I could see nothing except a man's hand and shirt-cuff on the edge of the door. The other voice was a woman's."

"Good gracious!" said Mrs. Hertford, glancing nervously at her two girls, who were frankly listening with all their hearts and souls. But there was no stopping the story now. Lady Risdon drew a step nearer to her semi-circle.

"They were arguing," she said. "The woman seemed to be trying to draw him inside again, because I heard him say: 'For God's sake, let go of me! Are you crazy?' I couldn't hear what she said, because he suddenly shut the door again, or else she forced him to." Lady Risdon moistened her lips: "I hurried past, of course. But I noticed which room it was: I noticed the flowers painted on the door."

"Ha!" croaked Sir Matthew, but whether in approval or derision nobody bothered to inquire.

"However," resumed Lady Risdon, weighing her effect carefully as she came to the climax, "a moment later the door opened again. I had just time to slip into my room when Major Lavering came out and almost ran down the corridor. He hurried past without seeing me. His hair was dishevelled and his tie was crooked. Whoever the lady was, she had given him a rough time." She laughed maliciously.

"And you don't know who it was?" said Sir Matthew impatiently. "Was it someone on our corridor? It must have been one of the guests—though I thought those rooms were empty."

"You face frontward, don't you?" said Clara. "Our rooms face the other way, over the garages. Those rooms on your side seem to be always wrapped up in dust-sheets whenever I catch a glimpse of them."

"Well," said Lady Risdon, "I haven't been able to look, of course, but if anybody cares to investigate, the door has a spray of lilies painted on it."

"Oh!" said Lucilla, coming forward again. "But that's one of the biggest rooms! It used to be Colonel and Mrs. Smith-Wilson's bedroom when the Colonel was alive—didn't it, Mother? I've seen inside: there's a huge four-poster bed in it, with a canopy, and lots of cupboards and bookcases. And isn't there a sort of private passage leading to it from the study? Anyhow, it's not occupied now!"

She turned to her mother for confirmation, but Mrs. Hertford did not answer. The others were silent as they considered the implications of all that had been said. But it seemed to be agreed that the subject had now better be dropped. Sir Matthew began to move towards the table:

"Tea's served, my dear. If you'll pour me out a cup, I'll go along afterwards and see if I can get any sense out of the police. We've been kept hanging about here all day for nothing, and if Mallett doesn't want us we may as well go home."

25

When tea was over, and Sir Matthew had gone indoors, Lady Risdon said to Mrs. Hertford:

"Shall we take a walk by the lily-pools?"

Mrs. Hertford meekly agreed. Clara and Lucilla were left alone.

"You *were* a fool to say all that in front of Rupert," said Clara cordially to Lucilla.

"Oh, shut up!" said Lucilla with equal cordiality. She was, to her sorrow, a little too old to kick Clara on the shins as once she would have done. "Rupert didn't mind: it flattered him. It was you others who made it all seem important and not funny at all. How can Rupert help it if all the women chase after him? He's so good-looking and so brave! I wish he weren't married. I'm sure Louise doesn't appreciate him. Look how she was behaving with Bernard last night!"

"I know," said Clara, her indignation deflected momentarily on to Louise.

Lucilla jumped up and clasped her hands excitedly.

"And what are *you* grumbling at, anyway?" she said. "If it hadn't been for me, you wouldn't have heard the rest of the story! Oh, wasn't it gorgeous, the way that old battle-axe was spying on him, peeping round her door! I wish he'd caught her. I've a good mind to tell him!"

"Lucilla! You wouldn't!" Clara looked shocked, but the idea was not without its appeal. She went on reflectively: "I wonder who it was, really. Do you honestly think it was Miss Bannermore?"

"Of course!" cried Lucilla. "She went to his room earlier on, and that didn't come off, so she lay in wait for him later. She wants to compromise him and get Louise to divorce him."

"But you don't really think she—got rid of Bernard?"

"Why not?" said Lucilla defiantly. "She gets the money, doesn't she? And her son gets it all in the end. If she's in love with Rupert, Bernard was only in the way."

Clara scrutinised her.

"I believe you're in love with Rupert yourself—and that's why you said what you did. You said it to provoke him!"

"Oh, don't be such an ass!" Lucilla, pleased, turned away and began picking the lichens off the balustrade.

"You're sure it wasn't you who waylaid him last night?" said Clara. "You were gone a long time, I thought, when you went to powder your nose."

Lucilla shook her head.

"I wish it had been!"

"Well, you'd better give up thinking that way. You won't get him, any more than I got Bernard."

"Pooh!" said Lucilla. "You weren't in love with Bernard."

"No," said Clara, "but I would have liked to have got away from home, into—this." Her gaze swept the façade of the house, the terrace, and the distant gardens. "Think of it, after all Mother's petty economies!" She sighed. "Bernard might have been more generous to us all in his will. He left more to some of his employees. Evidently he never took us seriously at all."

Lucilla came forward.

"Clara," she said, in a new tone of conspiratorial urgency, "I have an idea! Let's go along and have a look inside that bedroom! You never know: people leave clues about, especially in the dark and in such—circumstances. We might find out for certain who was there!"

Clara sat up, rigid.

"Oh, no, we can't!"

"Why can't we? Nobody's about upstairs at this time of day. We know which room it was—the one with the lilies painted on its door.

If we just strolled past casually, well, then, if nobody were about we could tap at the door, and if there were no answer we could just peep in. Come on! If you won't I'll go by myself! I feel sure it's awfully important, somehow."

Clara rose, still anxious, yet attracted.

"Promise you won't say anything to anybody else if we find anything!"

"I won't promise anything of the kind!" said Lucilla, dancing on ahead. "Come on! Don't be such a coward! You're as keen as I am to know who it was—except that I'm mad on him and you're not. Or are you?" She came back to her sister with a new light of battle in her eyes.

Clara shook her head.

"Don't excite yourself. I like Rupert very much, but I prefer something more solid for keeps."

"Oh, good heavens!" said Lucilla in disgust. "Anyone would think you were Mother's age!"

26

"Those are two fine girls you've got there," said Lady Risdon firmly, as they walked beside the lily-pools.

"You must have married very young."

"I was married at eighteen," said Mabel. "Clara's age. Sometimes I can't believe they're my daughters at all. We seem just like three sisters."

"Splendid!" said Lady Risdon, thinking what a bore it must have been to be saddled with two young children throughout the best years of one's life, and in such straitened circumstances that one would have to do everything for them oneself. "Matthew and I put it off too long: that's why we never had any children, I suppose. Were you left a widow very early?"

"Oh, yes," said Mabel, "when the children were only toddlers. That's another of the things that makes us so united."

"And haven't you ever considered marrying again? I should have thought a woman like you needed a man to—protect her."

Mabel smiled, rather dreamily.

"Yes—but it has to be the right man, hasn't it? I mean, the first time one marries, it's because it seems the right thing to do, or one wants to leave home, or one's rather proud of being asked. One doesn't realise what marriage means. But the second time one would marry for choice, I think, don't you?"

"Huh!" said Lady Risdon. "Don't ask me! Once is enough for me! If I survive Matthew, there won't be a second. But then, of course, I've been married for forty years—about as long as you've been born—and that makes a difference, no doubt. Still, I think you should consider it.

You'll want to get your girls off your hands first, no doubt. Have you any ideas for them, or have they any ideas for themselves?"

Nothing could have interested her less than the answer: her thoughts were running on Mabel herself. But Mabel began conscientiously:

"Well, Clara may have had her little fancies; but Lucilla, my younger girl—she's too young to have begun to think of such things. All in good time, I always say…"

27

Clara and Lucilla stood outside the door with the arum lilies painted on the panel. The corridor was deserted: up here not a sound was to be heard. The blinds of the windows at each end were drawn, and only a dim orange electric lamp overhead gave light. Yet the thick red carpet glowed, and the white paint gleamed, as did the small brass knocker in the shape of a grinning gargoyle above the lily-spray.

"*You* go first!" whispered Lucilla, pushing Clara from behind.

Clara resisted.

"It was your idea," she whispered back resentfully. "It's just like you to start something and then be afraid to go through with it."

"You were just as keen," retorted Lucilla. "Well, all right, if you're afraid—"

"I'm not afraid."

Clara seized the gargoyle-knocker, lifted it and let it drop as if it were too hot to hold, so that it fell with one smart rap that sounded loud in the empty corridor. But there was no answering sound from the other side.

"Perhaps the door's locked," she said hopefully.

"Of course it isn't!" Lucilla, recovering her boldness, pushed past her and opened the door a little way; but before entering she, too, lifted the gargoyle and gave a series of raps. "There! Now we know there's nobody inside!"

Clara gave a last look up and down the corridor. Then she, too, stepped inside.

28

Holmes sat hunched up in the chair opposite Mallett. He had been allowed to sit, because his pallor suggested faintness; but his two guardians loomed over him, ready to pounce. Olivia, by her own wish, leaned against the mantelpiece, a little behind Holmes's chair and out of the line of his vision.

"Well, Miss Bannermore?" said Mallett. "This fellow says you encouraged him in his activities, so far as misappropriation was concerned. Don't answer unless you wish, of course."

"Complete rubbish," said Olivia nonchalantly, flicking cigarette-ash at the empty grate. "As if he needed any encouragement!"

"He also says it was by your advice that he disobeyed Mr. Smith-Wilson's orders in these transactions. Is there any truth in that?"

"None whatever," said Olivia. "Why should I want my son's father to lose money?"

Holmes twisted himself round in his chair, in spite of the heavy hand on his shoulder.

"You deny you spent an hour with me in my room last night, between eleven and twelve?"

"I certainly do," said Olivia. "What are you trying to prove? An alibi?"

Holmes sneered. "You need one as much as I do."

Olivia turned away angrily.

"All right, Miss Bannermore: you'd better go and leave him to us." Mallett stood up. "We'll be leaving ourselves now, and taking him with us. We'll be back here tomorrow at ten. You might inform Mrs. Smith-Wilson and the other members of the household."

As Olivia reached the door, Mallett called out:

"By the way, has Mrs. Smith-Wilson's personal maid turned up yet? I'd like to see her. If she doesn't appear by the morning, I shall have to take steps to find her."

"I'll inquire," said Olivia indifferently, and left.

Mallett turned to Holmes again.

"Maybe *you* can enlighten us," he said, "as to this woman's whereabouts?"

Holmes stared at him with stubborn ideological hatred.

"What woman?"

"Mrs. Smith-Wilson's personal maid. You were friendly with her, weren't you?"

"Me?" Holmes sounded genuinely astonished and outraged. "I never exchanged a word with her. Why should I?"

"Oh, come!" said Mallett with heavy humour. "You were fellow-workers, weren't you? It was natural you should unite."

"Ignoramus!" muttered Holmes between his teeth.

"Well, let's see," said Mallett. "You know her name, I suppose?"

"Yes: Barke or Barker," snapped Holmes.

"And you'd know her by sight? You'd recognise her if you saw her again?"

Holmes looked uneasy.

"I might. It would depend how she was dressed. I never saw her except in Mrs. Smith-Wilson's room, wearing her disgusting uniform. What are you driving at, anyway? Is she trying to fasten this poisoning on to me, too? You think you're very smart, using these women against me, don't you? You'd do better to try pinning it on to one of them. How about *her*? She had access to the old woman's medicine-chest, which was full of junk belonging to mother and son."

"Oh! So you knew that?"

"Who didn't?" said Holmes scornfully. "They were always tinkering with themselves. They could afford to." He gave a hoarse laugh. "It's a good idea I've offered you, to pin it on to the maid! We can't have Bannermore involved, now we know she's the mother of the son and heir! Anyhow, so long as it lets me out, I don't care which of them you choose to hang. They're all as bad as one another, and no loss to the world."

"Not to your world, maybe," said Mallett. "So you deny all knowledge of Barker's movements?"

Holmes swore.

"Oh, for God's sake leave me alone!" he said. "How can I know anything about Barker's movements? I haven't been here, have I?"

"No," said Mallett. "Neither has Barker."

"Good for her!" said Holmes. "I didn't know she had it in her. All the people here have flunkeys' souls, like yourself."

One of the policemen made a menacing movement towards him, but Mallett checked him.

"Like yourselves," emended Holmes, twisting himself round to leer at his would-be tormentors.

Mallett made an impatient gesture.

The two men jerked Holmes to his feet and began to lead him to the door.

29

It took Rupert some few minutes to persuade Louise to leave the library and come with him to their own room, but his manner was so agitated and so urgent that at last, rather grudgingly, she agreed.

As soon as they were alone:

"Look here, Louise," he said, pacing up and down and ruffling his hair, "there's something I really must tell you—something that happened last night here, before I left. I ought to have made a clean breast of it before; but I didn't know if you'd understand."

A chill of fear shot through Louise. What was she going to hear? Not a confession! Rupert was hurrying on:

"You see, it involves another person. Perhaps that's why I didn't tell you as soon as I arrived this morning—or is it just that it makes me look and feel such an awful fool?"

He paused in his walking to consider this problem; but finding it insoluble and therefore unprofitable, he went on:

"Last night, as you know, I came up here, after the row with Risdon. I was determined to leave at once—"

Louise, sitting on her bed, said coldly:

"Yes, I know—on Olivia's advice. You've told me she brought you coffee and ice-cubes. We've been through all that, *ad nauseam*. She's told me, and you've told me. Well, what of it? Did she make love to you after all? Is that what you're trying to tell me? If so, don't bother to spare my feelings. I can stand most things—except being asked for my blessing on the event."

"Louise!" Rupert stopped in front of her, exasperated, while she swung her foot and looked this way and that, trying to avoid his eye.

"How can you be so blasted crude? How can I tell you what happened when you take such a ridiculous attitude! What I have to say has no concern with Olivia, damn her! I wish it had, in a way: she would have been easier to deal with."

Louise stopped her foot-swinging and stared at him with a new interest.

"Are you trying to tell me it was someone else?" she said.

Rupert put both hands on her shoulders, and said through his clenched teeth:

"If you would stop talking for just two minutes and let me speak! Listen: this matter is serious. The police are on to it. Mallett questioned me stiffly just now, as to where I was between ten and twelve last night, before I left. I couldn't tell him the whole truth. Why? Because it meant dragging somebody else in."

"Between ten and twelve?" said Louise wonderingly. "But you were here, lying on the bed! You said so yourself!"

"Oh no, I didn't!" said Rupert, releasing her now that he had captured her attention. "You assumed that. I hoped you would. Actually I was here only half an hour or so. I wasn't nearly as drunk as Olivia thought. I decided, therefore, I'd go along before I left and have a talk with Bernard. And so I did go, along the corridor and down that way to his study. But when I arrived, I heard voices, so I came away. That much I did admit to; but I couldn't tell Mallett what happened on the return journey."

"Go on," said Louise, when he paused.

"Well——" Rupert stood, hands in pockets, staring out of the window, and Louise could see the back of his neck turning red. "Well, I had to come back here to get my despatch-case, and as I was coming along the corridor from the head of the stairs a door opened and somebody called my name. The door was ajar. I was surprised, because I'd thought all those rooms were empty; the Risdons are a little farther along, I know, but whenever one saw inside any of the other rooms they seemed to be all covered up in dust-sheets. I glanced at the door: it's the one with the spray of lilies painted on it; and as I thought I recognised the voice, I pushed the door open and went in."

He paused again, for so long that Louise thought he had changed his mind about revealing the rest; but she dared not prompt him, lest he should harden in that decision. Presently he turned and came back to her.

"I can honestly say that the next quarter of an hour was the worst I've ever experienced in my life. I got away, of course. But—my God—it was indescribable! And then, to think I may have to depend on that for an alibi!"

"But, darling," cried Louise, by now nearly beside herself with curiosity, and throwing caution to the winds, "you haven't told me who it was!"

"Haven't I?" said Rupert miserably. "I thought you'd have guessed. It was—" He told her.

Louise stared at him in incredulity. Then she began to laugh. She laughed, throwing her head back, till the tears ran down her cheeks; and yet in her laughter there was a note of insincerity, covering up, not jealousy, but an embarrassment, almost a prudery, to which she did not care to admit.

"You won't mention this to anyone," said Rupert anxiously, "unless I say you can?"

"Oh, I don't know," said Louise, "I would if it were to save you from the police." She grew serious again: "But, darling, it means we must get away from here as soon as possible. I shall be afraid to let you out of my sight. Don't you think you could persuade the Superintendent to let us go?"

"He can't really stop us," said Rupert. "He has no powers to—"

Suddenly, from the corridor came a piercing scream, then another and another. Rupert flung open the door and ran out, in time to catch Lucilla in his arms as she threw herself into them.

"The lily-room! The lily-room!" she gasped, pointing.

Rupert handed her over to Louise and ran.

He found Clara leaning against the closed door. She said with ominous calm:

"Fetch the police. There's a body in this room—on the bed. I thought it was a pillow. I pulled back the sheet. I—"

Her eyes closed, and she fell with a thud at his feet.

Rupert pushed open the lily-painted door.

He knew what he expected to see. His teeth chattered, the soles of his feet tingled, and every muscle stiffened as he braced himself to meet the inevitable.

But what he saw was a face, blue, with open mouth and staring eyes, and the sheet drawn back to reveal, incongruously, a black collar edged with white: not the face he had expected and dreaded to see, but the face of Barker, Mrs. Smith-Wilson's personal maid, and round her throat was a thin pale evening scarf.

30

"M adam," said the breathless and terrified maid who reached Lady Risdon and Mrs. Hertford beside the lily-pool, "will you come at once, please?" It was to Mabel that she spoke, but her glance strayed to the taller and more imposing lady. "They've just found another body!"

"Whose?" said Lady Risdon sharply; and when the girl told her, she snapped again: "Where?"

Lady Risdon looked across the pool, and saw Sir Matthew hurrying towards them. When he had joined them and the maid had withdrawn, both women turned to him for confirmation. Even Lady Risdon was glad to see him.

"My dear," he said to her, avoiding Mabel's eye, "this is a dreadful business, and I'm afraid it's going to involve *you*."

"Me?" said Lady Risdon, outraged.

"Yes. Unfortunately you're going to be a principal witness. You heard the altercation in that room last night. You know who the man was—and I suppose we must assume that the woman was Barker. H'm." He turned to Mabel. "But first—Mrs. Hertford, don't be too much upset, but your presence is urgently needed up at the house. I'm sorry to say it was Clara and Lucilla who found the body. For some reason—following on our conversation, no doubt—they unfortunately had an impulse to explore the lily-room, as everybody calls it. Naturally they're both suffering from shock."

Mabel uttered a thin, wailing cry, and hurried away.

Sir Matthew stared after her, as with her gauzy scarf fluttering behind her she ran along the path beside the pools and up the stone steps to the terrace.

"Stupid girls," he said, "of a stupid mother," and for once Lady Risdon was able heartily to agree with him.

"This is a very awkward business, Margaret," he went on, feeling not a little awkward himself. He was sorry for his wife, because she had become entangled in this dreadful affair; but they had become such great strangers to each other that he did not know how to express sympathy. He was sorry for Lavering, who so soon after his triumphant return had got himself into such a predicament. But above all he was sorry for himself, because he was now condemned to pay heed for still longer to something that fundamentally did not interest him, and to deny himself the routine of pleasure and pleasurable business that he so dearly loved.

"You'll have to go at once and see the Superintendent," he said. "There's no avoiding it. I'd go for you, of course; but you're the witness, and he'll want to have the evidence direct from you."

Lady Risdon stood thinking.

"But Matthew," she said at last, "what am I to say? I should be sorry to think my evidence condemned poor Lavering."

Sir Matthew stroked his smooth, well-covered jaw-bones with finger and thumb.

"A pity you told that story, my dear," he remarked. "I thought so at the time. But since you have told it, there's no avoiding the consequences. If you don't tell what you saw and heard, Mrs. Hertford or the girls will."

"Yes, I suppose so," said Lady Risdon, still lost in thought. "And that wouldn't do—wouldn't do at all." She looked at her husband speculatively, as if wondering whether she should confide in him further; and then, deciding against it, added resolutely: "You're right. I must go myself at once, before anybody else queers the pitch."

She set out, and Sir Matthew, not without admiration, followed.

31

The hubbub in the house was considerable. Poor Barker's death seemed to be causing more stir than Bernard's, but Lady Risdon marched past everybody and straight upstairs. Ignoring the policeman who guarded the door and taking him by surprise, she walked into the room of death, giving a smart preliminary knock with the gargoyle as she passed through.

Mallett and Rupert were still standing beside the bed, though the body had again been covered. Mallett regarded the intruder beneath bent brows, but she went at once to the point:

"Sorry to interrupt you, Superintendent, but I think I can save you some trouble."

She had been so intent on her purpose that she had not taken in Rupert's presence; when she saw him, she stopped short.

"It's all right, Lady Risdon," said Rupert. "I suppose you overheard what went on in here last night. I thought I noticed your door ajar as I went by."

"Well yes, Major, I did," said Lady Risdon in her deep voice. "I'm glad you've saved me the trouble of telling the Superintendent. I felt compelled, for your sake as well as everybody else's, to come here at once and say what I'd seen. I'm afraid it's owing to my action—perhaps 'indiscretion' would be a better word—that those two poor girls have been the victims of a most unpleasant shock, though of course," she concluded, recollecting what their object must have been, "they brought it on themselves."

Mallett came forward, round the foot of the bed to Lady Risdon. He looked angry.

"What exactly *did* you see, madam?" he said. "You needn't be afraid of repeating Major Lavering's story. Major Lavering isn't willing to tell me what he was doing here last night." He cast a sour look at Rupert. "I've warned him, it's true, that what he says may be used in evidence."

Rupert made an irritable sound.

"I've told you I *was* here," he said, "and that I know nothing of this poor woman's death. I never saw her. She wasn't here when *I* was."

"Then who was?"

Rupert turned away, distressed and angry. Mallett turned disgustedly to Lady Risdon.

"Suppose *you* tell me!"

"I?" said Lady Risdon. "*I* didn't see anybody. I merely heard some kind of altercation, and I saw Major Lavering coming along the corridor looking—well, 'dishevelled' is the word, I suppose." She glanced towards Rupert, but he made no sign. "And I must say, Superintendent, I'm quite sure Major Lavering had no time to murder anybody. He simply shook himself free and came away."

"But you heard the other voice—a woman's. You mean to say you have no idea who it was?"

"I do."

"Then it surely can't have been one of your fellow-guests. You would have recognised the voice of, say, one of the Miss Hertfords."

"Oh no, I wouldn't. The door was shut, and I could hear nothing distinctly. The only distinct remark I heard was when the door opened for a moment and I heard Major Lavering say, 'For God's sake, let go of me! Are you crazy?' Then the door was shut again. Then, a moment later, it opened and he came out."

"So it could have been this woman Barker," Mallett pressed her, "for all you know to the contrary."

"Oh no, I don't think so," said Lady Risdon dubiously, and glanced at Rupert. "In fact, I feel sure it wasn't. Major Lavering would never—"

"We're not interested in your surmises, madam," said Mallett. "All we care about are facts. Have you ever heard Barker speak?"

"I may have," said Lady Risdon. "I don't remember."

"Well, I needn't detain either of you any longer. You both give me negatives. Major Lavering here says the woman who intercepted him was not Barker, but he refuses to say who it was. You, madam, say it was a woman, but you didn't really hear the voice. Odd, I must say!" He glared, bull-like, from one to the other: "If you are protecting someone, I warn you to be careful—you especially, Major. You're in a very dangerous position, and you'd be well advised to speak the truth. I suppose, however, you think you know your own business best."

Rupert, without answering, followed Lady Risdon to the door.

As they walked down the corridor together, she said:

"Hadn't you better speak out?"

He looked at her, startled.

"Do you mean to tell me you *know*?"

"Of course I do!" said Lady Risdon derisively. "I recognised the voice at once. I'm not *quite* such a fool, my dear man! Did you think I had come to denounce you? I came to tell the Superintendent that the woman you were trying to get away from was *not* Barker. I was going to say who it was. But I thought, as you were there and you apparently wished to conceal the truth, I'd better hold my tongue until I found out what your reason was, if any. Though I warn you, I don't promise to keep silent if things go too far. Does anyone else know?"

"Yes," said Rupert with relief. "I told my wife, luckily, a short while ago—just before they made this discovery."

"Then she'll tell the Superintendent."

"Not unless I say she can."

"She will, if she has any sense, with or without your permission," said Lady Risdon with finality. "Not that that will do you much good. Probably he won't believe her; he'll think she's protecting you."

"Yes," said Rupert, "and if you add your evidence later, he'll think you're in the plot, too, as you denied all knowledge just now."

Lady Risdon stopped short.

"Shall I go back and tell him?"

"No, no, please!" Rupert in his agitation laid a hand on her arm. "Not yet! We must give her a chance to go to him herself and explain."

"I agree," said Lady Risdon, "for the moment, anyway."

"Do you think she will?" said Rupert.

"I think she may."

"What makes *you* think so?"

"Oh," said Lady Risdon, "certain signs of—agitation I've observed. You see—it was very wrong of me, but I couldn't help it—I told the story in front of her just now, though without letting her know I knew it was she. Of course, her agitation may be due to fear of discovery. I had no idea about Barker when I spoke. Or it may have been compunction—or shame. She may not know about Barker, either. Everything depends on that, doesn't it? Well, we shall see."

They were standing now outside Lady Risdon's door.

"Do *you* think she killed Barker?" said Lady Risdon.

"I don't know," said Rupert. "I should hate to think so."

"Could she have had any motive?" Lady Risdon pressed him. "Could Barker have been spying?"

"I don't know," said Rupert again, "but I believe the answer has something to do with Bernard's death."

"Very likely. One tends to forget that. Well, you'll want to go and confer with your wife. And I'll have a talk with my husband and see what he thinks. I shall have to tell him what I know; but I promise you I won't act without warning you. After all, it's your affair, and you're entitled to first option!"

She went into her room, and Rupert hurried along the corridor to Louise.

32

The scene that confronted him when he opened their bedroom door completely daunted him.

Lying on the bed was Clara, with Lucilla sobbing at her feet, and Mrs. Hertford holding a wet handkerchief to Clara's forehead. Louise, a little apart, looked on unsympathetically, taking each handkerchief as it became warm and steeping it again in cold water, suggesting that Clara's head should be on a level with her feet instead of uplifted on Mabel's bosom, trying from time to time to calm Lucilla. She herself remained perfectly calm. Rupert made signs to her to come outside and join him.

"Well?" she said, when they had closed the door on the tableau of distress inside. "What has happened? Is it true?"

Rupert nodded.

"Barker's body was lying on the bed in that room. She looked to me as if she'd been strangled."

"How dreadful!" said Louise mechanically, and then, with lively concern: "What are you going to do?"

He drew her farther away from the door.

"Nothing, at the moment."

"Why not?" Louise retreated a step to look at him with suspicion. "Have you told Mallett about——?" She nodded in the direction of the door.

"I said I was in that room last night—and why. But I didn't say who it was that waylaid me."

"For heaven's sake, why not? Are you mad? He'll suspect you!" She looked round resolutely. "Where is he? I shall go at once myself and tell him. If you're such a fool, somebody must protect you!"

Rupert caught her by the arm.

"Not yet, darling! There's no need. For one thing, I don't think Mallett does suspect me. He pretends to, to get me to speak. But I have a powerful feeling that he doesn't really. And even if he did, I've a witness on my side: Lady Risdon saw and heard the final *fracas*, and she knows it wasn't Barker, and even if it had been, she knows I wouldn't have had time to strangle her."

"But I don't understand!" said Louise. "Why don't you tell Mallett the truth?"

"Darling, I can't. I simply can't bring myself to act as informer—and that's what it amounts to."

"Why not?" persisted Louise. "She's dangerous. She has to be stopped. She knows *you* know—and you'll be the next victim. She's bound to hate you, anyway, after what happened last night. She'll never forgive you for having turned her down."

"Maybe," said Rupert. "But, darling, what proof is there that she murdered Barker? She may be as innocent as I am. She could say she left that room soon after I did; and unless we can pin it on to her, we're no better off than before. What *we* want to know first of all is, who killed Bernard?"

"She did, of course," said Louise. "That's obvious. And Barker knew."

"But that's pure guesswork! You've no proof!"

"Well, my guess is as good as Mallett's. And I won't have *you* acting as decoy-duck—not to mention myself, for she'll assume you've told me."

"She can't kill us all. There's safety in numbers."

"Good heavens!" said Louise. "And they say women are illogical! What do I care about statistics if she picks on you?"

"And yet," insisted Rupert, "if we don't get proof—proof good enough to convince a jury—she'll be at large for the rest of her days, however guilty."

"There's something in that."

"There's everything in that," said Rupert, pressing his advantage. "Meanwhile, we've got to watch—be on our guard—keep together. If she should strike again tonight—"

Louise shuddered. She took his arm and drew him away.

"Do you think Mallett would mind if we went off somewhere and got a meal? I'd be afraid to eat anything in this house in case it were poisoned."

"We'll risk it," said Rupert, drawing her hand into his. "I'm sure he won't mind. He's a good sort, really."

"Darling, your optimism is ridiculous," said Louise affectionately, "but it does bring you through things. Let's go, just as we are. I can't face that woman again. Or no, I must have my coat. *You* fetch it, darling! And my handbag. And my ear-rings. They're on my dressing-table. Or no—I think they're in my handbag…"

Rupert fled.

33

Superintendent Mallett faced Mrs. Smith-Wilson.

She did not look in the least put out by the discovery of Barker's death; she sat upright as usual in her stiff-backed chair, while Mabel Hertford hovered behind her looking anxious and with red and swollen eyes, and Olivia Bannermore leaned against the window-frame, sardonically watching the scene. Mallett, furious and baffled, looked as if he would like to clap them all into gaol.

"We don't know," he said, "whether this woman Barker was killed before or after the death of your son. The body has lain there since late last night."

"I thought you had exact methods of telling the length of time since death has occurred," said Mrs. Smith-Wilson scornfully.

"That, madam," said Mallett, "is one of the commonest myths believed in by the public. We can tell, but not to within an hour. There are too many factors involved. And in this case, it is a matter of an hour or two—no more."

"Then I'm to be left here," said Mrs. Smith-Wilson grimly, "in this great house, with a murderer at large—for you don't seem to be in any doubt about *that*, this time, as you were over my poor son."

"No, madam," said Mallett. "Your servant Barker was undoubtedly murdered—struck on the head, and then strangled; and therefore there is an even stronger presumption than ever that your son also was murdered. And it is a strong probability that Barker met her end because she knew something about the poisoning. I have questioned the servants, and they are all agreed that she was in the kitchen at ten-thirty last night, and then she left, saying she was going to take her glass of milk up to her room and wait until all the guests had gone. She also was heard to say that it was no use for her to undress because you'd ring for her before you yourself went to bed."

"Well," snapped Mrs. Smith-Wilson, "that's what she was paid for, wasn't it? And a preposterous amount too, for anyone so inefficient—always losing things." She turned to nod at Mrs. Hertford, and Mrs. Hertford nodded eagerly back. "You know how she said she couldn't find my eyedrops yesterday; and there they were all the time on the dressing-table. The doctor found them at once."

Mallett nodded, too.

"Yes," he said. "But there may be another reason for that. Somebody may have taken the eyedrops, used them, and put them back again; so, too, with the liniment, which also contained atropine."

Mrs. Smith-Wilson tossed her head. She was unwilling, even now, it seemed, to listen to any excuses for Barker. Perhaps she still felt resentful because Barker had not come when rung for: it was somehow *like* Barker, no doubt she would have said, if her injustice had been challenged.

"Well, but what are you going to *do*?" she said impatiently. "We don't seem to be a bit further on, so far as I can see. And here we are, everybody suspecting everybody else, and meanwhile the murderer is at large. Or is he? You've got that young man Holmes in custody, I believe—and Miss Bannermore here thinks he's undoubtedly guilty: don't you, Olivia?"

"I do," said Olivia, folding her arms as if she were pronouncing judgment.

"A criminal type, certainly. No respect for property usually means no respect for life either, in the long run. He's no longer in this house, you say? I'm thankful to hear it."

"Holmes is locked up in Chode gaol, madam," said Mallett, "protesting his innocence, and accusing Miss Bannermore of every crime he can lay his tongue to." He gave Olivia a shrewd look. "He persists in saying that you were the instigator of his thefts, because of your hostility to Mr. Smith-Wilson. He also sticks to his story that you spent some time with him in his room last night while he made his preparations for departure."

"An easy excuse!" scoffed Olivia.

Mallett gave her another shrewd look; but she returned his look unflinchingly. Mrs. Smith-Wilson, too, gave her a hard stare, then she turned instead on Mabel, who started guiltily when she spoke:

"You've got some views, too, haven't you, Mabel? Come on: speak up! Now's the time! The Superintendent would like to hear, I'm sure."

"Oh, please!" said Mabel, her blue eyes opening wide. "What interest can *my* silly little opinions have?"

"Any opinion's interesting," said Mallett, "if it's based on fact."

"Well," said Mabel diffidently, "I hate to say it—such a brave man—but don't they perhaps lose all sense of values on the battle-field? I should, I feel sure."

"You're referring to Rupert, I suppose," said Mrs. Smith-Wilson scornfully. "Then why not say so? The Superintendent wants to get away."

"Well—of course one knew about the rivalry between him and Bernard. And though you'll be angry with me"—she addressed herself to Mrs. Smith-Wilson—"I must say I always thought Rupert had a good deal to complain of. Bernard did take his invention, you know, and exploit it—"

"Rubbish!" snapped Mrs. Smith-Wilson. "If Rupert was such a fool, it served him right. However, I don't doubt Rupert feels he has a grievance: weak people usually do when they have to pay for their mistakes." Her contemptuous look made it clear that she included Mabel in this category.

"Is that all you have to say, madam?" said Mallett to Mabel. "You have no definite reason for suspecting Major Lavering—nothing except your belief that there existed some bone of contention between them?"

"Well, no," said Mabel rather doubtfully, with her head on one side; and then, as if making up her mind, she added firmly: "No."

"Very well." Mallett turned to Mrs. Smith-Wilson. "I am leaving here now, to confer with two of my colleagues who are coming down here to assist me. The body of the maid Barker has been taken to the mortuary, and Dr. Fitzbrown is already busy on the post-mortem. After that, we shall confer again, and I shall return here tomorrow morning. Meanwhile I have made arrangements for all possibilities. My men will be on duty inside this house and outside. Everybody here is under suspicion and everybody will be under guard. You needn't be afraid, madam: there will be a police officer on duty all night outside your room, and"—he looked from her to Mabel—"in the corridor on to which all the guest-rooms give, as well as the room in which Barker's body was found."

"Oh, but," said Mabel, "I shouldn't dream of leaving Mrs. Smith-Wilson alone. I can easily sleep on one of the settees out here. She'll need someone, especially now that poor Barker has gone." Her tone suggested that Barker, contrary to her own interests, had left to take up an inferior situation.

Olivia came forward from the window, and said incisively:

"If anybody stays here tonight, it'll be myself."

Mabel, flushed and nervously determined, protested.

"Pardon me, Miss Bannermore; I think I have known Mrs. Smith-Wilson a good many years longer than you have, and I claim it as a *privilege* to be near her in her time of trouble."

"Pardon *me*"—Olivia imitated her maliciously—"but I'm a near relative. I'm in the fortunate position of being the mother of Mrs. Smith-Wilson's grandson. Why don't you go and look after your daughters?"

The two women, one short and flustered, the other tall, cool and exulting in her power to be offensive, faced each other like two incongruous combatants disputing possession of a small piece of territory.

Mrs. Smith-Wilson smiled grimly, but gave no indication of her wish; it was as if she were enjoying the combat and wanted it to be prolonged. Olivia looked the likelier winner, though Mabel held her ground gamely, when Mallett intervened:

"Excuse me, ladies, but I must ask you both to stay in your own rooms tonight. Mrs. Smith-Wilson will be adequately protected, as I have already explained. What's more, I've felt myself obliged to institute a kind of curfew. I shall ask all guests to assist the police by being in their own rooms not later than ten o'clock tonight, and remaining there until they're called tomorrow morning. In fact, I have already given instructions to that effect, both to the domestic staff and to my own second-in-command here, to see that these arrangements are carried out." He picked up his hat from a nearby table. "You understand that these things are being done as much for your own protection as for our convenience."

He had almost reached the door when there came a tap on it.

"You're wanted on the 'phone, sir," said the messenger. "There's a call from the south lodge. I had it put through to the study."

Mallett bade the three women a perfunctory good evening, glad to leave them to their bickering. He reached the study and picked up the house-telephone. The lodge-keeper said:

"Major Lavering and his wife are at the gates, sir, in their car. The Major says he wants to take his wife out to dinner this evening, somewhere in the neighbourhood."

"Why didn't he come and inform me?"

"He said you were engaged, sir, and he was sure you'd be quite agreeable."

"Agreeable!" Mallett's impulse was to interfere; but realising that this could not be done, he said:

"Wait two or three minutes; then open the gates and let them go." He replaced the receiver. "Tell Bridges to follow them," he said to the constable at his side, "keeping out of sight, of course. I must know what these people are up to. And ask Sergeant Coles to come here."

When Coles arrived, Mallett closed the study door and began giving him detailed instructions as to the disposal of his men, and what they were to watch for. At last, when he had finished and was about to go, he was recalled by another ring on the house-telephone bell. Coles picked up the receiver.

"It's the south lodge again, sir," he said, covering the mouthpiece with his hand. "They want to know if they are to open the gates for Sir Matthew Risdon."

Mallett snatched the receiver from Coles's hand.

"What's this?" he said. "You've only just let Major Lavering through, haven't you?"

"Yes, sir—and one of your plain-clothes men on a motor-bike. But as soon as I'd shut the gates again, Sir Matthew drove up in his car with Lady Risdon. He said they wanted to get away for a couple of hours and have a meal; they were sure you would have no objection."

"You haven't got a son with a motor-bike, have you?" said Mallett.

"No, sir," said the lodge-keeper, surprised. "My youngest son has a push-bike, but he's not here at the moment."

"Never mind," said Mallett resignedly. He placed his large hand over the mouthpiece and said to Coles: "We can't spare men to go chasing after these people all over the countryside. What's come over them all? They'll spoil my little game. Ah well, I suppose they'll come home to roost all right." He uncovered the mouthpiece: "Let them through."

34

"Oh, darling, this is lovely!" said Louise as they drove along the country road leading away from Fairfield House. She pressed against him, her shoulder a little behind his, and a new strength and pleasure filled him. "What a difference it makes to get away from there! I won't spoil it yet by even beginning to discuss what we've got to do. I'm just content to drive on and on like this beside you for ever."

Rupert said:

"It reminds me of that first drive we had together: remember? But then it was winter—January. I was afraid you wouldn't come. I thought perhaps you belonged to Bernard."

Louise laughed.

"And I was afraid you'd be terribly chivalrous—towards Bernard—and not ask me. You *are* far too chivalrous, darling: it's your only *real* fault." She stopped short, because she did not want yet, as she had said, to spoil things by touching on what had to be decided between them. "But what a wonderful fault to have!" she added in all sincerity. "And how poor and small it makes everybody else look in comparison!—including me." She sighed, content now that she could truly believe in and pay tribute to his nobility, however foolish and unprofitable it might be, and however little intention she had of allowing him to exercise it.

"Where are you taking me?" she said after a while. "Not that I care. I should like never to go back. I suppose we must go back."

"I'm afraid so," said Rupert. "It would look rather bad if we didn't. Besides, we're being followed."

"What!" said Louise, shocked as the uninitiated always are when this threat to their freedom of movement is for the first time revealed.

"Look behind."

She did so, and saw the motor-cycle some fifty yards behind them.

"You mean to say that man is following *us*?"

Rupert nodded.

"Why do you think the lodge-keeper took so long to get the key? He was putting through a 'phone-call to Mallett up at the house, and Mallett told him to keep us there until he had time to send a sleuth in pursuit."

"But I thought you said he didn't suspect you!"

"I don't think he does, on the whole. But naturally he's not sure. I was in that room last night. And think what a fool he'd look if I were guilty and he let me vanish! He's up against it now, with this second murder on his hands."

Louise having recovered from the first shock and sense of outrage, looked out of the back window with lively interest.

"There's another car coming up just behind him," she said. "It's overtaking him. Don't say they've sent a police-car after us as well!"

Rupert had been driving, for him, rather slowly, enjoying his freedom and Louise's praise. He touched the accelerator:

"We'll give them a run for their money!"

Ten minutes later, Rupert drew up in the paved courtyard of the Winking Eye, with the long nose of his car almost touching one of the bottle-glass-paned, chintz-draped windows of the dining-room. A minute later, Sir Matthew Risdon's car drew up beside his; and before the two couples had time to greet each other, Bridges came roaring in on his motor-cycle and drew up alongside with a scream of brakes.

Rupert swung the car-key on his index finger, almost under Bridges's nose as he sat astride his machine.

"Good evening, Bridges. Look here, old chap, don't worry about me. Go round to the bar and have a drink at my expense. I give you my word of honour I won't leave without letting you know."

"Thanks, Major," said Bridges, grinning. "I could have told the Super. I was wasting my time—but you know how it is: orders are orders."

"That's all right, Bridges," said Rupert. "Superintendent Mallett is a fine chap, but he doesn't know everything: a certain café in Nauplia, for instance, where the *ouzo* put the Brigadier-General under the table—what?"

The two began to laugh.

Louise looked on for a moment. She felt completely excluded, and yet completely happy. Smiling to herself, she walked away to join Lady Risdon. She heard Rupert's high laugh, and Bridges's deeper one, as Rupert said:

"And a certain Spartan damsel called Angelica—not so very Spartan, nor so very angelic—eh?"

"Well," added Rupert when they had finished laughing and had withdrawn themselves unwillingly from the olive-groves and the blue skies of Greece to the soft evening sunset light of England, "you go along and make yourself happy here. I shall be about an hour and a half. I've got my dinner to eat and something damned unpleasant to decide. But don't give me a thought. This is your lucky day."

"Very good, Major," said Bridges, getting off his motor-cycle and saluting.

Rupert walked slowly away to join the ladies, who waited in the porch while Sir Matthew fumbled with the car-keys.

"We recognised your car ahead of us," called out Lady Risdon triumphantly as Rupert approached, "and my husband said we couldn't do better than follow you: he was sure you knew exactly where to go for a good meal!"

"There can be no greater tribute," murmured Rupert, "coming from Sir Matthew. Well, come on, girls: let's have a drink!"

He put an arm round each of them and drew them inside, into the cosy dining-room, where the ceiling was so low, and the woodwork so heavy and dark, that there was always an excuse for having the shaded lights on.

35

Sir Matthew, content after a good meal and sedulous service, leaned back in his chair with his cigar poised and regarded his companions with benevolent omniscience.

"And so I told Margaret," he said, "that she'd have to disclose what she knew, promise or no promise; and she agreed. But she felt she ought to let you know first, in case you preferred to do it yourself. And when we sent someone to look for you, we were told you'd gone out to dinner; so we thought, what you could do we could do. And presently we saw your car ahead of us, with Bridges trailing you on his motor-bike; so we thought we'd join the procession." He oozed a laugh. "And a splendid idea, too, from our point of view!"

"And ours," said Rupert. He always enjoyed company, even when it meant temporary separation from Louise; and this evening it meant postponement of that tiresome discussion, and a softening of the tone of the discussion when it began, as it soon must.

Lady Risdon, flushed and happy ever since Rupert had grouped her with Louise as a 'girl', smiled her compliments. Only Louise looked thoughtful. She could not forget what it was that Rupert had to do—for she was determined that Rupert should do it, no matter what the Risdons might offer in their good nature, or whatever it was. She knew just how Rupert felt: the chivalry—or sentimentality—that made him hate betraying anyone, even a possible criminal, especially when that person was a woman. And wasn't there always, she wondered, in his chivalry a touch of egoism also, an enjoyment of the grand feeling it gave him to shield the weak? He was, she thought for the hundredth time, a thousand times better than herself; but if she sat back, as she was doing now, and regarded him with a touch of critical hardness, this sprang not only from her own nature, that wasn't easily convinced, but from her very love of and admiration for him. For instance, wasn't he using the Risdons, exerting all his charm to make them laugh and talk, in order to postpone the inevitable decision—in order to evade *her*?

"Of course I'll go and tell Superintendent Mallett if you like," Lady Risdon was saying. "I held back at the time merely because—"

Louise interrupted.

"Rupert knows *he* has to do it," she said quietly. "It's just a question of choosing the right time—or, rather, of overcoming his natural objection to playing the informer."

Sir Matthew waved his cigar, but gently, in order not to disturb the ash.

"My dear fellow," he said rallyingly, "I can't understand why you feel all these scruples—not on behalf of this woman, anyway. I can quite understand your not wanting to be mixed up in it. But you *are* mixed up in it, and so your course is settled for you. Your responsibility, my dear boy, is to the Law and Society."

"Oh yes," said Rupert dubiously.

"You ought to get in touch with your lawyer."

"Oh, good heavens!" said Rupert. "Need I do that? He'll at once assume I'm guilty and begin preparing me an elaborate defence."

"But meanwhile"—Sir Matthew leaned forward a little—"what exactly did happen? It'll do you good to tell us first—a sort of rehearsal—and you can decide then exactly what you're going to say to Mallett."

Rupert looked exceedingly uncomfortable. He cast a glance at Louise, as if hoping she would suggest a way of escape for him; but Louise showed no signs of helpfulness.

"Well," he said, leaning his elbows on the cleared table and looking down at his clasped hands, "as you know, after I left the smoking-room

I had a talk with Olivia Bannermore, and she told me that Bernard's plan for depressing West United wasn't going to succeed. She advised me to leave at once and go up to town so as to be there in time to cope with any new developments. I was feeling rather muzzy, so I went and lay on my bed for half an hour, and Olivia came in with some coffee and ice. I heard her come, but I pretended not to."

Again he cast a look at Louise. He knew that this episode annoyed her out of all proportion to its significance, and yet he seemed to be always referring to it, as if from perversity. The glint in her eye showed him once again exactly how little she believed in Olivia's *bona fides*. He was aware, even without looking, that the Risdons didn't believe in it, either. He went on:

"After she had gone, I drank the coffee and stayed there for another half an hour or so, until I felt perfectly clear-headed and able to drive. Then it came over me that I'd like to speak to Bernard before I left, and find out why he had been trying to play such a peculiar game with me. So I started off down the corridor towards the staircase at the end, the one leading past his mother's room and down to the study. When I arrived outside his door, I could hear him talking; so I decided to come back again and wait a while. On my way back, as I came opposite the room you know of—the one with the lilies painted on the door—I heard someone calling me."

"This was after eleven?" put in Sir Matthew.

"I suppose so. The door was ajar, and there was a dim light inside—not the ceiling light, but one of the bedside lamps, as I found out. Of course I instantly stepped inside. I recognised the voice."

"What exactly did she say?" asked Lady Risdon curiously.

"Oh, something like 'Major Lavering, could you come here a minute? There's something I want to ask your advice about.' I thought, naturally, she'd heard the rumour about the shares, or even heard the discussion an hour earlier between you and me." He turned to Sir Matthew.

"H'm," said Sir Matthew. "Oh, I don't think any of the ladies heard, my boy. After all, it was just a passing remark of mine, meant for your ears only."

Rupert could not be bothered to combat this legend.

"So I stepped inside, and she closed the door, looking very mysterious and rather elated. I was taken aback to find myself in a large bedroom which obviously wasn't in use, and it did flash across my mind as odd that she should have chosen such a place for a conference. But then I had no reason to suspect her of any——"

"Designs, darling," supplied Louise, when he hesitated.

Rupert accepted the word, though he would not repeat it.

"I thought of her as a woman much older than myself—a mother— whereas I suppose she sees herself as young."

Lady Risdon turned avidly to Louise:

"What age would you give her?"

"I think," said Louise, "she's not much over forty."

"And, of course, that's young nowadays. With her fair colouring she could pass for thirtyish, if she hadn't to go about with those two great girls."

"Well," said Louise. "she does rather like to give the impression that they're sisters."

Lady Risdon nodded.

"Yes, I've noticed that. Go on, Major—I'm sorry to have interrupted you."

As the moment for being specific drew nearer, Rupert grew more and more restive.

"At first," he said, "she began saying rather excitedly that in spite of what was being said about those shares, she at any rate had every confidence in me, and would stand by me whatever happened. Then she went on to attack Bernard."

"She attacked Bernard?" Lady Risdon was more interested still.

Rupert said, looking down:

"She said he was treacherous and had a distorted outlook, especially since his illness, which had given him a grievance against the whole scheme of things. She said he was betraying me—once again, as she put it. I had no idea she had taken such an interest in my affairs: one doesn't suspect people of being interested in one, when one has never paid them any attention or even noticed them. But it seemed *she* had followed *my* career with the closest attention. She knew all about the Thasson and how Bernard had appropriated it when I went into the Army. I don't know how she knew. I suppose she got it from his mother. She's always been very friendly with her, I believe. In fact, I've noticed, now I come to think about it, that she was often there when I visited them; and Bernard left them a small legacy for looking after his mother."

"She's after the old lady's money, I suppose," said Sir Matthew.

"She *was* after Bernard for one of her daughters," said Lady Risdon.

"Well, I know nothing about that," said Rupert. "I thought the legacy Bernard left them was very small, considering what he had. Still, I suppose Mrs. Smith-Wilson will put that right."

"I doubt it," said Lady Risdon. "She always struck me as one of the tight-fisted kind. You should see her at bridge! She'll be the same after death as she is in life. And I'm sure she's not at all grateful for attentions and services. She'll throw Mabel Hertford out, now the Bannermore woman has come into the picture."

"She'll be making a mistake," said Sir Matthew. "Or—I say! Good lord, my boy! Do you realise, if what we think is true, the old lady may be in danger this very night? Go on: carry on with your story."

"I reassured her," said Rupert. "I said she needn't worry about the money invested in West United, as I had reason to believe that all would be well—that some mistake had been made, and they were quite safe. I told her I was in fact leaving for town as soon as possible to keep an eye on the situation. And as for Bernard and the Thasson, I said, if he had profited, he had also helped, and whatever had been done had been done with my knowledge and consent, so I had only myself to blame. I talked a lot because I could see she was excited, and I wanted to soothe her so that I could get away. But the more I talked, the more I noticed a sort of gleam in her eye. She seemed to be hanging on my words and yet not really taking in what I was saying, if you know what I mean. I don't know of anything more exasperating. It's—it's a sort of liberty."

He frowned at the recollection; then, as if anxious to get it over, he went on with a rush:

"Suddenly, to my horror, she threw herself at me and hung round my neck. She begged me to take her with me. She said Louise didn't value me as she ought: that she was obviously allowing Bernard to pay her marked attention, and Bernard was in love with her and determined to get her away from me and marry her: that he would ruin me if I didn't give place to him; that she had heard him tell Louise all this in the library earlier in the evening. She had happened to be passing—"

"So that was the noise I heard on the stairs!" said Louise. "I thought it must have been Holmes, as he came in a few minutes later. It was only a slight noise, and Bernard said it was a mouse. She must have slipped back to Mrs. Smith-Wilson then, because she was there when Bernard took me up to see his mother."

"And *did* Bernard make those suggestions to you?" said Lady Risdon.

"He certainly did!" retorted Louise. "And I told him that nothing he could do would make the slightest difference to me. But Mrs. Hertford evidently didn't stay long enough to hear that." Louise's anger, flashing all round like a sword, challenged any to disbelieve her.

"By this time," Rupert resumed, "I realised that she was crazy. I tried gentle means at first. I said I was honoured by her confidence and so forth, but I was sure she was speaking under a momentary impulse which didn't spring from her real wishes, and I suggested she should go to bed and forget about it. In the morning, she'd feel quite differently. At that, she went completely hysterical." He shuddered at the recollection. "She said, if I rejected her, she'd kill herself.

"Of course I didn't take her seriously. And anyway I didn't much care what she did so long as she left me alone. But the more I tried to disentangle myself, the worse she got. I remember she had on one of those fluttering scarf-things that women wear, and every time I tried to push her off, this blessed thing seemed to cling to my coat and get mixed up with me, round my arms and even round my neck at one point. Oh, lord!" He struck his forehead brutally. "I can't bear it, really I can't! There's nothing so utterly caddish as repeating such a story, in my opinion—and to think I should be condemned to do it, even for the sake of Law and Society!"

"Yes," said Lady Risdon thoughtfully to Louise, "she does rather favour a tulle scarf, doesn't she? This afternoon she was wearing a pinkish one. I remember: I noticed it as she left me, after we'd been walking together round the lily-ponds." She turned to Rupert. "Was the one she was wearing last night pink, do you remember?"

"I've no idea," said Rupert with another shudder.

"I have," said Louise. "It wasn't pink: it was beige."

"Is there a great difference?" said Sir Matthew.

Louise smiled at him and did not deign to reply.

"Why do you ask, Margaret?" said Sir Matthew.

"Because," said Lady Risdon, "they say Barker was strangled."

"Oh, I see! And you think a flimsy affair like that could do it?"

"I'm sure it could. If she used the pink one to strangle Barker, she'd hardly be so callous as to wear it again today. I wonder what's become of the beige one: she surely didn't leave it behind!"

"Let Lavering finish his story," said Sir Matthew.

"There's really nothing more to tell," said Rupert. "When I realised she was impervious to reason, I'm afraid I became desperate. I flung her off. She fell on the bed. I made for the door. She bounded after me and caught hold of me again. I tore myself away."

"That's where I came along," said Lady Risdon. "I heard you say 'For God's sake let me go!' and I heard her say 'Rupert, Rupert, don't leave me like this!' You shut the door again. Then after a minute you came out, looking rather ruffled, in all senses of the word."

"I went back to our room," said Rupert, "and changed my clothes, and wrote a note to Louise. Then I went once more along the corridor and to Bernard's study. I knew he was still there because I had seen the light from the windows of that beastly bedroom. However, it was still no good: he still seemed to be talking to someone. So I gave it up, and went to the garage for my car. I left soon after midnight. That's all I know."

"And you saw nothing of Barker?" said Lady Risdon. "I mean, she couldn't have been hidden anywhere in the bedroom, could she—in one of the wardrobes, or perhaps a cupboard? That would suggest a motive for her murder—if she overheard the scene between you and Mrs. Hertford and threatened to blackmail her."

Rupert considered.

"But how could she?" he said. "After all, what did it matter if the story did come out? Mrs. Hertford's a widow: she has no irate husband to worry about. Beyond making her look rather silly, I don't see what harm it could do her—not sufficient to make her want to murder a witness, surely! I should have thought, if Barker had overheard the scene, she'd try blackmailing *me*. But no: I'm sure she wasn't there. It's absurd to think she could have known what was going to happen and thought it worth while to hide in a cupboard, even if she saw Mrs. Hertford going into that room."

"You're right," decided Sir Matthew. "No: I'm convinced that the killing of Barker was the second of the two—a consequence of the killing of Bernard. Barker knew something about the poisoning. She followed Mrs. Hertford into that room after you had left, and taxed her with it—and Mrs. Hertford strangled her."

"Aren't you forgetting one thing?" said Lady Risdon.

"What?"

"Major Lavering has just told us he heard Bernard talking in his study shortly before midnight. Therefore you have to assume that Mrs. Hertford left the lily-room, gave him the poison, and then went back to the lily-room, where Barker followed her. Now why on earth should she do that? I would have thought any woman who'd made such a fool of herself would avoid even passing the door if she could. No, no, it's contrary to human nature. She wouldn't go back, whatever else she did—not after *that* episode!" Lady Risdon laughed confidently.

"Well," said Sir Matthew, "it's up to Mallett to work everything out. By now he'll have a pretty clear picture of everybody's whereabouts during those hours. He'll be able to fit your statement in. But you must make it, and at once. What will you do? 'Phone him from here? We'll come with you. My wife will have to make her statement at the same time."

"Let me see," said Rupert, "I shall have to tell Bridges if I don't go straight back. He might get into trouble otherwise. Waiter! Ask the motor-cyclist in the bar if he'll come here a minute, will you? Bridges is his name."

When Bridges came, Rupert rose and drew him aside.

"Look here, Bridges, I've got to see Superintendent Mallett at once. I've got to make a very important statement. So I shall have to go on into Chode instead of back to Fairfield House. You can follow me if you want to. Sir Matthew will be coming too."

Bridges looked exceedingly uncomfortable. He glanced to right and left at the other diners, and towards the table that Rupert had quitted. Then, making up his mind, he said:

"This puts me in a very awkward position, Major."

"Why?" said Rupert, surprised, and taken aback at Bridges's apparent mistrust. "You don't surely think I'm trying to give you the slip?"

"It isn't that, Major," said Bridges. "But—it means breaking strict orders. I was told you were to be back there by ten. Everybody is to be in their rooms by ten: that's what the Super. said."

"But my dear chap," said Rupert angrily, "we're not under arrest! You've no right to interfere with our liberty!" Then, calming down: "I realise your difficulties, but don't you understand, I must see the Superintendent immediately? He'd be the first to agree. I tell you what: go and ring him up and tell him what I say, and get his permission. Is that all right?"

Bridges heaved a sigh.

"It's no good: I'll have to tell you," he said, "though we were all given the strictest instructions to say nothing. The truth is, Major"—he sank his voice to a whisper and spoke behind his hand—"the Super. isn't in Chode. He's at Fairfield House. He's spending the night there."

"Good lord!" said Rupert. "Why?"

Bridges shook his head.

"We don't ask. But he wanted people to think he'd left, and that's what we were all told to say."

"I see," said Rupert. "Can I tell my friends, if I swear them to secrecy?"

"I'd rather you didn't, sir, if you don't mind. I'd get into a very nasty mess if anything went wrong there tonight and the Super. found out I'd talked."

"Will you leave it to my discretion?"

Bridges looked him straight in the eye.

"Yes, sir, I will."

"Right. Wait for us outside."

Rupert went back to the table. He leaned both hands on it:

"We're going straight back to Fairfield House," he said.

"What!" said Sir Matthew. "Anything new?"

"Not that I know of. But we're going back there."

"But Rupert," protested Louise, "you must see the Superintendent tonight! It's all settled! Why do you keep changing your mind? I'm tired of arguing. I won't go back to Fairfield House. I'll get a taxi and go on to Chode without you."

Her voice was sufficiently raised for those at the nearer tables to realise that there was a difference of opinion; heads were turned towards them. Rupert said under his breath:

"You'll do no such thing! You'll come straight back to Fairfield House with me!"

His tone was so peremptory that Louise wavered.

"But why?" she lamented, as Rupert turned away and began to thread his way past the tables. When they reached the door, he turned back to her and said:

"You'll see why when we get there."

Sir Matthew and Lady Risdon, seeing Rupert's face and dreading a scene, followed without protest.

When the procession, with Rupert's car leading, was on the main road heading back towards Fairfield House, Louise said icily:

"You realise, darling, I shall never forgive you for this? I didn't know I'd married a man who could turn back in the face of—not even danger, just a temporary discomfort." She wrapped her white lamb's-wool coat more closely round her as if to avoid further contact with him.

"Don't be ridiculous, darling," said Rupert incisively. "We *are* heading for the temporary discomfort you covet so much for me, at the rate of forty miles an hour. Mallett is at Fairfield House, if you must know. But keep it to yourself, will you, when we arrive? I don't want to bring trouble on my old friend Corporal Bridges. God! I wish I were back with him in Crete! We had some peace there!"

Louise pulled up the collar of her coat high over her small, diamond-studded ears.

36

The procession—car, motor-cycle, car—moved slowly up the lane and stopped as Rupert's car was challenged at the lodge gates. Then again it moved slowly on like a funeral, stopping outside the porch. Rupert ran up the steps and spoke to the man on duty:

"Where's Superintendent Mallett? I want to see him immediately."

"I'm sorry, sir," said the policeman. "The Superintendent isn't here."

"Oh yes he is!" said Rupert impatiently. He glanced in through the open front doors into the hall and saw Sergeant Coles crossing the tiled floor. He ran towards him. Coles, waylaid, looked annoyed, as if he would have liked to charge his opponent head down; he also looked, Rupert noticed, furtive. Coles was not good at play-acting; he preferred direct methods.

"Coles!" said Rupert. "Where's Superintendent Mallett? I must see him at once."

"He's gone," said Coles surlily. "You can't see him."

"Oh no he hasn't!" said Rupert. "Don't try to put that across me. I know he's here."

Coles gave him a glare so forbidding that Rupert realised he was beyond persuasion.

"All right," he said, "you'll regret it. I've got something important to communicate." He brightened as he thought of a new argument: "All right, then! I'll go back to Chode and see him there."

Coles stepped at once between him and the door.

"Oh no you don't!" he said; and then, remembering that he had no power to detain Rupert, he added more conciliatorily: "You wouldn't be able to see him, sir—not tonight. He's busy."

"Well, I'll have a word with him on the 'phone."

Coles shook his head:

"You won't get him. Now look here, sir: you go to your room and stay there till morning, and then you can speak to the Superintendent first thing, when he arrives." He essayed a cajoling smile ill-suited to his red and angry countenance: "Please go along, and your good lady, too!" The other three had now reached the hall and were watching the colloquy: "We want to shut this place up for the night."

Rupert reflected for a moment, then he nodded.

"All right," he said. He called out brightly to the others: "We'd better go to bed. Mallett isn't available tonight. After all, it can wait till the morning."

They all moved off towards the stairs.

"What will you do?" said Lady Risdon as they went up.

"Do?" said Rupert. "Well, there's nothing I can do, is there? I'll just have to wait till the morning, as Coles says."

At the head of the stairs, they said good night and parted.

"Do you really think he's gone?" said Louise as he and she walked away towards their own room.

"Of course he hasn't gone," said Rupert. "I could see consciousness of Mallett's presence written all over Coles's honest face." He sounded elated at his discovery. Louise realised with trepidation that he was carried away by a new idea. "Mallett is staying here to see that nothing happens during the night—and so he ought, since we know there's a murderer prowling round!"

"What will you do?" said Louise. "Let him wait till the morning?"

"Do?" said Rupert. "Exactly what you're so keen on my doing—look around till I find him. He can't be far."

"But darling," said Louise, by now greatly alarmed, but trying to conceal her unease, "do you think you ought? You know they want us all to stay in our rooms after ten, and it's several minutes past already!"

They had reached the door of their bedroom. When they were inside, Rupert rounded on her furiously.

"Darling," he said, "I wish I understood you! Just now nothing would satisfy you but that I must see Mallett and humiliate myself by informing on this wretched woman. Well, you succeeded in convincing me—though I'd never have agreed—if that meddlesome old Risdon dame hadn't made any other course impossible for me. I'll bet she was peeping round her door in the hope of hearing what she shouldn't! " He laughed angrily. "And I'll bet she was mightily disappointed!"

Louise turned away and went to the dressing-table.

"Where do you expect to find him?" she said, as coolly as she was able.

"Oh, I don't know! I shall wait till the house is quiet, and then go on a tour of exploration."

"But there'll be men on guard, won't there?"

"I'll manage to get past them somehow. It's a sort of reconnoitring trip. I'm used to it."

"Yes, darling, but there aren't any shell-holes here."

Rupert threw himself on to his bed.

"I'll wait till midnight," he said, lighting a cigarette. "God! I wish I had a drink!"

"Or some black coffee?" said Louise.

He did not answer. He lay looking up at the plaster mouldings of the ceiling, while Louise finished her toilet, and, arrayed in silk and lace and perfume, got into the other bed and turned her back and went to sleep.

37

D id you believe that yarn of Lavering's?" said Sir Matthew, sitting up in his bed with his spectacles on and his white hair ruffled, reading the *Financial Times* while Lady Risdon tormented her own scanty hair into many curlers. "I thought it was a tall story myself."

"Well," said Lady Risdon in her deepest and most judicial voice, "I know it was Mrs. Hertford he was talking to, but whether his explanation was the true one is another matter—and where poor Barker came into it, too. What struck me was how reluctant he is to speak to Mallett. His wife, poor girl, had to urge it on him—and I believe, if I hadn't happened to come along and overhear, he would never have mentioned he'd been there. That doesn't look like complete innocence, certainly."

Sir Matthew grunted acquiescence.

"And then of course he stood to gain twenty thousand pounds by Smith-Wilson's death. I wonder if he and Holmes were hand in glove over the business of those West United shares? Smith-Wilson seemed positive they were falling when I spoke to him yesterday evening."

"I wonder why Lavering insisted on coming back here after all," said Lady Risdon, busy with her fringe. "He spoke so violently to his wife, I thought he was going to strike her."

Sir Matthew laid down his paper.

"You should have seen him yesterday evening when I mentioned quite mildly—as I had every right to do—that he had grossly misled me. These fellows get like that, you know: they lose all ordinary standards of civilised life. They have to, of course. One can't altogether blame them. It's partly the result of all they've been through." His voice took on a tone of great fairness and even magnanimity. "I expect he went along later to see Smith-Wilson, and Smith-Wilson said something to annoy him, and it all happened like that."

"But Matthew—poison!"

"I know—I know. But Lavering was dead drunk. We all have a lower nature, you know, which takes control when our higher centres are depressed. These psychological fellows say our lower nature is often the exact opposite of our higher nature, because it's a sort of rubbish-bin containing all we've discarded and don't like in ourselves. Well, then," he finished, proud of his reasoning powers, "what could be more likely than that a fellow who's outstandingly brave should resort to cowardly actions when his lower nature's in control?"

"All the same," said Lady Risdon, "I find it hard to believe. I could much more easily believe he strangled Barker, who was a very tiresome person according to Mrs. Smith-Wilson. She certainly sniffed; I've heard her."

"Well, anyhow," said Sir Matthew, folding up his paper and taking off his glasses, "your best course is to go straight to Mallett tomorrow as soon as he arrives, and tell him what you know, without bothering about Lavering." He lay down and rolled over. "You should have done it six hours ago."

"I know," said Lady Risdon, getting into bed, "but we don't always do what we should." She snapped out the light above the beds: "And we don't always regret it, either. Good night."

"Good night."

Soon, back turned to back, they were snoring.

38

Louise, too, was sleeping soundly when Rupert, still fully dressed but wearing slippers, opened the bedroom door and peeped out. There seemed to be no one on duty in this corridor: the lights were still on, but they were small and orange-shaded, and placed at intervals of twenty yards or so; deep shadows lay in the intervening doorways. Yet Rupert relied on his trained perception—his quick ear and eye. He knew that the corridor was empty.

The spirit of adventure surged up in him. This was something to do. To be sure, it was only a game—'Spot the Super.'—but it reminded him of other times when, although it had seemed like a game, one mistake, one forgetful moment, might cost one one's life. Those were the days! What a bore it was, he thought, sitting at a desk, talking, thinking about figures, going home to Louise, who was also feeling the strain, and so seeking relief in constant quarrels!

After a quick look to the right, in the direction of the main staircase, he set off on tiptoe, along the wall, in the shadows. He even amused himself by stopping occasionally in one of the doorways and looking back, as they do on the films. But behind him, as before, the corridor, with its orange glow-worms on the ceiling, was empty.

Where should he look for Mallett? He had tried to think out the probabilities as he lay on his bed listening to Louise's gentle breathing. The person Mallett was most concerned to protect was obviously Bernard's mother: she was an obstacle in the way of Olivia, whom Mallett probably suspected; and she had probably made her will, giving various people reason to wish her dead, if they didn't already. One of the beneficiaries was almost certain to be her devoted friend Mabel

Hertford, though Mallett might not have thought of that. But one thing was sure: no matter whom Mallett suspected, he was bound to assume that Mrs. Smith-Wilson was next on the list after her son. And so, instead of watching every inmate's door, he would use the much more economical and efficacious method of protecting the person in danger. But naturally he would not do this himself: he would station a reliable man on guard, and himself retire somewhere within call.

Then would he not be found in Bernard's study, as before? It was possible; but Rupert did not think so. Mallett would surely want to get some sleep; and he would not sleep on Bernard's own divan, surely. It did not seem proper. That room would be left as nearly as possible untouched. Anyway, one could not find out, because there were only two ways to Bernard's study: past the door of his mother's rooms, which would be guarded, or through the library, which meant passing through the main entrance-hall where Rupert had last seen Coles.

Rupert, lying on his bed, had pondered this possibility from all angles. He could not be sure that Mallett was not in Bernard's study; but the more he thought about it, the less he wanted to believe it, and the more reasons he found for not doing so. Then, from nowhere, came a flash of inspiration: of course, he thought, Mallett would spend the night in the room with the lilies on the door! There were two beds in the room: the large four-poster, on which Barker's body had been found; and a smaller one nearer the door. Mallett could sleep on the latter. Policemen have strong nerves; and since Mallett would want to use one of the bedrooms, why not that one, so that if by any chance the criminal returned, as criminals are said to do, to the scene of the crime, Mallett would be there. People with guilty consciences probably think they've left some clue behind, and go back to look. That was why Mallett had given it out that he himself was leaving, and that everyone was to stay in his or her room after ten: so that the criminal should think he had a clear field in which to wander. And that was why this corridor was empty.

When Rupert had arrived at this conclusion, he felt elated. His elation was increased when he remembered that his flask was in his suit-case, and that he had filled it that very morning with best dry gin. Tiptoeing across the room to the case, he had managed to extract the flask noiselessly—Louise did not even stir—and to slip it into an inner pocket. Now, half-way down the corridor, he pulled it out and took a little—nothing excessive, but it helped the illusion of the reconnoitring trip, and amused him. He almost laughed aloud. Especially he wanted to laugh when he thought of Mallett's face, supposing he, Rupert, were correct and he discovered Mallett's hiding-place. What he, Rupert, was doing might be thought silly by some; but Louise, he thought now, had been right: the sooner he saw Mallett, the better. In this way he, Rupert, would ensure that Mallett did not first hear some garbled account of events from Mrs. Hertford. After all, poor woman, if she were guilty, she would certainly be adjudged insane; so that it was misplaced chivalry to try to protect her. She should be under control, for her own sake as well as everybody else's.

He took another tot of gin; it was good, but it made his head swim, since four or five hours had now elapsed since he had eaten. Then he stepped carefully across from his side of the corridor to the opposite wall. He had not forgotten that one of these doors concealed Sir Matthew and Lady Risdon. But this was of no interest, except that one mustn't wake them. He moved on from door to door, drawn now irresistibly towards the door with the lilies. It happened that there was one of the orange glow-worms in the ceiling just above the door, so that no mistake was possible.

Once inside, he had thought, he would switch on the light beside the door and prove himself right or wrong. If the latter, he would just creep away quietly and no one would know he had made a fool of himself. In fact, he wondered if he had better give up the chase and go quietly back to bed. But the moment he stepped inside and listened, all other thoughts were banished from his mind by the certain knowledge that he was not alone.

So he had been right after all! What a thing is instinct!—though he believed someone had told him one shouldn't call it that. He listened again: somebody was in this room, and if he was any judge, that person was not asleep. He could hear no breathing: merely the creak of a board, the movement of—what? A foot on the carpet? A hand brushing the bedspread? The sound was too faint for him to decide. But he was pretty sure that whoever was in here did not know he had entered; and that was odd, because one would have expected a little light to glimmer in through the opening of the door.

He began to move very cautiously: first to press the door to though without latching it because that would make a noise, and then to creep across the floor towards the window, so that he could dominate the room. He knew that between him and whoever it was there was the large bed, and if he switched on the light near the door, he might not get a clear view to the other side. So he tiptoed across towards the dressing-table, feeling meanwhile in his pocket for his torch.

He stopped, afraid lest he should collide with the dressing-table. The faint noises also had ceased. Could he have been mistaken, he wondered. Floor boards creak sometimes without anyone touching them, when the wood contracts after the warmth of the day; and there are always mice. But no: there came the sounds again, the faint creaks and rustlings; and this time he thought he could hear breathing. But it was not the sort of breathing one would have expected from Mallett, who was a heavy man, apt to breathe loudly even when awake. Rupert stood there, tense, listening, straining his eyes; but there was not the faintest glimmer of light, now that the door was closed. Someone had drawn down the blinds.

The sounds came nearer.

Yes, there was no doubt: someone was in the room, crawling about on the carpet, crawling towards him. He felt for his torch again; but before he could use it, the door was thrown open so that it banged against the bedside table; a large form, with another close behind it, filled up the doorway; a torch was shone in Rupert's face.

"Ah, Major!" said Mallett. "And what, may I ask, are you doing here?" He came forward.

Rupert shone his own torch into Mallett's face:

"Believe it or not, Superintendent, I was looking for *you*."

Mallett spoke across his shoulder to the man behind him:

"When did he come here?"

"Two minutes ago, sir."

"Smart work," said Rupert. "But not smart enough. There's somebody else in here you seem to have missed."

He walked round to the far side of the large bed, and from behind its surrounding valance he dragged up by the wrist, before Mallett's astonished gaze, Mabel Hertford.

39

Mabel stood there blinking into the beams of the two torches. She looked frail and pathetic in her nightwear, with her hair in two plaits, one over each shoulder, and with a bow of white ribbon on the end of each plait.

"Switch on the light," said Mallett to his man. "Now, madam, will you kindly explain how *you* got in here?"

Mabel looked from one to the other of the three men, and then, fearfully and uncertainly, behind her.

"Didn't you know," she said, "about the secret passage? I thought you detectives found out everything—by tapping walls and so on."

She turned to the built-in cupboard behind her and pushed open a sliding door.

"Colonel Smith-Wilson—Bernard's father, that is—had it put in. He liked that sort of thing." She pushed open an inner sliding door. "There's a wooden partition making a passage along the wall, behind the dressing-room and through the rest of the bedrooms, behind the wardrobes. It comes out on to the private stairway opposite Bernard's study. There's no point in it that I can see. Colonel and Mrs. Smith-Wilson used to sleep here in the old days—and he liked sometimes to go straight to and from his study without meeting any of the servants. He was a shy, secretive sort of man."

"He must have been," said Mallett. He walked round the bed to look at the sliding door, and stepped into the cupboard and shone his torch down the passage. Then he stepped out again.

"How did *you* know about it?" he said.

"I?" said Mrs. Hertford innocently. "Oh, it was no secret—at least, it wasn't in the Colonel's day. I believe the staff has all been changed since then, and nobody bothers."

"Did Barker know about it?" asked Mallett.

"I'm sure I don't know. She must have, mustn't she? Perhaps Mrs. Smith-Wilson told her. There are still some of Mrs. Smith-Wilson's frocks hanging up in the cupboards. I daresay she may have sent Barker here on errands sometimes, as she did me."

"And was it Mrs. Smith-Wilson who sent you here tonight?" said Mallett, still with apparent kindness. His tone changed suddenly. "Or were you looking for something of your own—something you dropped last night, for instance?"

Mrs. Hertford's mouth opened and shut. She looked uncertainly at Rupert, and then back again defiantly at Mallett. Then, drawing herself up, folding her hands and throwing back her head, she said in the tone of one too disdainful of bad manners to resist their rude demands:

"I have no intention of denying it." She turned a look of even greater hauteur upon Rupert: "Perhaps you will ask Major Lavering what *he* is looking for also."

"All in good time, madam," said Mallett. "You both left your clues here last night. But Major Lavering has admitted he was here, and you have not, though you've had every opportunity."

Mabel's dignity fell from her. She let out a thin wailing cry.

"Oh, Superintendent," she said, clasping her hands tightly together, "how could I tell you what happened here last night? How could I? It's all very well for a man—but a woman—and the mother of two grown-up daughters! I assure you, it had nothing to do with me!" She sank on to a low satin-covered gilt chair and gave way to weeping.

"*What* had nothing to do with you?" Mallett pressed her. "Do you mean Barker's death? That's what interests me."

Mabel raised her tear-stained face.

"Oh, no, oh, no," she cried. "I know nothing about that! I came here last night to get a book, after I left Bernard. I didn't want to go downstairs to the library—I wasn't feeling like company, so I came here. Mrs. Smith-Wilson keeps all her books for lighter reading here." She indicated the glass-fronted bookcase between the two long windows. "I came along the passage. I was going to leave the other way and go to my room; but when I opened the door, I saw Major Lavering coming along the corridor. He was walking unsteadily."

"Oh, I say!" protested Rupert. "Nobody has seen me do that for the last ten years!"

Mallett motioned to him to keep quiet.

"He had been drinking," went on Mabel rapidly. "He has been drinking now. Can't you smell it? The room's full of it." She applied a lace-and-tulle handkerchief to her nose.

"Not everybody who smells of drink is drunk, madam," remarked Mallett, "unless he's involved in a motoring accident." And he cast a look at Rupert that was not far removed from a wink.

"When he saw me," went on Mrs. Hertford, undaunted, "he staggered across the corridor towards me. I thought he wanted to speak to me about the money I had invested on his advice: there had already been a scene about these shares, downstairs in the smoking-room, between him and Sir Matthew Risdon; and I thought Major Lavering wanted to reassure me, knowing how I and my girls had trusted him with our all. But no." She looked down, biting her lip.

Rupert, somewhat reassured by Mallett's near-wink, had ceased to interrupt. He gave himself up to the pleasure of listening—for it was a sort of pleasure, though not perhaps to everybody's taste, to hear someone deliberately, shamelessly falsifying the scene in which he had been the other participant. The pleasure perhaps came from one's amazement at the glibness of the lies, the smooth art of the liar, the comparison between the facts which one had witnessed and acted, and the narrative told with such an air of authenticity. It was better than a play.

Mabel continued, as if with an effort:

"At first he did talk about the shares. And then—well, Superintendent, you won't expect me to describe what followed."

"You mean the Major made advances towards you?" said Mallett, pulling a very long face. "Well, well, who would have thought it?" This time, as he glanced at Rupert, he did wink unmistakably. Rupert began to enjoy himself more and more. "And then what happened? You fought? You struggled? You called for help, no doubt?"

"I didn't call out," admitted Mabel. "I couldn't. The house was full of guests. I had my daughters to think of. I couldn't create a scandal in Mr. Smith-Wilson's house."

"I see," said Mallett. "But you were able to shake off the Major and get away. No doubt that was how you came to leave your evening scarf on the floor in here: it came off in his hands. And Major, you left a pocket-handkerchief behind. At any rate, it has the initial L on it, and it corresponds with others among your luggage."

"I never noticed," said Rupert. "I changed into other clothes before leaving, and I suppose I took another one."

Mallett turned back to Mabel.

"You must have thought we were very negligent, Mrs. Hertford, not to have seen a thing of that size." He crossed the room, round the end of the bed, and stood looming over her. "You know where we found it?"

Mabel, frightened, could hardly give back a negative or shake her head.

"Round the neck of the maid Barker," said Mallett savagely, "wound several times round her neck and pulled tight round the left-hand upper bed-post, after she'd been stunned by a heavy blow on the head. Someone made certain of killing her, in case the blow failed. It's amazing how strong these apparently fragile materials are. You can't tear them—and if you remember that union is strength and use several coils, they're strong enough to hang a heavy man from. You didn't know that, of course."

Mabel had been listening with bowed head; but now she jerked herself up.

"I know nothing about it! You must ask Major Lavering about that! I went back the way I came. I don't know what happened after I left. But he's a man—and he can be violent. He was violent to *me*!"

The three inside the room had become so intent on each other that they had either not heard, or had refused to heed, a slight commotion outside. But now it intruded: the voice of Mallett's attendant constable became audible, trying to forbid someone's entry; and a woman's voice insisting:

"It's no use your trying to stop me. I intend to see Superintendent Mallett this time. If he wants to know the truth, he'll want to see *me*."

It was Louise. She gained her point, and entered on Mabel's last words.

"Oh, what a lie!" she exclaimed, stopping so suddenly in full career that the folds of her full-skirted dressing-gown swirled round her. She was pink with anger and interrupted sleep; but in spite of her speed to save Rupert, she had found time to powder her nose, and not one of her golden hairs was out of place, except in so far as this was allowed.

Rupert, watching her entry, smiled. Louise was always spectacularly pleasing to watch. Tonight she was marvellous. She continued her interrupted passage across the floor to where Mabel sat cowering, as if expecting a blow.

"How can you—how dare you say such a thing?" she raged; and to Mallett: "Superintendent! You're *not* going to listen to a word this woman says? You *know* she inveigled my husband into here last night and tried to make love to him? And now, because he wouldn't listen to her, she'll try to pay him out by pretending he did this murder. I expect she did it herself. She arranged to get him here to cover her own wickedness. Rupert wouldn't hurt a fly!"

"Darling!" murmured Rupert deprecatorily, "aren't you perhaps exaggerating?" And Mallett added:

"I expect he's hurt more than flies in the past six years, ma'am!"

Louise rounded on them both.

"How like people," she stormed, "who've stayed at home all these years and had their fighting done for them by men like him, to use his very war service against him! Those things haven't made him violent. Nothing could!" And then, to Rupert, just as he was beginning to expand and sun himself in this unexpected praise: "Rupert! I don't believe you've told the truth *yet*! Your sentimentality amazes me—and all in defence of this woman who's only too ready to try to ruin you! It's more than sentimentality—it's sheer cowardice!"

Rupert cast an appealing look past her at Mallett. But Louise was not to be stopped. She made for the door again, at the same speed as that with which she had entered.

"This has got to end," she said. "If you won't speak, we must call the other witness." And in a moment she was off down the corridor, and hammering at the Risdons' door.

"Lady Risdon!" she called out imperiously. "Will you please come at once? You're urgently needed."

Lady Risdon sat up in bed and switched on the light.

"Coming!" she called back.

Sir Matthew stirred and muttered: "Eh? What's that?"

"It's all right," she said cheerfully. "Things are coming to a head at last, I think! I've a good ear for voices. That's Mrs. Lavering outside. I believe they've caught the murderer!"

She sprang out of bed.

40

The commotion increased as Louise and Lady Risdon, talking volubly, swept together up the corridor. Heads looked round bedroom doors: first Clara appeared, then Lucilla, and finally Olivia, who came strolling across towards the lily-room. She arrived just after Louise and Lady Risdon had gone inside. The policeman at the door pulled it to after them.

"What's going on in there?" said Olivia. "Another body?" She lit a cigarette.

"I don't think so, miss," said the policeman. "But there's a spot of bother. I should advise you to go back to your room. And you too, ladies," he said, as Clara and Lucilla came hurrying up. "No, no, you can't go in there!"

"But we must!" cried Lucilla. "I heard my mother's voice. I'm sure I did, when you opened the door! Why should Mrs. Lavering and Lady Risdon go in if we can't? I insist! Come on, Clara! They can't stop us!" And she made a dive for the door-handle, under the policeman's outstretched arm, while Clara began hammering on the panel.

"Go it, girls!" Olivia, standing apart, egged them on. "Oh, well played!"

The policeman, hard put to it to guard the way without handling the scantily-clad girls too roughly, shot Olivia a resentful look. He had managed to interpose himself in an impregnable position between them and the door when suddenly it opened, causing him to fall backwards into the room with Clara and Lucilla after him.

"What the devil are you doing?" said Mallett to his discomfited assistant. "Can't you keep people out of here?"

But it was no use: when the door was shut once more, Clara and Lucilla were inside. They rushed upon Mrs. Hertford with heart-rending cries of "Mother darling! What has happened? What are they doing to you?" and one on each side of her, they faced the audience in attitudes of defence. Mrs. Hertford, seizing her advantage, wept unrestrainedly into her handkerchief.

Louise, baffled, cast a look of inquiry at Lady Risdon. Lady Risdon shrugged her shoulders.

"Can't be done," she said, "in front of the girls."

"Oh, damn the girls!" said Louise; but even she could see that one could not accuse a mother in front of her two daughters of having tried to seduce one's husband.

Mallett, stroking his chin, looked on.

"You'd better take your mother to her room," he said curtly to Clara. "I'll see her in the morning."

The girls conveyed their weeping mother away, past Rupert at whom they levelled resentful looks, past Louise and Lady Risdon whom they ignored; past Mallett at whom they tossed their heads; through the door and past the policeman and Olivia, who were now reconciled and looking on with scepticism.

"So she has got away with it again!" said Louise in exasperation. "How does she do it? I wish I knew! It must be wonderful to be never in the wrong!"

She swept out, without a glance at Rupert, and Lady Risdon followed her.

Mallett and Rupert were left alone. Mallett came towards him.

"Major," he said earnestly, "are you prepared to declare on oath that this woman inveigled you into this room last night and made improper advances towards you?"

"Well," said Rupert, distressed, "she certainly got me here and talked a lot of nonsense about wanting me to take her away. I don't honestly think the poor woman's right in the head."

"That would be for a jury to decide, on medical evidence," said Mallett. "It didn't occur to you that her object might be very different—that she might, for instance, be planning to cover herself in advance in connection with something she proposed to do later? When we examined this room after the discovery of the body, we found—lying on the floor just where you're now standing—"

Rupert looked hastily down at his feet, as if expecting an adder to raise its head from behind one of the cabbage roses on the carpet.

"We found your handkerchief, the one I referred to just now. It was a simple matter to show that it was yours. What was not so simple was to decide on its significance. We knew you'd been here: you yourself told us. But Mrs. Hertford has consistently attempted to deceive us. Therefore we asked ourselves, wasn't it possible that she had pulled the handkerchief out of your pocket while pretending to embrace you, and left it lying on the carpet?"

"It's possible," said Rupert doubtfully. "I hadn't thought of that."

Mallett shook his head.

"You haven't thought very hard, I'm afraid, Major. You should have come to me at once with this story. As it is, I've been compelled to keep an eye on you as well as on the others, because although you admitted having been in here last night with a woman, you refused to explain how it came about or even who the woman was."

"Yes, but," demurred Rupert, "I knew, if I named her, you'd instantly suspect her of this murder, and I didn't want to be the one to put a rope round her neck."

"Not even if she put a rope round somebody else's?" said Mallett.

Rupert was silent.

Mallett walked over to the cupboard and pulled back the two sliding doors.

"We knew about this, too, of course," he said. "There was no great secret about it. Mrs. Smith-Wilson herself directed our attention to this passage, which she said was one of her husband's ideas for getting from this bedroom to the study without meeting anybody. He had a great objection to being seen by the servants in his dressing-gown, and yet he liked to go to his study whenever he felt inclined, early in the morning or late at night. She said that the present staff didn't know about it, with the exception of Barker, who often went that way from her room to fetch things from the cupboards, or books from this case here. She also mentioned that Mrs. Hertford knew of it. So you see, quite apart from anything you may have contributed, there are already a number of fingers pointing at Mrs. Hertford."

"I'm sorry to hear that," said Rupert. "I mean, Mrs. Hertford's nothing to me, and after what happened here last night and the fact that she seems to have tried to use me to shield herself, I suppose I ought to be glad. But I always dislike seeing people caught out and humiliated, or worse. I suppose you're certain, now, she killed Barker?"

Mallett regarded him appraisingly.

"Well," he said, "there's nobody listening, so I don't mind answering your questions, Major, up to a point. The truth is"—he put one of his feet up on the bedroom chair in front of him, and addressed Rupert like a counsel dealing with a witness—"we don't make up our minds until we've got all the evidence." Then, seeing Rupert's obvious disappointment, he added: "Why don't you join us, if you want to know how we work?"

"Oh," said Rupert, turning away, "I wouldn't have the patience. I can't settle down to anything these days."

"Well, think about it," said Mallett. "It's just the job for a man like you. It'd keep you out of mischief." He walked to the door. "Meanwhile, just leave things to us, will you? It's difficult enough without people getting in the way."

Rupert left.

When he reached the bedroom, Louise sat up eagerly.

"What did he say?"

"Exactly nothing," said Rupert disgustedly. "He suggested I should join the police force."

"Oh, but, darling," said Louise, "that's ridiculous! You'd never be any good at that!"

"Why not?"

"Because you're much too sentimental."

"For once, darling," said Rupert, "I'm inclined to agree with you."

41

Next morning, when Mrs. Hertford tapped at the door of Mrs. Smith-Wilson's sitting-room and entered, she found Mrs. Smith-Wilson already up and dressed, standing by one of the long windows, leaning on her silver-topped ebony stick and gazing out across the lawns.

She was not aware at first of Mabel's entrance; and Mabel was shocked to see the ravages that grief had wrought in her appearance. Her dress was immaculate, her hair was fixed in the high coiffure she favoured, which looked as if it were never disarranged even in sleep. Her attitude was as upright as ever. But on her face it seemed as if age had bitten deep lines overnight; and this was all the more shocking because, although she had always affected an old-fashioned style, a dignity and formality strongly opposed to modern laxness, she was not really old in body or in mind. The strength of her character upheld her still; but the struggle to overcome her despair showed itself now in a sudden ageing, the end of a long process that had been going on unseen during her son's illness, when she had known in her heart that even if he could recover, he could never again live the full life of a young and vigorous man.

'No,' she was thinking as she looked out over the garden that he had taken such great pleasure in restoring, 'Bernard's life was over. He could never have been resigned to living the life of an invalid. Every move he made would have had to be watched. He would have had to watch himself, to check himself at every turn. He would have come to hate us all—himself—even me. The better we looked after him, the more he would have hated us. Glasses of milk, indeed! That last night of celebration was a pretence to himself that he had returned to life and normal health again. But it wasn't true, and he must have known it. I was against the idea. I knew he'd find out, if he persisted in it, that he wasn't any longer one of them. He'd watch them all at dinner, eating, drinking, not having to think, as he had to do, about their health; and he'd know that for him, and him only, in all that gathering the banquet was over…

'And then, there was that wretched girl he brought here to me. Ha! I kept her away from him, away from all the fun, very cleverly! To think that Bernard should care about a woman like that, a perfectly ordinary woman, pretty enough, no doubt, if you like that style, but *ordinary*: excellently well-suited to the young man she has married. But not to Bernard—not to Bernard! To think he should so far forget his pride, he, the most self-willed creature on earth—so far forget himself as to run after a woman who had dared to reject him!'

At that thought, her face contracted into an expression so grim that Mabel was frightened, especially as at that moment Mrs. Smith-Wilson turned round and saw her, so that she received the full force of that forbidding look not meant for her. When Mrs. Smith-Wilson recognised her, the look changed from bitter anger to contempt.

"Ah, there you are, Mabel!" she said, hobbling towards Mrs. Hertford, leaning heavily on her stick. "I thought perhaps you'd been scared away from this house of—insecurity. Well, how's Clara? I hear she gave herself a bad shock yesterday. She won't be quite so ready to go prying round other people's houses another time." She paused in front of Mabel and eyed her up and down: "And I hear you've been making a complete fool of yourself. Ha!" The exclamation was a scornful laugh.

"What do you mean?" said Mabel, bridling and reddening.

Mrs. Smith-Wilson was delighted to tell her:

"Throwing yourself at the head of that young Rupert Lavering! A woman of your age, with two grown-up daughters! I'm surprised at you!"

"I should like to remind you," said Mrs. Hertford, quivering with indignation, "that there's less difference between his age and mine than between my age and yours."

Mrs. Smith-Wilson waved her free hand impatiently.

"I'm not good at arithmetic. I only know that a woman of forty with two daughters of marriageable age is making a fool of herself if she sets her cap at a man ten years younger than herself, even if he's a bachelor. If he had been, you'd have done better to have tried to get him for Clara or Lucilla. As it is, he's married already, and to a woman quite suitable for *him*." She turned away. "Well, you know your own business best, I suppose; but I wish you wouldn't choose *my* house for your absurd activities."

Mrs. Hertford followed her. Her mouth opened and shut, but at first no articulate sound emerged. By the time that Mrs. Smith-Wilson had installed herself in her chair, with one foot on a beaded footstool and one hand on her silver-topped stick, Mrs. Hertford was managing to utter the words:

"Such ingratitude! Such ingratitude!"

Mrs. Smith-Wilson contemplated her balefully.

"Whose?" she said. "Mine—to you? You came here to please yourself, not me! You like hovering round people who don't want you, offering to do things they don't need. And didn't you really come here because you hoped to marry off one of your daughters? Well, you've had your recompense: Bernard has assessed your worth—a good deal higher than I would have done, I must say. Well, you needn't hover any longer. My son's dead, and you'll get nothing out of *my* will. I've still got something better to do with *my* money, thank God!"

Her savage delight in hurting staggered Mrs. Hertford, angry as she herself had been. She withdrew a step, as if in alarm, and gasped:

"I can hardly recognise you! You've changed—changed completely!"

"Changed, have I?" said Mrs. Smith-Wilson grimly. "Well, perhaps I have. Perhaps something has happened—not to change me, but to make it not worth my while to pretend any more." She leaned forward. "For instance, Mabel Hertford, I've always thought you a fool, and I've often treated you as such; but I never before gave myself the satisfaction of saying so."

Mrs. Hertford, after a great effort, had recovered herself. She said quietly:

"You don't know what you're saying. You're not yourself. After all you've been through, it's natural. I forgive you."

Mrs. Smith-Wilson did not answer. She seemed not even to be listening; so Mabel moved a step nearer.

"But I *should* like to know," she said, "where you got the garbled version of what happened between me and Major Lavering. From Miss Bannermore, I suppose." Her voice took on a self-pitying tone. "I realise you don't need me any longer, now you have her. But I never would have thought you'd have believed such things against me on the mere word of a stranger!"

Mrs. Smith-Wilson turned and regarded her with some slight interest and even amusement.

"Well, go on," she said. "What's *your* version? I'm always willing to listen to both sides."

Mabel, encouraged, came forward another step.

"I know it must be painful to you, now," she began, "and I wouldn't have dreamt of mentioning it if you hadn't asked me. But—well, I know you well enough, dear Mrs. Smith-Wilson, to know you'd rather have the truth.

"You remember, on Wednesday evening, just after Barker left you, you asked me to go along to the lily-room and get you a book? Well, I couldn't find it in the bookcase, so I thought I'd look for it in the library. When I reached the door at the bottom of the small staircase, I thought I heard voices. So I opened the door just a tiny way, and I heard poor Bernard telling Mrs. Lavering the most terrible things. He said he'd ruin Rupert if she didn't give him up. I didn't wait to hear what she said. I came back to you, and I was going to tell you, but in a minute or so Bernard brought Mrs. Lavering here and went away again. You and she began playing cards. I thought how sly it was of her to sit there knowing what had just happened, and yet be able to look so innocent and unconcerned."

Mabel pursed up her lips in an expression of righteousness. Mrs. Smith-Wilson nodded several times, slowly, as she watched her, but whether in agreement or whether at some secret thought no one could have told.

"Go on," she said.

Mabel, further encouraged, proceeded:

"My next thought was that all this excitement must be doing Bernard harm, and it struck me that they'd have forgotten about his milk in the kitchen. He ate very little at dinner, so the girls told me later, so I was glad I had been able to do this little thing for him. I went and got the milk and carried it up, but when I reached the study door I heard voices—men's voices; and I knew they'd hate to be interrupted. So I put the milk just inside the sliding door in the passage and went away.

"I went along to my own room. On my way back I met Miss Bannermore carrying a Thermos flask and some ice-cubes on a tray. I saw where she went: she went straight to the Laverings' room. I knew that Mrs. Lavering was with you. Then I saw my own girl, Lucilla, at the end of the corridor. I didn't feel I wanted to speak to her just then, so I hurried away back to Bernard's study."

Mabel breathed fast, as if she were covering the distance again with all her original haste and nervous agitation.

"When I got back," she continued, "Sir Matthew Risdon was just leaving. I waited until he had gone down the stairs. Then I fetched the milk and took it to Bernard.

"Bernard really did look dreadfully excited. I was quite taken aback. His face was flushed, and he gesticulated a good deal, which he doesn't do as a rule. When I first went in, he was standing with his back to me at the window, but he was muttering something to himself and jerking his head and his hands. When I spoke—I said: 'Bernard, I've brought you your milk. Now do take it! It will do you good.'

"At first he didn't seem to recognise me. Then he came forward to the desk, frowning and muttering, and he said something that I took to mean: 'Put it down and go away!' There was a glass with some whisky in it on the desk, and another empty glass on the mantelshelf.

"When I said again: 'Do drink your milk!' he seemed to misunderstand me. He took the half-finished glass of whisky and drank that, and then walked away again to the window, taking no notice of me. His manner was so odd that I didn't like to stay longer. Still, I felt I owed it to my girls to say something about the shares. I thought, if he ruined Rupert, there was really no need why *we* should suffer too; and I knew, you see, that everything depended on what Bernard did. So I said: 'Bernard, is it true that those shares we bought through Rupert on your advice are falling?'

"At that, he turned round on me so violently that I was quite frightened. He said: 'Of course they're falling—and they will fall. The bottom's dropping out of them, this very moment!' He waved his arms and seemed to be arguing with someone else, not talking to me. He said: 'I've given instructions—given instructions—' and then he stopped and stared at nothing, as if he weren't quite sure what he'd been saying. So I said, just to remind him: 'But you won't forget about me and the girls, will you, Bernard? *We* can't help what has happened between you and Louise!'

"I thought, the moment I had spoken, perhaps it wasn't very wise of me to have mentioned her name, especially as he might guess I'd overheard what he'd been saying to her in the library. But then again, I had Clara and Lucilla to think of. Bernard didn't respond, even to that. He simply stared at me as if I'd been a stranger, and he said very rudely: 'Get out!'

"I assumed, then, that he must have taken a little too much to drink. So I picked up the two whisky glasses and went away, leaving the glass of milk on the tray on his desk. He didn't drink it while I was there."

"No," said Mrs. Smith-Wilson. "He drank it later."

There was a pause.

"Well?" Mrs. Smith-Wilson roused herself from her thoughts and spoke sharply again. "You haven't told me about the rest of the evening. Go on: I'm interested."

Mabel sat down at last, on a low gilt-legged chair, and turned her face away, so that Mrs. Smith-Wilson could not see it. She said in a low voice:

"I don't expect you to understand."

"Oh!" retorted Mrs. Smith-Wilson vigorously. "And why not, pray? I shall understand well enough, if you speak the truth. But don't bother to make up a story for *me*. You can tell that man Mallett anything you please, but I'm not so easily deceived!"

"I should like to tell you—or somebody," said Mabel slowly, as if driven against her will, and to her own surprise, into speaking. "All along I've struggled—but what's the use? So long as the girls don't know—"

"Oh, the girls!" said Mrs. Smith-Wilson contemptuously. "*They* won't know—and what if they do? You pay far too much heed to them, Mabel—always measuring yourself up against them, trying to seem as young as they are. There's nothing disgraceful in being middle-aged. If you'd accepted the fact and looked around you for a man of your own age or older, you'd have got married again years ago—and a very good thing too! Well, it's not too late, provided you give up all thoughts of a dashing romance. Rupert Lavering! Why, he's just an ordinary young fellow, with the glamour of the war on him! He wouldn't suit *you* at all!"

Mabel sighed.

"I know, I know. I can't imagine what came over me. Looking back, I feel as if I had dreamt it all, or as if it weren't myself. Or perhaps there were two of me, and one looked on and the other acted. I suppose you won't believe me if I tell you that *you* were the first cause of my unusual mood that evening."

"I? Impossible! How?"

"Because you *would* keep me with you," cried Mabel passionately, "when I wanted to be happy and enjoy myself! You don't understand what my life has been like! When I was a girl, I was sociable and gay. And then I married, and there were the children. Then, when they were getting big enough not to need all my attention, the war came. I was still young—still fond of pleasure—still hoping for the fun I'd some-how always missed. That was eight years ago—and now I've passed the border-line, into middle age. I know it. But it's hard to accept. And then, on Wednesday night, there was this party.

"It meant nothing to you. In fact, you didn't approve of it. You thought Bernard was forcing the pace after his illness. You were grudg-ing and ungracious about it, even to him. You wouldn't receive his guests. You wouldn't preside over his dinner-table. You pretended it was to please him—but it was to please yourself. You didn't like to see Bernard enjoying himself in company. You liked it better when he was an invalid—in bed—at your mercy. Didn't you?" Her voice trembled in spite of her sudden boldness.

"Perhaps you're right," said Mrs. Smith-Wilson, with an utterly unexpected reasonableness; and then, in a lower voice, to herself: "Perhaps you're right."

"And so, because you wished to take no part in it, you wouldn't let me either. You pretended that I was the same age as yourself and didn't want to. You blame me for trying to be as young as my daughters—but where's the difference? You were trying to make me as old as yourself, and yourself twenty years older than you are! Your crime's as bad as mine!" She crisped her fingers together in the intensity of her emotion.

"Crime?" murmured Mrs. Smith-Wilson ominously. But Mabel was beyond caring.

"And so you wouldn't let me dine with the company—as if they were all young and we were out of the running! What about the Risdons? If they could be there, why not I?" Tears sprang into her eyes at the recollection of this injustice. "Still, I stayed with you and did my best to be resigned—once again.

"And then—I heard Bernard making love to Louise in the library. It excited me. I wished, in a way, I were in her place: not with Bernard, of course, but—young again, young enough to be kissed, even by a man I didn't care for. She had everything, more than she wanted. I had nothing. I never had had anything, really, for I was married and a mother before I knew what love was all about.

"I stayed. I listened. It was dangerous. I ought not to have, for my own sake. But I pretended it was because of his talk of shares and prices, and because it affected us—myself and the girls. Oh, yes, I lied to myself, as usual! But I knew, really: one does, you know, even after a lifetime of pretending.

"I managed to get back just before they did. I left you and her together. And then—I had an irresistible desire to take another look at Bernard. I don't know why. I never found him very attractive. I suppose it was because I knew he was trying to steal Rupert's wife. And I was interested in Rupert—I always have been. I thought my interest was just friendly and almost maternal. And yet—I never felt maternal towards Bernard, though I thought of them as being much the same age.

"I didn't really go to get the milk for Bernard's sake, you know. I've said so, I know, to myself and everybody else, up to now. But that was just an excuse. I didn't go to ask him about the shares, either. I knew he wouldn't let us lose in the long run, whatever happened."

"That's the first sincere good word I've ever heard you utter about Bernard," said Mrs. Smith-Wilson. "He was always fair, in the end. I'm glad you recognise it."

Mrs. Hertford went on more rapidly:

"I went because I wanted to look at Bernard. I knew he was in love with Louise—and I wanted to look at him. I can't explain any better than that. I wanted to look at *him. She* didn't interest me: *she* wasn't at all moved, I could see that. But he—well, I've told you. I went away wondering—marvelling. I thought she was a very lucky woman."

"She was," said Mrs. Smith-Wilson grimly, "a great deal luckier than she deserved."

"I went away," said Mabel. "I wanted to be by myself—to think. I thought I'd slip through the passage to the lily-room and get the book you wanted, and one for myself—a love-story—and then go to my own room and read for a while. I was restless—not myself. When I reached the end of the passage-way to the lily-room, again I heard voices—a man's and a woman's, talking on the other side of the sliding door. I stayed where I was, and again I listened."

Mrs. Smith-Wilson leaned forward in her chair and rapped impatiently on the floor with her stick.

"Well, go on! What are you waiting for? Who was it? Was it Barker—and Holmes?"

"You knew?" said Mabel.

Mrs. Smith-Wilson nodded.

"I guessed. Nothing much escapes my eye."

Mabel went on more hurriedly:

"They were talking—or, rather, *she* was talking in a low voice, and very fast; and he was answering surlily. I couldn't hear all they said; but I think—I think she was trying to keep him, and he was telling her he had to leave." Mabel's face grew solemn and shocked. "They'd been using that room as a rendezvous, you know, for a long time, whenever Holmes's duties brought him here."

"The slut!" interposed Mrs. Smith-Wilson furiously. "To think that she dared—in my house—in my room!"

"At last," said Mabel, "Holmes broke away. I heard Barker calling out something, saying he'd regret it if he went without her. He came back into the room and began arguing again, trying to reason with her, saying she could follow him later. She began to cry. In the end he left her there. He went out by the farther door, into the corridor. As soon as the door closed behind him, she jumped off the bed and began raging up and down the room, muttering to herself. I was afraid she'd come back through my passage—but she didn't. To my relief she followed Holmes, out through the door.

"In a few moments, they were both back again, arguing more furiously than ever. At last I heard him say: 'All right, then: meet me here at one o'clock. I promise I won't go without you.' Then they went out again, she first this time, and he a minute or so later. And I came out of my hiding-place into the room.

"I was terribly shaken by all that I'd heard. I knew I should have to tell *you* in the morning—and I knew how angry you'd be. I wondered if I ought to go at once and tell Bernard—but I didn't dare, after the way he'd spoken to me. I thought I must get away, out of this room, before anything else happened: perhaps they might come back again. So, scarcely knowing what I was doing, I went to the door.

"I saw Rupert coming along the corridor. I called out to him, I don't know why. From then onward I acted, as I've told you, like someone else, or like myself in a dream.

"He came. He was very kind at first, very polite—but puzzled. I asked him about the shares, and he began reassuring me. But I wasn't listening. I was watching him, thinking how he was all I'd missed, all my life—and yet that girl Louise, who could have had Bernard, had got Rupert as well. By now I knew—I knew what had happened to me. But I didn't care. I began talking, telling him about Bernard and Louise, and what I'd overheard in the library.

"He was angry—but not with her: with *me*. I began to get angry, too. I told him how I'd seen Olivia going into his room.

"This time he was more than angry: he was disgusted. I saw that I was failing—failing again. I saw how he regarded me—as a woman to be pitied—rather absurd and terribly embarrassing. At that, I should have withdrawn—pretended he'd misunderstood me. But a sort of panic made me go on.

"I let him see how I felt about him. I asked him to give up Louise, to let Bernard have her and take me instead. I heard myself using some of the very words I'd heard Barker using a quarter of an hour before. I knew that it was madness; but for once in my life I chose to be mad. I made a mistake. It doesn't pay—not even once. Once you've chosen the wrong path in life, there's no going back—and life goes by so quickly! They ought to tell us all that when we're young."

She sat with head bowed, looking down at her hands.

"You left your scarf behind," said Mrs. Smith-Wilson at last.

"I know. I never gave it a thought, really, until they told me Barker's body had been found in that room—on that bed. And even then, nobody mentioned my scarf. I didn't know it had been used to strangle her. I thought I must have dropped it somewhere, perhaps in the passage-way where I'd been standing when I listened. I went back to look. That was a mistake, too. My judgment's always at fault." She sighed. "So Holmes killed her after all, when she met him there at one o'clock that night. What a stupid woman, to drive him so far! I don't think I need tell all this to the police, do you? They've caught him, and they can prove it all without my help."

"You ought to have told them at once," said Mrs. Smith-Wilson. "Instead, you tried to throw suspicion on Rupert. Why? I suppose you hated him, because he rejected you."

Mabel blinked defensively:

"Did I?" she said. "I forget. I must have had an impulse to protect myself. I thought he'd tell the police about what had happened between us in that room."

"Rupert isn't a coward," said Mrs. Smith-Wilson. "I should have thought even you would have noticed that. What did you do after Rupert got away from you?"

"I went downstairs to the drawing-room," said Mabel, "and met the girls coming up. We had our usual little chat before going to bed. Clara noticed I wasn't wearing my scarf. I went back to my room and looked for it, and when I couldn't find it, I came along to you. You know the rest. After I left you and was in my own room again—it was then after one o'clock—I was looking out of my bedroom window and I saw someone driving out of the garage. I knew it must be Holmes. I thought he was alone, and I decided he hadn't taken Barker with him after all. When she didn't turn up next morning, I thought I must have been mistaken: she must have been in the car. But I dared not tell you what I'd seen and heard, in case you asked me how I knew."

"*Your* cowardice," said Mrs. Smith-Wilson, "cost my son his life. I hope you'll remember that for the rest of your own life."

The door opened and Olivia Bannermore entered.

She took no notice of Mabel, still sitting dejected on the low chair. She walked straight across to Mrs. Smith-Wilson.

"Holmes has committed suicide," she said without preliminary. "It appears they were questioning him until about four o'clock this morning. When they came for him again at seven, they found him hanging. So I suppose that's that."

"I suppose so," said Mrs. Smith-Wilson, unemotionally. "Olivia, I feel tired. Help me to get back to bed again, will you?"

"You'd better go," said Olivia to Mabel.

Mabel went.

42

The two doctors left the gaol together.

"This is a bad rap for Mallett," said Dr. Jones, "though I suppose it solves his problem for him."

"I suppose so," said Dr. Fitzbrown.

"Otherwise it's the best thing that could have happened, no doubt. You were there throughout, weren't you? Did Mallett get anything out of him?"

"Yes," said Fitzbrown, "I was there. I was supposed to be observing his mental condition. I don't like these man-baiting scenes. That's no part of our job."

"Pooh!" said Jones. "One can't feel much sympathy with a killer— and he practically admitted his guilt by committing suicide."

"Not necessarily," said Fitzbrown. "I should have called him an obviously suicidal type myself. His whole life was a sort of self-immolation. One has heard of people who have an urge towards death. It's an idea which I personally find incomprehensible, but there's no doubt that it does exist, and I think we have an example of it there in Holmes. As to whether he did these murders: however likely it seems now, it still isn't proven, you know. In fact, it worries me a good deal."

Dr. Jones shot his colleague a sharp glance.

"You're overtired," he said. "Come and have dinner with me this evening and tell me all about it."

43

'It still isn't proven…'

Fitzbrown sat at his desk, waiting for his morning patients, staring ahead, envisaging the scene of a few hours ago. Mallett's quarry had escaped him, by the easy way. An underling's carelessness had set Holmes free.

Fitzbrown thought of the long hours of questioning. Could anyone be blamed for this man's death? He did not think so. In such a case, time was of the utmost importance: other lives might be in danger, if one were on a false trail. One had every right, and, indeed, it was one's duty, to try to squeeze the truth out of a prisoner. Mallett had not used any unduly harsh methods. He had simply pegged away with question after question, trying to break down the man's resistance. And if Holmes had had to do without some sleep, what about the rest of them, the guardians of the law?

Fitzbrown rubbed his smarting eyes.

He could see again the familiar setting: the bare room, the prisoner seated on a bench, and two impassive men, the semi-circle of watchers: himself, Mallett, Coles, Detective-Inspector Smayles from the Broxeter laboratory, a stenographer, someone in charge of a table of exhibits. Holmes was paler than ever, with several cuts and bruises showing up on his face as a result of the previous day's struggle. His hair was tousled, his clothes were awry, his hands, which he clasped in front of him, were dirty; but he was as uncompromising as ever. On the whole, he stared at the ground; but when he did look up, he managed to infuse a remarkable degree of contempt and hatred into his glance. There was no room for anything else in his mind, not even the self-pity which usually, in Fitzbrown's experience, was the most powerful emotion of the criminal. Holmes owned no duty to any existing institution, any moral code, any convention: only to the crazy dream which was the absorbing passion of his distorted soul.

Since he had heard of the discovery of Barker's death, he had, so they said, sat humped up in his cell like a hedgehog, refusing to speak. But now he answered Mallett's questions readily enough. In fact, he would have embarked on tirades from time to time if he had not been prevented. At first, he seemed inclined to be difficult.

"Did you kill Smith-Wilson?" Mallett began.

"No."

"Did you, with intent to kill him, introduce the poison known as atropine into the glass of whisky which you knew Smith-Wilson was about to drink?"

"No."

"Have you ever seen this?" Mrs. Smith-Wilson's blue liniment-bottle was held up.

Holmes, without looking up, said: "No."

"Or this?" The bottle of belladonna eyedrops was exhibited.

Holmes did not reply.

"You categorically deny having extracted or used any of the contents of either of these bottles at any time?"

No answer.

Mallett tried a new line:

"You know that Smith-Wilson died of atropine poisoning?"

"Yes." A flicker of feeling that might have been interpreted as pleasure, if ever Holmes could have felt anything so futile, passed over his face and was gone.

"You don't appear to regret his death," remarked Mallett. "That's odd, isn't it, seeing that he paid you, and paid you well, and, so far as I know, treated you with every consideration?"

"Consideration!" Holmes jerked up his head. "He used me, as he used everybody else, with the consideration necessary to squeeze the last ounce of work out of me. Men like you, who fawn on the tradition of wages for work—which is the historical derivative of slavery—you're so blinkered by habit that you can't see the criminality of giving power to men like Smith-Wilson! He was a weakling—soft inside, like a crab. What we want in key positions is the hard man, the man who can't be deflected by personal desires like the craving for fine food, fine houses, fine clothes—and women!" His contempt reached its acme. Mallett interrupted:

"We don't want to hear your political views."

"I'll bet you don't!" sneered Holmes. "You think our régime wouldn't suit you! And yet you'd be no worse off than you are now: you'd be a cog in the machine, a lackey as you are now; but it'd be a better machine—and a more worth-while master!"

Mallett said patiently:

"Well, what exactly *had* you against Smith-Wilson?"

"Nothing personal," said Holmes. "I didn't want his woman, or his house, or his money."

"You helped yourself to the latter," said Mallett, "all the same."

"Not for myself: for the cause. But you wouldn't understand that. You think, if a man has money, he's a strong man and everybody should obey him. I think Smith-Wilson lost all right to wield power when he lost his physical health. He'd already shown himself spiritually a weakling over a woman—two women. He'd have done better to poison himself six months ago."

"That's what *you* think," said Mallett. "Are you sure you didn't help him over the border?"

Holmes gave a sneering laugh.

"I had no time to bother about him! He wasn't worth it, to me! I wanted to get away, to fresh spheres of activity. He'd have been swept away with the rest of his crazy social system when our ideas were victorious! It's a waste of energy, dealing with individuals. One strikes the tree at the root."

He looked murderous enough as his eyes flashed with the joy of this idea: it was as if he saw the great tree falling, crashing to the ground, humiliated, finished. He waved a hand.

"What good could Smith-Wilson's death do me? It could only ruin me and all I stood for. Look what the mere suspicion has done for me—tied me here by the leg when I meant to be far away! Do you think I'd bring this on myself deliberately for the sake of one miserable life, not worth twelve months' insurance anyway? As it is, he's got me, out of the grave, he and"—he stopped, but no one spoke; he added in a whisper—"whoever killed him."

There was a pause. After a moment or two, Mallett resumed:

"Now, Holmes, so far as Smith-Wilson's death is concerned, the position is this: he was perfectly normal at dinner. After dinner, he had some conversation with Mrs. Lavering in the library—"

"Pah!" said Holmes.

"—which you interrupted," continued Mallett. "You then went to him in his study. That was at five minutes to ten. You left five minutes later, to fetch Sir Matthew Risdon. Sir Matthew reached the study at about ten minutes past ten."

He paused, but Holmes said nothing.

"Sir Matthew instantly noticed something different about Smith-Wilson. His manner was excited, whereas normally he was the reverse: in fact, I gather he took a pride in always appearing calm and unruffled in any circumstances. Now: what had happened to change him in the interval?"

Holmes sneered:

"Hadn't you better ask Mrs. Lavering?"

"Are you suggesting that Mrs. Lavering gave him atropine?"

"No—something stronger, to a weak constitution like his."

Mallett said sternly:

"I am putting it to you that between the time when Sir Matthew Risdon saw Smith-Wilson at dinner and the time when he entered the study, Smith-Wilson had been given a small dose of atropine, not enough to kill him, but enough to create a condition of excitability. And I am further suggesting that as you were the only person who visited him in the study before Sir Matthew saw him there, you were responsible for this preliminary dose. I suggest that you took the opportunity, when Smith-Wilson's back was turned, to let fall a few drops of belladonna into his whisky, knowing as you did that he was allergic to this drug, and believing that it would poison him. Your motive was to get rid of Smith-Wilson before he discovered your activities, as he was bound to do the next day. You got the belladonna from Mrs. Smith-Wilson's bottle of eyedrops, which was given you by the maid Barker. Later, when you found they were insufficient to kill—"

Holmes held up a hand.

"Listen," he said with an air of resignation, "if it's the eyedrops you're talking about, why didn't you say so before? Certainly he had eyedrops. What's more, he got me to put them in his eyes."

"What!" said Mallett. "You admit you put them in his eyes?"

"Why not?" said Holmes. "That's what they're for, isn't it? Why should I put them in his whisky, especially with him looking on?"

Mallett controlled himself with difficulty.

"Tell us exactly what happened," he said.

Holmes, for once, complied:

"I was waiting for him in his study, as directed. He came down the private staircase from his mother's room, after taking Mrs. Lavering there. When he came into the study, he said to me: 'Holmes, look here, my eyes are smarting like hell after all that smoke. I can hardly see." He was blinking and his eyes were red and full of tears. He took out a small bottle labelled 'Eyedrops' from his waistcoat pocket. He said he had picked it up off his mother's dressing-table, and he asked me to put a couple of drops in each eye. He sat down and lay back in his chair like a man waiting to be shaved. I did as he asked."

"Did you know the drops were belladonna?"

"I never thought about it. I knew they were the drops his mother used to brighten up her eyes before a bridge-party. Women of that class are all decadent, whatever their age."

"Did you know that belladonna contained atropine?"

"Not I! And if I had, I wouldn't have known what atropine was, so what difference would it have made?"

Mallett turned to Fitzbrown.

"Would you like to ask any questions?"

Fitzbrown said to Holmes:

"Do you know if Smith-Wilson had ever used these eyedrops before?"

"How should I?" said Holmes contemptuously. "I wasn't his nurse."

"What exactly did he say when he handed you the bottle?"

"I've told you. He said: 'I picked this up off my mother's dressing-table. I don't know if they're any good. But we might as well try. Just put a couple of drops in each eye, will you?'"

"What did you use?"

"He gave me a fountain-pen filler."

"Did he make any comment afterwards?"

"He said 'Damn!' Apparently he didn't like the feeling when the drops fell in his eyes. Then he jumped up and began walking about. I waited. Then he said, 'Damn it all, they've made things worse!' He walked about a bit more. Then he went to the cabinet and poured himself a glass of whisky. He drank some. Then he put the glass on the desk and stared at me. Then suddenly he shouted: 'Well, get out, can't you?' I said: 'You haven't told me what you want.' He said: 'Go and tell Sir

Matthew Risdon about West United shares. And sell the lot—sell the lot!' I went. I never saw him again."

Mallett leaned over to Fitzbrown and said in an undertone:

"Is that possible? Could eyedrops have such an effect?"

"Yes," said Fitzbrown, "they could, in rare cases—people who are allergic to atropine. I've never met one myself, but I've heard of them."

"You didn't mention the possibility in Smith-Wilson's case."

"No. We found so much atropine in the bladder that it was clear he died from a dose taken by the mouth. I did suggest that there might have been a small initial dose causing excitability and perhaps confusion. Ask Holmes what became of the bottle labelled 'Eyedrops', will you?"

Mallett turned back to Holmes.

"Did you notice what happened to the bottle containing the eyedrops?"

"No. I left it on the desk."

"You didn't take it away from the study?"

"No."

"Nor hand it to anyone else?"

"No."

Mallett glanced round the attentive semi-circle of his assistants.

"Very well: we'll leave that for the moment. Now before we consider the second dose of poison—the one that caused Smith-Wilson's death—I want to deal with the murder of Mrs. Smith-Wilson's maid Barker. It's only fair to you, Holmes, to repeat the customary caution: anything you say may be used in evidence. You understand that clearly."

At the mention of Barker's name Holmes's manner underwent a change. Before, while Bernard's death was being discussed, he had seemed indifferent, as little touched by fear as by regret. But now he became subject to an agitation he found it impossible to conceal.

"I know nothing about that!" he said. "I refuse to answer any questions!"

"You were on intimate terms with her, I believe?" said Mallett.

"Intimate!" shouted Holmes. "If you mean I couldn't shake her off, yes, we were intimate—about as intimate as a boa constrictor and its dinner!" He jumped up, and the men at each side of him stepped forward hastily to restrain him; but Mallett signed to them to leave him alone. "To think I let myself be taken in by a woman—a couple of women! And I talk about Smith-Wilson and his affairs! I was as bad as he, but without any excuse, because I'd been warned. 'Never trust a woman even when she's dead': that's an article of our creed. In the Anticratic State, 'back to the harem' will be the cry—and they'll take it and like it!" He wiped the saliva off his lips with the back of his hand.

Mallett remained impassive.

"Do you deny," he said, "that you planned to take this woman Barker with you when you left for abroad?"

"Planned!" said Holmes, subsiding on to his bench. "It wasn't planned—not by me. I was trapped into it. I thought the woman was ill-used—put upon by her employers. I thought she'd be grateful to be shown a way out. I explained our ideas to her. I taught her the Thirteen Points of our creed. She accepted it all. She seemed transformed." He made an exclamation of disgust. "I might have known! They're not capable of ideals. All they have is their petty personal cravings, which they call love."

"So Barker professed an attachment to you," said Mallett. "But you were unable to reciprocate. Is that it?"

Holmes did not reply. He was absorbed in some inward self-chastisement.

"I take it you met sometimes where you couldn't be seen or heard," suggested Mallett. "In the lily-room, for instance. And I suppose it was Barker who showed you the short cut from the study across the private staircase through the so-called secret passage to that room?"

Holmes still did not reply.

"And your contact with Miss Bannermore?" pursued Mallett. "Was that purely for business reasons?"

Holmes spared him a hostile glance.

"She was Smith-Wilson's woman," he said. "She'd have served me up fried with onions for his breakfast if it would have pleased him. More fool she! He didn't care for her. He only cared for that blonde doll, the hero's woman. They're a decadent lot—blown about like thistle-down. In the Anticratic State they'd be put to some more useful purpose than—"

But Mallett had had enough.

"Listen to me!" he said, banging down his fist on the table, so that Holmes started and shrank back. "Did you or did you not meet Barker in the lily-room on the night of the thirtieth?"

Holmes didn't answer.

Mallett, conscious of an advantage, pressed him more closely.

"Did Barker, during that interview, give you the bottle labelled Poison, containing liniment, from Mrs. Smith-Wilson's medicine-chest? And did you then proceed to Smith-Wilson's study and by some means or other induce him to swallow a large dose of this poison—this time, enough to kill him?"

Holmes had now looked up, and was watching him closely with glittering eyes. His throat worked, but still he did not answer.

"And after that," said Mallett, "did you return to the lily-room and continue your interview with Barker—an interview in which she claimed her reward, and you refused it. Did she threaten that if you didn't take her with you she'd expose you—ruin you and all your crazy schemes? Did you finally lose all control of yourself in your desire to escape? Did you strike this woman down, and then pick up the scarf you found lying on the floor and strangle her? Is that the true story? If it isn't, can you account for your movements between the time when you left Smith-Wilson's study—that is, shortly before ten—and the time when you left Fairfield House in your car—that is, shortly after one o'clock in the morning?"

There was a long silence.

They waited, watching Holmes twisting and untwisting his hands, looking not at Mallett now, but at the floor. In the end, when Mallett had almost given him up and was about to dismiss him, Holmes spoke in a low, rapid voice, as if to himself:

"I didn't kill Barker. I don't know who killed her. She said she'd ruin me, and she has—she and the Bannermore woman. But it's no use talking. It was my fault for trusting them. I was false to myself. It serves me right."

His lips went on moving for some time, but he seemed unable or unwilling to make his voice heard. His head sank on to his chest, and his whole body sagged forward as if in unutterable weariness. The two policemen were just in time to catch him as he fell. But when they touched him, he roused himself at once as if from sleep.

"Take him away," said Mallett. "It's no good going on now."

44

Fitzbrown and Jones sat on the veranda outside Dr. Jones's house, looking out over the dark square of moss and daisies that served as a lawn. The golden sunshine caught the tops of the highest trees.

"Well, that's how it was," said Fitzbrown. "What do you make of it? It wasn't very pleasant to watch. Mallett has it a little on his mind, too, I think, that he may have driven the man too hard."

"Pooh!" said Dr. Jones. "The fellow was crazy. He'd have committed suicide somewhere, somewhen, for some crazy reason, anyhow, as you said yourself just now. It seems to me there's nothing to worry about. The jury'll have an easy job."

"I suppose so," said Fitzbrown. "Still, there's no actual proof that he did these murders—not even that he killed Barker, much less Smith-Wilson. There's not enough evidence to hang him if he were alive."

"Well, he's saved us the trouble," said Jones, "and saved the world a lot of trouble, too, perhaps. Who knows?—in these crazy times, he might have blossomed into a new Führer with a bit of luck and plenty of showmanship. Personally, I'm glad the business is over; I was afraid it was going to mean a great deal more work."

"I thought so, too," said Fitzbrown. "But I wish I felt more satisfied about it all."

Jones pushed across the whisky bottle.

Epilogue

I

It was six months later, in Switzerland.

Rupert, with his red scarf flying, came skimming across the lake to Louise and took her arm. They went on together, keeping perfect rhythm. The glorious air whipped their cheeks to redness and filled their spirits with the sparkle of the untouched snow on the mountain-side above them. They were alone on the lake.

"Darling, isn't this heavenly?" said Louise.

"It is, darling," said Rupert.

"And it *is* so clever of you to have got me here, too," she said. "I know heaps of women who've been refused a permit."

"We're partners now, darling," said Rupert, laughing. "You've as much right to come as I have. I merely said I couldn't manage without you, and it worked, because it happened to be true."

Louise pressed his arm, and they swept round the end of the lake in a wide curve.

"What exactly are we supposed to be doing, darling?" she said, as they began on the return run.

"The firm of Lavering and Company, my dear," said Rupert, "is visiting Zürich for the purpose of investigating certain methods of cheap generation of electricity. One of the partners, Mr. R. Lavering, is here because he understands the technical side; the other partner, Mrs. R. Lavering, is here because, having been educated at an expensive school in Switzerland, she can act as interpreter and translator of recent technical publications."

"I see," said Louise. "Together we make a formidable combination. Divided we fall." She gave him a push away from her, and he went skimming away, laughing.

From the hotel on the edge of the lake they could see a boy starting out with the letters in his hand. Rupert skated towards him and took them, and came back to Louise. Reversing before her, he tore open the letters, cramming them, as soon as read, into his pocket. When he came to the last one, he frowned.

"I say!" he said in a tone of concern, "listen to this, darling. It's from Olivia. It's addressed to both of us:

DEAR RUPERT AND LOUISE,

Thank you for your postcard. How lucky you are! Hugh thanks you for his, and says will you please bring him a cuckoo-clock if you can keep it quiet as it comes through the customs?

Mother is not at all well. Dr. Fitzbrown says it's her heart. She had a sort of little seizure yesterday, and today her speech is not so good and she can't use her right hand. Dr. Fitzbrown says he thinks she may recover; but I have the feeling she doesn't want to. So she'll probably die. You know how self-willed she is.

Come and see us when you get back.

OLIVIA.

"What do you make of that?" said Rupert, handing it to her. Louise, skating forward slowly still, read the letter gravely. Rupert skating backward, continued to watch her face. She looked up.

"I think it's—oh, look out, darling!"

But it was too late. Rupert had already collided backward with the bank, and he sat down, laughing. She helped him to his feet; laughing, too. When they skated away, arm in arm again, towards the hotel for luncheon, neither said any more about the letter, though they both were thinking of it. But they did not want the shadow of the past to cast even a momentary gloom on this bright day.

"Poor Bernard," murmured Rupert at last, as they mounted the wooden steps, with their jingling skates in their hands.

"Yes, darling," said Louise gently.

<h2 style="text-align:center">2</h2>

Mrs. Smith-Wilson lay on a bed in the window of her first-floor sitting-room that overlooked the terrace and the garden and the now bare trees. Below, she could see Hugh Bernard Smith-Wilson, his red hair gleaming in the afternoon sun, kicking a football up and down the terrace with several other boys from the village school.

"I shall never get used to it," said Mrs. Smith-Wilson, "seeing him playing with those ragamuffins. It won't pay!" Her voice was older now, and querulous rather than critical. "You'll find I'm right!"

"Perhaps," said Olivia. "But the world's changed, and he's got to take it as it is. One can't fight the whole world."

"No, I suppose not," said Mrs. Smith-Wilson, falling back on her pillows. "But I would never have allowed Bernard——" She gazed past Olivia's dark, sleek head towards the door, as if expecting to see Bernard enter. "Bernard was a wonderful man, with all his faults."

Olivia said nothing.

Tea came and went. The curtains were drawn. Olivia still sat there, writing letters by the light of a shaded table-lamp; the only other light was that from the glowing log-fire on the other side of the room. Mrs. Smith-Wilson dozed, muttering sometimes in her sleep. At last she opened her eyes, and after studying Olivia for a moment or two with great intensity, she said:

"You know I avenged his death, don't you?"

Olivia, *distraite*, looked up.

"Now, my dear, lie down and go to sleep again," she said. "All that's past and over."

"I know, I know," said Mrs. Smith-Wilson. "I suppose, now, even you won't believe me. But I've a mind to tell you the truth. Don't pass it on, though, especially to Hugh."

Olivia took off her horn-rimmed glasses.

"Would you like me to read to you for a while?" she said.

Mrs. Smith-Wilson gave an irritable laugh.

"You think I'm wandering!" She struggled up in her bed. "No, I don't want you to read to me. I can make up my own stories. You go on with your writing, and I'll talk. You can listen or not, as you please."

Olivia put on her glasses again, and pretended to write. But she was listening; and as Mrs. Smith-Wilson talked, old habit came back to Olivia. She began, since she could not continue with her own letter-writing, to record in shorthand what she heard. Mrs. Smith-Wilson saw what she was doing, and lay back, gratified. She said:

3

It wasn't Holmes who killed Bernard, you know. It was Barker. And that was why *I* killed *her*.

"It was true, what they later came to think, that the dose of poison was, as it were, accidental. Bernard borrowed my eyedrops that evening in the casual way he had, because his eyes were feeling inflamed with the smoke; and he got Holmes to put the drops in for him. He had forgotten he was allergic to belladonna. I could have told him. He had been given it in an injection before his operation, and it caused such disturbance that the operation had to be postponed. So when Holmes dropped the belladonna into his eyes, it excited him terribly, as everybody who saw him noticed. Sir Matthew Risdon and Mabel Hertford saw him soon afterwards, and they noticed it. Then you remember, both the Laverings said at the inquest that they heard him talking round about midnight in his study. That was true. What nobody realised was, he was then talking to himself. It was the effect of the drug. It makes you talkative if you have only a small dose—and he was upset and excited to begin with.

"It was nearly one o'clock when Mabel Hertford left me. Before that, I had seen Bernard's light still on, and I was worried. But when I sent her to see, she came back and said the light was out and the door locked. I was still more worried. I waited until she had gone. Then I went along myself.

"I saw Barker come out of the study. I heard her turn the key in the lock and come out. She looked up and down the stairs. Then she crossed to the sliding door and went in through the passage, the way my husband had built between the study and the lily-room. I waited till she was gone. I went in to Bernard.

"He was lying on the floor. He knew me. All he could say was 'Water!' I gave him some, out of the carafe. He died a minute or two later, in my arms. There was no time to call anyone. I don't think he suffered as much as people said, in spite of his appearance. He wasn't strong enough to put up such a fight as a healthy man would have done.

"When I saw he'd gone, I looked round. On the desk was an empty glass that had contained milk, and a smaller medicine-glass. I picked them up without realising what I was doing, and smelt them. I knew then, when I smelt the medicine-glass, what had become of my liniment that Barker had said she couldn't find. On the desk, too, I saw my bottle of eyedrops lying. I wiped the milk-glass carefully, since I had touched it, and put it down. But the medicine-glass and the bottle of eyedrops I took with me, and followed Barker along the passage to the lily-room.

"I found her there, lying on the bed—my bed. She was wearing Mabel Hertford's evening scarf, which she'd picked up off the floor.

When she saw me she got off the bed. I confronted her with the medicine-glass. I said to her: 'You've killed my son. Why?' She was terrified—but still insolent. She said: 'I'm not going to be the only one to suffer.' I said: 'What has my son done to you? He never noticed your existence.' Then she said: 'I did it to get my own back—on Ralph Holmes. They'll think *he* killed him. He's run away—without me. Now they'll get him back.'

"I said: 'You killed my son—*my son*—merely to revenge yourself on your lover? Where did you get the poison?' She said: 'Out of your medicine-chest.' I followed her glance—and I saw the bottle that had contained my liniment, standing on the dressing-table. But I pretended I hadn't seen. I said: 'When did you take it?' She said: 'I meant to give it to Ralph Holmes, if he broke his promise to me. But I couldn't. Then I thought of a better way—to get him back.'

"I said: 'Why are you wearing Mrs. Hertford's scarf?' She said: 'I didn't steal it, if that's what you think! I found it here. I never took anything that wasn't mine, all the time I've been here!' The wretched creature was quite indignant with me for accusing her of dishonesty!

"I said: 'Only my son's life!'

"She came at me, then, in a fury. I raised my stick. I struck her with all my strength. She fell across the bed. I tied the ends of the scarf to the post at the bed's head and covered her up. She must have been still alive, for they said she died of strangulation. I suppose she struggled and couldn't release herself.

"I went back to my room, taking the medicine-glass and the two bottles. It was the glass in which he always took his cough-mixture. She must have gone to his room late that night with the poison in this glass, and said it came from me. Bernard would take anything to please me. He used to laugh at me, but he'd gulp it down. And he wasn't himself. The excitement, the party, and then the effect of the eyedrops, confused him. He wouldn't even know what time it was.

"As soon as he'd taken it and she saw the effect, she turned out the light. She was still there, behind the locked door, when Mabel Hertford tapped. She waited, then, till Mabel had gone and all was quiet again.

"But she didn't see me.

"I didn't go back to the study. I didn't call anyone. What was the use? I knew he was dead. The police were puzzled because they couldn't find any finger-prints on the milk-glass in Bernard's room. I'd been too clever there. As for the medicine-glass, I took it back to my room and washed it and put it away; and I took the liniment-bottle and put it at the back of the medicine-chest. The eyedrops I put back on my dressing-table. And so I waited for the morning to come.

"I played my cards pretty well, I think.

"When Barker didn't turn up, I pretended to be surprised. And when they found her, nobody suspected me. Luckily there was Holmes to take the blame for everything. If suspicion had fastened on to Rupert Lavering or Mabel Hertford, I'd have had to intervene."

She leaned back and closed her eyes:

"Ah well, I'm tired now. You can read to me a little. I think I can sleep."

4

Over luncheon the white-coated waiter handed Rupert a newspaper in its wrapper:

"Your copy of *The Times*, sir."

Rupert opened it.

"Good heavens!" he said. "She's gone."

He handed the paper to Louise and pointed to a small paragraph among the obituary notices, where the peaceful passing away of

Bernard's mother recalled the tragic death of the head of the great Smith-Wilson Engineering Company.

Louise read it and handed it back.

"I somehow didn't think she'd survive Bernard for very long," she said. "I always felt she never quite forgave *me* for the part I'd played in his life, however unwillingly. Do you remember how she kept me beside her all that night of Bernard's banquet? She wanted to find out what on earth Bernard saw in me—but she never did. What a good thing she had the boy there, after all!"

"And Olivia," said Rupert.

"And Olivia," echoed Louise dutifully. "Darling, isn't it awful, but there was a time when I wondered if it were she who had killed him? And do you remember how for a long while Mallett seemed to suspect *you*? What a good thing the real murderer revealed himself!"

"It was indeed," said Rupert.

But he did not want to think of these things. He wanted to be with Louise, outside in the sunshine, and on the dazzling snow.